Nature of the Beast

Other Books by S. L. Kassidy

Warrior Class
Sky Cutter
Taming the Wind
Blood Rain

Please Baby

Scarred Series
Scarred for Life - Book 1
New Cuts, Old Wounds – Book 2
Bandages – Book 3
First Degree Burns - Book 4
Learning to Walk Again – Book 5

Nature of the Beast

S.L. Kassidy

Desert Palm Press

Nature of the Beast

by S.L. Kassidy

copyright© 2022 S.L. Kassidy

ISBN-(book): 9781954213289
ISBN-(epub): 9781954213296

    This is a work of fiction - names, characters, places, and incidents are the product of the author's imagination or are used fictitiously. Any resemblance to actual persons living or dead, business, events or locales is entirely coincidental. All rights reserved.

    No part of this publication may be reproduced, distributed, or transmitted in any form or by any means, including photocopying, recording, or other electronic or mechanical methods, without the prior written permission of the publisher, except in the case of brief quotations embodied in critical reviews and certain other noncommercial uses permitted by copyright law.

    For permission requests, write to the publisher at lee@desertpalmpress.com or "Attention: Permissions Coordinator," at

Desert Palm Press
1961 Main Street, Suite 220
Watsonville, California 95076
www.desertpalmpress.com

Editor: Kellie Doherty
Cover Design: Jamani Hawkins-El

Printed in the United States of America
First Edition June 2022

Dedication

This book is dedicated to my family, who supported my writing long before I thought it was worth anything, and to my friends, who helped me believe in myself and my work. Thank you all.

Chapter One

CITLALI SIGHED AS SHE stared around the space, illuminated by overhead lights. She studied every inch of the room. It wouldn't work. She flicked back the lapels of her pomegranate-colored suit jacket and then pressed a hand to her forehead. *Think. You got this. Just think it through.* With a sigh, she threw her head back, shoving her fingers through her long hair.

A dull throb in her skull grew with every second as the orange and cream room stared back at her. The scent of cleaning products hanging in the air didn't help. *There has to be a way to make this work. The show must go on.* The design of this place was terribly irksome, even though it worked best for everyone to see the show.

It was a mix of stadium and balcony seating, hosting couples and larger groups. Each set up was blocked with a small barrier wall that curved at the top to give the sense of privacy, and everything centered around a stage no bigger than a public hockey rink. It was optimal if no one ever changed anything, but Citlali wanted change, damn it. She always wanted change. The table set up, the stage, sometimes even the specials. Change was good.

The show worked best if it could be seen at all angles. When she and Daphne viewed it live, they actually circled the stage to take the video for reference to plan around the show. The video didn't do it justice, but if they didn't figure this out, the patrons would end up with the video version, flat, 2D, even though the performers were right in front of them. *That will not do.*

"We can't do it," Daphne said, her Trinidadian accent creeping out, as it did when they were alone. It was tragic she couldn't let her accent fly, but apparently people frowned upon any accent from the West Indies; they thought the person speaking was less educated. Daphne's business and marketing degrees would say otherwise. Citlali saw the same nonsense from people dealing with her father, and Daphne's business and marketing degrees would say otherwise.

Daphne's brow wrinkled as her hazel eyes, behind wire framed glasses, swept the area. Her boot heels clicked on the tiled floor as she turned, trying to make sense of things.

"I refuse to accept that." Citlali took a breath and straightened her crimson tie as she would straighten out this mess of a room. They would figure it out. They always did, but this might take a little longer than usual. "But why the hell did he set this place up like this? How are we supposed to accommodate a large party?"

Daphne had the nerve to laugh, like this wasn't annoying to her as well, and twisted her long, caramel hair from one side to the other. Citlali could almost see the gears shifting in Daphne's mind. "I'm sure it served him well when he first opened the place."

Citlali scoffed. "Yes, well, that was fifteen years ago. We have to constantly innovate to stay ahead of the times. He hired us because he knows he needs upgrading."

A smile lit up Daphne's slender face. "Li, didn't he hire you the second you told him you speak three languages?"

Citlali shrugged, as that was probably the truth. Raul Rafe had almost jumped out of his chair when he learned she spoke English, Spanish, and Cantonese. He also liked her business degree and was familiar with her father, having worked with him on several deals. He gave her a chance with an idea she had for The New Moon, and he liked it so much he let her hire her best friend as another manager. The rest was history...frustrating history.

Like right now, they were stuck.

"We could change the show." Daphne turned to the stage.

Citlali shook her head. "The show is amazing as is. We've sold out the house. And who are we to tell them to change their performances because our building situation is inadequate?" Even she looked forward to seeing the show, and she never looked forward to these things. Even the best of performances got stale after the fifteenth review.

Daphne walked down the stairs next to the larger tables. "I'm not suggesting *change,* change the show."

Citlali had no idea what that meant. "Then what are we supposed to do?"

"What were we thinking when we booked this?" Daphne twirled around like she was a ballerina, only she had on a powder blue business suit rather than a tutu.

"Celebration that we sold so many tickets, probably." Her gaze went back to the center of the room and then to the leveled tables. She groaned.

Daphne took off her glasses to pinch her nose. She seemed to have a developing headache as well. "You'd think we were new at this."

Citlali chuckled. "Has it been a year?"

"It has been a year. Have we ever moved the tables?" Daphne replaced her glasses and then walked back up the stairs, like she needed to keep moving to stop the creeping insanity.

"Obviously not." Citlali tilted her head back, stared at the ceiling with its multitude of lights glaring back at her, and the solution struck her. It was so simple. "We'll put mirrors on the ceiling."

Daphne looked up, pursing her maroon lips. "Would that work?"

"It'll also add to the effect."

"Agreed!"

Citlali held up her fist and Daphne gave her an appropriate bump. "Now to check with the kitchen. Did the chef hire new staff?"

"He said that was handled, but you know him."

She frowned, her headache working its way down to her teeth at the thought of dealing with the damn chef. "If he lied again..."

"I want him to lie to me again right before we have this damn event." Daphne smiled in a way that showed all of her teeth. With her shade of lipstick, it looked like she had blood around her mouth. She wanted the excuse to curse the man out. "I hate that he thinks he's special because he's been here for five years."

"I'm going to strangle him to avoid hearing another speech about how he single-handedly turned that kitchen from a strip club to a five star restaurant." She rolled her eyes. It was true, but no one wanted to hear that literally every conversation with the man.

Daphne groaned. "You have to do the talking. I took the deliveries."

Citlali sucked her teeth, but she would do that. She was sick of their usual deliveryman. He and the other delivery people had the gall to beg her for tickets to the show. She'd possibly oblige if they weren't so creepy about it.

"What decor do you want to go with now that we're doing the mirrors?" Daphne mused, staring around the room.

"I'll leave that to you." Citlali rubbed her face with her hand.

It felt like there was still so much to do, but they only needed to finalize matters. Amazingly, the chef hired people like he was supposed to. Their kitchen had been light for a couple of weeks, which was fine for a regular night, but they needed their special menu complete for this show. Tickets cost way too much money, and they spent too much time promoting things to half-ass it.

"If people complain about how they can't see the penetration, I'm blaming your mirrors," Daphne said.

Citlali arched an eyebrow. "We've both used mirrors enough to know this will work. I'm more concerned over new people exposing themselves."

The worst was when people who had never been to The New Moon came. They thought the place was some cheap strip club or sex shop where they could do whatever.

Daphne curled her lip. "I hate having to police the audience. Who wants to get fingered in the middle of a four-course meal?"

"Oh, please." Citlali couldn't help gawking at her. "You've been eaten out in the middle of a meal." College was a wild time, especially when Daphne fully embraced her bisexuality. Some stories she could've kept to herself, but sometimes, to this day, they both got excited and over-shared.

Daphne held up a finger. "Not in front of people."

Citlali scoffed. "Only because you hate an audience."

"So much pressure to perform. I have so much respect for all of our shows and the cast. You'd probably enjoy an audience."

Probably. Citlali's cheeks burned. "The mirrors will show everything, including any and all penetration. Everyone should be able to see both the stage and the mirrors. This show will keep The New Moon as the hot spot it is."

Daphne and Citlali had turned what had been an overtly sexual burlesque-type business into something unique. They were certain everything they presented in the club was nothing short of performance art.

Daphne snapped her finger. "We have to do a waitstaff inspection again."

Citlali groaned and led the way to the backroom. It was a beehive of activity, as always. The staff primping, preening, and fixing each other up. Dozens of smells clouded the area, dust from makeup, and noise of overlapping conversations.

Citlali's eyes almost fell out of her skull as she caught sight of one of their best waiters. The throb in her skull was close to splitting her head apart now.

"What the hell?" Citlali managed to say through her disbelief.

"Ryan, what is that?" Daphne asked, voice very controlled, accent all but gone. She moved to poke the model-cum-waiter in his slightly flabby gut. People fluttered about in the background, probably trying to get out of the line of fire.

Ryan giggled and put his big hands over his bare abdomen, abandoning the black boxers he had been adjusting. "My old trainer moved. I didn't realize the new guy was bad soon enough."

"No, no, no." Citlali clutched her hands together and put them to her mouth. "Please tell us you've switched trainers. You have to have your cuts and definition. That's your spot." Their waitstaff were all models or aspiring actors with wait experience. They had a variety of body types, and Ryan was supposed to be the slender, toned muscle. His torso was losing its definition, one of his hallmarks. They had a strict system about body types to make sure every guest had eye candy.

All of the color drained from his olive-toned face. "Are you going to fire me?"

Citlali gawked. Was he out of his mind? "We're not going to fire you, but we won't be able to use you as often if you break body type."

"But I need the tips!" Ryan protested.

It was not unheard of for the waitstaff to get tips over five hundred dollars a table, and that was without dancing at all, just looking nice and serving food and drinks. A few of them even built reputations on bad attitudes. People paid for the experience. So some came to be yelled at by staff while others preferred waitstaff who catered to their every whim with a bright grin.

"I'm sure you do," Citlali said, and she would've gone on, but Daphne screamed.

"Erika, what happened to your hair!" Daphne's voice had gone up so high, Citlali was scared to look, but she had to. She winced. Typically, Erika kept her hair fairly short, but someone had gone savage on her. Her usually stylish blonde locks had been butchered.

"I know!" Erika wailed, crying from her seat in front of the long vanity. Makeup tracks marred her sienna cheeks. "She cut it all wrong. It's way too short."

Daphne went over and wrapped her arms around Erika's shoulders. "It's okay."

Erika's voice pitched higher. "I look stupid!"

Citlali turned to Genevieve. "Please fix her up with a good wig."

"Girl, why did you get your hair cut the day before the show?" Genevieve, another member of the waitstaff, gave an exasperated sigh.

"I always get it cut before the show! A fresh cut sells." Erika bawled even louder. Daphne rubbed her shoulder, but it didn't seem to help.

"I got her." Genevieve opened her arms and Daphne gently pushed Erika to her.

Citlali and Daphne made their rounds. They made sure certain tattoos were covered, or certain tattoos were on display. They checked that everyone was on the same page about makeup, tie-dyed bathing suit uniforms went with the colors of the show, and that everyone understood the pacing.

"Are we dancing in between?" Kwame asked, standing by a mirror and checking the cut of his shorts. They were too long. It was possible he mixed up his uniform with someone else. Citlali frowned. Time to be on the lookout for above-the-knee shorts.

"We're not going to stop you," Citlali replied.

"You do have to pull in tips," Daphne said.

Ryan curled his lip as he slipped on his uniform. The way they hugged his thighs, they were probably Kwame's, and they switched so more attention would go to his legs than his abdomen. Good idea. "You know how the performers get with the shows, though."

"We've made it very clear to the performers that you're going to dance. It's how to engage the audience," Daphne said.

Citlali nodded. "Not to mention, they're being paid for the show. It's not like you're stealing their tips."

After driving themselves crazy with the staff, Citlali and Daphne were as prepared for the show as they would get. It was such a rush putting the whole thing together, but they barely got to see the show. Hell, the whip sounds barely registered to Citlali. She glanced up once to check on the mirrors. She could definitely see the penetration. *I knew that would work.* Success.

***

Tala was confused as hell from her dark blue beanbag chair tucked in the corner of her tiny living room. Her one bedroom apartment wasn't the place for some couple's spat. *Yet, for some weird reason, Kyra and Raina are always fighting here.* She paused her video game and then put the controller down next to her tumbler of water.

"Why the hell can't you be happy for me that I got the job!" Kyra stomped her small foot, which barely made a sound on the oak floor, and glared daggers at Raina, despite the fact that she had to look up several inches. Her sun-colored gaze was as hot as a supernova, but Raina hadn't flinched.

"What's going on here?" Tala asked, rubbing her hands on her black sweatpants. There was no way she'd try to make sense of it on her own.

Kyra looked at her, brown face flushed from shouting. Dark umber curls trembled as she shook her head. "I got a dream job and this ass isn't even happy for me!" She motioned to Raina. Raina's much-too-large college hoodie seemed to drown Kyra's thin frame with even that slight movement.

Raina choked for a moment, her burnt umber face going red. "I'm sorry, I didn't know your dream job was to work at a strip joint!"

Tala's ears perked up. *What's my sister doing?* "Kyra, why the hell would you need to work at a strip club? You make a decent living down at Good Taste. I know it's not great, but you shouldn't need to strip."

"I'm not stripping." Kyra growled at her with a flash of teeth, white and glinting. Bold, but telling of her rage. This argument must have been going on long before they made it to the apartment.

"That's good to know," Tala replied. One problem solved, but then there was another, much bigger issue. "Then why the hell are you two here?" They lived in a palace compared to her little hole in the wall.

Kyra blinked and regarded Tala as if she was out of her mind. Like they weren't having a full-blown argument in her living room, like they lived there and not her. Her sister was all too aware how much Tala hated surprise company. And loud surprise company was the worst.

"This is neutral ground," Kyra replied.

Neutral ground? Tala used the edge of her gray couch to push herself up on the beanbag, certain she heard wrong. "I'm sorry. This is what?"

"Neutral ground," Kyra replied, like Tala was a moron, and then had the nerve to wave her hands around the apartment.

"You guys have an argument and leave your negative energy all over my house, so you can go back home and make up there?" Tala couldn't believe what she was hearing. The disrespect to her whole energy. Kyra was better than this, and yet here they were.

"You're also the best tie-breaker for us," Raina said, which was better, but still not what Tala wanted to hear.

Tala bit back the desire to gnash her teeth, but her stomach twisted. *I just want to be alone and play my damn games while I have the time.* "I know I'm going to regret asking, but what tie am I breaking?"

Kyra folded her arms. "Raina thinks you'll agree with her and try to stop me from working at The New Moon. It's a huge step up. A five-star restaurant!"

Tala's eyes widened. That was definitely a step up for her little sister.

"It's a strip club!" Raina looked like she wanted to rip her hair out, but the neat, tight coils of black hair wouldn't be much to get her fingers on.

Tala scratched her chin. "The New Moon?" It sounded familiar.

"It's that big black building down by the boardwalk. It looks like an arena," Raina replied.

Tala squinted as she went through her mental map of the area. "By the rich hotels and casinos?"

"Yeah," Kyra replied.

Tala pursed her lips, not sure what Kyra thought went on there. Not that sex work or stripping was a problem, but Kyra didn't seem to understand where she had decided to work. "Pup, that's a strip club." That didn't match up with what Kyra wanted in life.

"It's not." Kyra gnashed her teeth.

Tala frowned. Kyra had one more time to do that and then Tala was going to get the hell up. Sisters or not and angry or not, no one was going to try to dominate her in her own home.

"Okay, it says it's a gentlemen's club, but that's just fancy talk for a strip club." Tala said. Well, she thought it said gentlemen's club, but she didn't pay much attention to it. It wasn't a regular restaurant.

Kyra practically ripped her purse open for her cell phone. She jabbed at the screen as if trying to break the damn thing in half. "See!" She shoved the phone in Tala's face.

Tala blinked several times and pulled back enough to see what Kyra was trying to show her. According to the search, The New Moon restaurant was a five-star dining establishment with unique staff, service, and shows. Images showcased the weird stadium for the tables and what looked like theater balconies on the side. The reviews praised the food. And the menu did look tasty, particularly the sweet potato risotto.

Raina made a noise somewhere between a scoff and a groan.

Kyra turned on her, pushing her phone toward her girlfriend's face. "Does this look like a strip club?"

"Just because you see a nice picture on the internet doesn't mean it's true!" Raina had to back up even more than Tala did. She frowned.

Anxiety flared in Tala's belly. Butterflies sparked to life, and Tala's muscles tightened. If Raina was still bothered, this could actually be bad. Kyra's view on nudity and sex was more open than Raina. While her own view was less open, Tala understood where Kyra was coming from. Still, that didn't mean she was okay with Kyra cooking at some funky strip club buffet, surrounded by musky sweat and skunky body fluids. Her sister was better than that.

Despite her anger, Raina cupped Kyra's hand and gently moved Kyra's phone out of her face. "It could be much different in person."

"But I was inside the place! This is exactly what it looks like." Kyra walked in a tight circle, barely avoiding the little box of a coffee table, before glowering at Raina again.

Raina didn't even flinch. That took a lot of trust.

"Were there strippers?" Tala asked.

"Of course not!" Kyra was so flushed it was like she had popped blood vessels in her whole face.

Raina didn't look any better. "It was daytime when you went. Strippers aren't hanging around their place of employment when it's closed."

It finally clicked. Raina's upset had nothing to do with Kyra taking a step back in her career by working at some grungy strip club. She was bothered by the idea of her girlfriend working in a strip club specifically. Probably bothered with stripping overall. While it wasn't Tala's thing, she didn't think there was anything wrong with it. Obviously Kyra didn't either.

"Raina, you act like she's stripping," Tala said.

"Of course I'm not!" Kyra curled her lip, probably pissed Tala even brought that up.

Tala scowled. "Why the hell are you mad at me? I'm trying to help you two annoyances." She could be doing a side quest in her game to level up right now rather than dealing with their crap.

"It's not about you stripping!" A vein throbbed in Raina's neck, and it sounded like her heart was about to explode. The escalating thump-thump-thump sounded clear in Tala's ears. They might need to calm Raina down before she passed out. "It's about you being in a seedy environment, possibly putting yourself in danger without realizing it. Strip clubs aren't known for being places of law and order."

Okay, that sounded more like Raina rather than her looking down on strippers.

"There's nothing seedy going on. You saw it." Kyra waved her phone.

Raina face-palmed with both hands and let out a loud groan. "Of course it's not going to look seedy on the website."

"It didn't look seedy when I went in for my interview."

"They want to put their best foot forward when hiring people!"

"Raina, why not just go check it out?" Tala asked before she realized what she was saying, but now that it was out there, they might as well just run with it. She wanted to get back to her games while she had the free time. Her eyes shifted to her coffee table with all of the textbooks and loose papers. School would be back too soon. Spring break didn't last forever, after all.

Kyra glanced away, and Raina glared at her. *Okay, curious.* Kyra's golden eyes were just a little less molten now. Her scent was not trying to dominate the whole area anymore, covering up a soothing lavender. She wasn't saying everything.

"What's wrong? Raina could just go up there, right?" Tala asked.

"Significant others of employees aren't allowed inside," Raina replied through gritted teeth.

"Okay, wait, that sounds super shady," Tala said. The hair on the back of her neck was at attention, and her stomach butterflies fluttered about like they owned her torso. She didn't want something to happen to her sister. "That's not shady to you?"

Kyra folded her arms, face twitching with tension. Her eyes begged for some leeway. "Of course it's weird, but do you guys not understand what a boost this would be to my career? This place has a world-class kitchen and is run by a world-renowned chef. It can't be that bad."

Tala's anxiety twisted. "It sounds weird." *I don't like it.*

With a huge sigh, Kyra rubbed her forehead, brushing dark curls from her face. She looked deflated and small. "I actually impressed the chef there. Me." She tapped her heart with her fist, tucked into the sleeve of Raina's hoodie.

Tala sighed. Kyra's dream was to be a master chef. *How could a strip club make that happen? How could the place be both a strip club and an amazing restaurant?* This all sounded impossible.

Raina closed the gap between her and Kyra. She wrapped her hands around Kyra's waist, then kissed Kyra's chubby cheek. At least they were about to make up, but that didn't help set Tala at ease with Kyra's job choice.

"I want you to soar in your career. I want you to be amazing, like I know you are," Raina said quietly. "I don't see how that's possible in a strip club."

Kyra huffed. "It's not a strip club. I wish I could prove it to you, but you can't come in and see for yourself."

"I know," Raina replied. "I trust you, and I know you can handle yourself, but still, I worry."

"Why can't you just lie? They don't know you're her girlfriend," Tala said. She'd feel better if Raina gave her stamp of approval.

Kyra shook her head. "I had to give her name when they hired me. They keep a list. If she shows up, I get in trouble." Suddenly, she popped up, looking like the ray of sunshine she generally was. *Oh, this isn't going to be good.* "Tala could go in!"

Tala tilted her head and blinked hard, twice. "Who could do what now?"

"Tala, you could see it's not a strip club." Kyra grinned.

"No!" Tala shook her head. She just wanted to play video games. *Is that too much to ask?* From the way Kyra and Raina looked at her, hope shimmering in their eyes, the answer was a resounding yes. *Damn it.* She'd have to stop letting them in. *You didn't let them in. Kyra has a key. Double damn it.*

Chapter Two

HOW THE HELL DO I let myself get talked into crap like this? Tala turned her motorcycle off into a shadowy spot of the street. Away from people. Perfect. It was hard to find places like this by the boardwalk considering how busy it was all the time. There were casinos, a carnival, clubs, and activities all over the place. Cars, bikes, and people were everywhere. Tala hated it so much.

Tala popped out the kickstand and groaned as she pulled off her helmet. She hated the damn thing, but the city fined riders without one. Her braided mohawk made wearing a helmet awkward. She pulled at the loose coils of her hair, hoping they weren't flat, then she glanced around, feeling self-conscious.

Dude, everything makes you self-conscious. This bullshit you're about to do makes you self-conscious. And the butterflies in her stomach were merely an exclamation point to the whole matter.

Tala knocked on her forehead with her fist a couple of times. "How the hell did I let her talk me into this shit?" Her stomach growled to remind her.

Food. Promises of so many dinners. Kyra had gone down a long, delicious list of items she would make if Tala did them "this small, teeny-tiny favor that doesn't even involve anything embarrassing because you just have to go in and look around." Tala snorted. Like anything was ever that simple. Anxiety set in.

"Stupid stomach. Always getting me in trouble and then being all upset," Tala grumbled as she dismounted her motorcycle. Kyra had always been able to talk her into the dumbest things, thanks to food. Sometimes, she was convinced that was the reason Kyra learned to cook, since Tala couldn't be bothered to even boil water much of the time. *Stupid metabolism, getting me involved in nonsense all the damn time.*

With a heavy sigh and a drop of her shoulders, Tala glanced up and down the street. Shop signs and hotels lit up the night along with the merry sounds of the fair down the boardwalk. The smell of cotton candy and popcorn hung in the air. A grand movie theater with flashing lights loomed down the way. The hushed sea whispered on the sandy beach not too far away.

Shaking her head, Tala moved to the sidewalk and almost got mowed down by a passing couple. Giggly and drunk, they muttered about going to the bowling alley. If only they knew they were headed in the wrong direction. Cars choked her with exhaust. Streams of people flowed around her.

She felt itchy already. Her guts twisted, and she had to resist the urge to get back on her bike and go home.

Trying to block everything out, Tala focused on a nearby building she typically ignored—The New Moon. Cobalt lights outlined the massive black building. Trimmed bushes decorated the front and cut off a large parking lot with a high wall. The heavy bass of music pumped from the place. It reminded her of those halls people rented for proms or wedding receptions.

Raina insisted it was a cheap strip joint, but it seemed too nice. Still, she couldn't see how it was the upscale restaurant Kyra claimed it was, either, not with thick music bumping from it. Well, it had to be something. She'd soon find out, and she could go home, give her impartial review of the joint, and never think of the damn place again, but she couldn't bring herself to move.

Frozen in place as The New Moon loomed before her like an alien beast, Tala took a deep breath and released it slowly. Her chest tightened. *Damn it, legs, move.* Her legs didn't listen.

"Just go in there," Tala said, trying to hype herself up. Each breath pained her. The rumble in her stomach didn't abate, and it had nothing to do with hunger. Her body threatened to pop as butterflies took over every available space. "Look around. Make sure Kyra is all right."

She had to make sure Kyra was okay or she would never be able to live with herself. *You're responsible for her. That's your little sister. You have to take care of her.* Those thoughts got her legs moving.

As she got closer, she could make out that it was a three-story building, but it didn't seem like there were windows. Weird. Turning the corner to get to the entrance, she saw The New Moon in cursive, backlit by blue lighting. Classy, kind of.

She expected onyx smoke to be pouring out from the building, like a horror movie. The wind whistled down the street behind her. Under other circumstances, she'd dismiss it as anxiety, but the feeling felt larger and heavier than that. Her heart thumped. She swallowed around a lump in her throat.

"Oh, ha, ha. You're scared in a horror movie." Tala shook her head at the ridiculousness of it all, discarding her butterflies as best as she could. She rapped herself on the forehead twice to remain focused.

Walking up the cut stone path to the door, the lack of a line didn't help set Tala's stomach at ease. *What kind of club doesn't have a line?* Low soca music hummed through her. The scent of cigars, cigarettes, and alcohol wafted from the area. Under all that, there was food. Not hot wings and fries, but steak and salmon. Utterly baffling.

The door opened and a tall, imposing blond woman met her. Dressed in a black designer three-piece suit with a gold vest and crisp white shirt, she wore an expensive, gold men's watch, and a stunning necklace of braided gold with a diamond in the center. A subtle sage cologne wafted from her. The New Moon must have some class if the bouncer looked like she could buy and sell Tala's sorry ass. Now she understood why Kyra picked out her clothes for this adventure. Underneath her leather jacket, she had on dark grey dress pants with a matching vest. A silver shirt highlighted the white of her hair.

The bouncer arched an eyebrow at her. "Name?" The bouncer held a small tablet up, illuminating several bits of jewelry in her face.

"Tala Grayson." She pulled out her slim wallet and showed her ID through the little window it was secured against.

The bouncer pressed on the tablet. "Go on in."

Stepping inside, Tala found herself in a well-lit, white lobby. It was warm, so she wasted no time taking off her jacket. She scanned the place, looking for any signs of strippers.

A fountain that might have come straight from Rome caught her attention first. Tables filled with diners were lined up against tinted windows. *So what appeared to be a wall outside was actually a big window. Restaurant there checks out.* Large, dark wooden double doors sat in front of her across the room, almost like she'd expect to see in a palace. A well-dressed man nodded to her from his desk by the doors.

The man at the desk smiled as she walked to the double doors and requested her ID. She showed him and he waved her in. *Please don't let me see something gross.*

Pulling one of the doors, she found herself in the main hall of the club, but it looked like a theater. High ceilings vaulted over her, dotted with expensive, crystal chandeliers that didn't provide much light. Cigar, cigarette, and vape smoke lingered, yet nothing was overwhelming—

not the smoke, or perfumes, or colognes, or the food. Despite that, her brain short-circuited for a moment.

Tala lingered in the doorway, unsure of where to go. The hum of conversation surrounded her as she took in the space and the people lingering in it. The atmosphere was purposely dim. Lights around the orange and cream walls seemed low, especially compared to the brightness in the lobby. Scenery artwork lined the walls, and koi ponds with color changing lights in the water were dotted between tables. It was actually pretty cool. People chatted on the couches that lined the ponds. Including women in corsets and panties! She yelped and her eyes went right to the floor.

What the hell kinda restaurant is this where people wear underwear around like that? How could Kyra not think this was a strip club? Women wandering about in lingerie was definitely a strip club thing.

The tile mosaics on the floor seemed classy. Maybe she imagined the corset and panties. She picked her head up. Balconies opened up on the sides like a theater, and in a sunken space at the center of the whole place, a stage had been cleared. She had a sneaking suspicion that if something happened on the stage, she'd definitely have to make a run for it.

A man brushed by her, carrying a tray and wearing assless chaps. Tala turned her head to avoid staring at his ass. That only led her to seeing more ladies in corsets and panties.

"Shit, shit, shit." She already felt in over her head. Everything else suggested the place was on the up and up. The patrons here acted so normally—eating, playing cards, reading, chatting—and most of them were dressed in semi-formal and formal wear.

The waitstaff were barely wearing anything at all. Some of them were dancing at the tables or shaking various body parts in front of customers. *What the hell sort of place is this?* The lights faded lower and she just knew she was about to find out. The chatter died down when performers came out on stage and...holy shit!

Four people were completely naked and wasted no time bending in various ways that hurt her joints just looking at it...while they also fucked each other! They just got right into it. No introduction, unless one performer going down on the other while then being flipped upside down counted. Shaking her head, she looked at the ceiling and followed it until a nice distant wall had her attention.

There's no way in hell Kyra saw any of this crap when she came here. She'd never lie to Raina like that. It didn't discount the fact that Raina was being nice when she said this was a strip club. *There's not even stripping. They're just already buck naked!*

A few servers stopped next to her, openly leering at her, and she took a step back. She gulped and tried not to look like a rabbit in a den of wolves. *Don't be stupid. You're no rabbit.* Sometimes, her anxiety made her feel that way.

Still, Tala put her best foot forward, stepping deeper inside. She felt out of place, like everyone was staring at her, trying to figure out why the hell she was there. As moans from the stage reached her, she couldn't help wondering what she was doing there, too. *Where the hell is the kitchen?* She needed to check on Kyra and then get the hell out. *I hope she's wearing more clothes than the performers and waitstaff.* It would be dangerous cooking with hot oil if she was practically naked.

***

Citlali's curiosity piqued. Her eyes had fallen upon a lesbian wet dream: short, stout, clearly an athlete, in a perfect grey suit. She had black hair braided up into an amazing mohawk with grey streaks. Her ends were left free, curling upward, and Citlali would have delighted in twirling her finger around a strand. The poor dear looked ready to bolt. *Well, time to go to work. The scared ones tended to shell out the most money, typically out of panic. I'll sit with her until someone else can get her going.*

Lone female clients tended to be older and sure of themselves. Successful and brazen, like their male counterparts. That was all well and good, if one wanted normal and boring. Change was good and filled out that suit almost better than Citlali did her own, and hers was tailor made.

"Oh!" Daphne cooed as she came over, pressing her hands together. Her eyes danced behind her glasses. "I knew I spotted your next project the second she walked through the door."

Citlali smiled. "Well, she looks like she could use a friend."

Daphne chuckled. "I'm sure you really want to get to know her in a more friendly manner." She wiggled her eyebrows.

"I am a professional, you know."

"I also know you have a thing for lost puppies. You better grab her before she makes a run for the door."

Daphne made a good point, so Citlali got a move on it. She stepped right in front of the woman and earned a yelp as the woman came to a halt. Up close, she was even shorter than Citlali thought hovering around five feet. *Adorable.* Citlali wanted to put her in her jacket pocket and carry her around. The wide-eyed expression helped.

Citlali slipped her hands into her pocket, giving the newbie a smile. "I'm sorry to startle you, but I don't think I've seen you around before. Are you new to our little club?" She made sure to sound affable and cheery, but not so much so that she sounded fake.

The young woman took a step back, her smooth brow furrowing. The woman had flawless skin in the most perfect shade of chestnut. No makeup, no lip-gloss, just a bow mouth. And then there were her strange eyes. Blue, but almost looked white, with red and green starbursts around her large pupils. Citlali would love to study them for a while, to understand how so many colors could play in one set of eyes. Those eyes narrowed on Citlali after a moment.

"Uh...yeah, I'm new. What's it to you?" the woman asked, clutching her leather jacket to her chest as if it were a shield.

Citlali smiled wider. She had to pour on the charm, but she didn't want to overdo it. There was a fine line between her professional persona and over-enthused. "Oh, nothing. Is there anything I can do or get for you to help you enjoy your stay?"

The woman glanced off to the side, as if seeking an escape, but then snapped back forward. "Uh...no. I don't need anything. I'm good, just checking the place out."

Citlali nodded. "Good. I hope things are to your liking. Has anyone seated you? Would you care for a drink?"

"No, no, no. I'm good," the woman replied as she took a step back.

Citlali reached out to grab her wrist, but the way those pale blue eyes cut to her hand let Citlali know she was about to lose it. The woman growled. Actually growled. *Just like a puppy.* The air around them seemed to crackle, like it was charged with static.

Citlali adjusted, holding the woman's hand instead, and then clasped her other hand on top, cradling a surprisingly large hand in both of hers. The anxiety pouring off of her in high waves was enchanting, but the wild, furious look in those blue eyes faded as quickly as it appeared. The atmosphere calmed, but Puppy still looked ready to bolt. Citlali grinned, hoping to set Puppy at ease. *Who the hell left this poor newbie to navigate The New Moon on her own?* She'd have to find them and thank them.

"My name is Citlali. Here, let me find you a seat and get you a drink. We can talk for a while. It'll be pleasant," Citlali promised. She never let anyone leave The New Moon with a bad experience. That was just good business practice, whether the person was cute or not.

Puppy made a strangled noise, but followed as Citlali strolled away, still holding her hand. She walked Puppy over to one of the small tables. Puppy put her jacket over the back of the chair and sat, relaxing as the leather armchair cradled her. The slim armchair provided some privacy, and the divider, solitude, which was more for allowing customers to enjoy themselves without having to worry about an audience. Now, it seemed to offer a perfect hiding place.

Citlali eased into the seat across from the woman. For all of her nervous energy, Puppy's muscles stretched the fabric of her shirt. Citlali relaxed, but made sure she could see several bouncers. While the new patron didn't seem dangerous, it was better to err on the side of caution.

"Allow me to order you a drink," Citlali said. She would get something to help soothe the woman, but also something on the pricey side if only to help get a little more money in case Puppy never came back.

"I guess cola would be fine," Puppy answered, hunched over a little. She seemed to be trying to make herself smaller, which was ridiculous since she wasn't that tall to begin with.

"Cute." Citlali couldn't help it.

Puppy glared at her, a hint of red staining her brown cheeks. Citlali waved over Sonya, one of the servers. Puppy eyed Sonya, but it was hard to tell if it was in appreciation or suspicion. The white bikini barely covered Sonya's full figure and the gossamer sarong hugged her waist, inviting eyes to feast on her.

"Oh, a fresh face," Sonya said, her voice a friendly chirp.

Puppy pressed herself deeper into her chair. Wow, being amiable was a threat.

Citlali sent Sonya off for the soda, and then turned her attention back to Puppy. Odd newcomer. *Is she some kind of criminal? Is she waiting for the police to raid the place? Has she set someone up or is she spying on someone?* Citlali came up with so many scenarios. Time to find out.

"So, what brings you here?" Citlali asked.

Puppy shrugged, trying so hard to be nonchalant. "Just checking things out."

Oh, she is too cute. She couldn't lie worth a damn. She couldn't be a criminal, wouldn't be able to pull it off. Maybe someone dared her to come here. Citlali nodded. "Do you frequently check out nightclubs, or did we just get lucky?" *Or did this poor dear draw the short straw?*

Puppy blew out a breath. "You got lucky."

Citlali laughed softly; it was a mix of her actual laugh and a giggle meant to set customers at ease. Puppy's face twitched. Possibly a smile.

"I certainly feel lucky, but I feel that way often. What about you?" Citlali asked.

A snort, then an eye roll. "I'm one of those people who if I didn't have bad luck, I wouldn't have any luck at all."

"I find that hard to believe." Citlali leaned forward.

"Oh, it's true. I was born under a whole constellation of bad stars. My mom says my terrible luck comes from the fact that I was born under a moonless sky."

Citlali wasn't sure what that meant, but she assumed it was cultural. "I'm sure she's just teasing."

"Hell, no, she's not. She's trying to make sense of my supernatural bad luck. Dad's pretty sure a god cursed me, but at least he takes the blame for that one."

"I don't believe your luck could be that bad," Citlali said to keep the woman talking.

Puppy didn't disappoint, going into a tale of misery and woe. Halfway through the story, the soda was delivered. For all of Puppy's earlier embarrassment, she snuck a peek at Sonya's ass, showing she at least had decent eyesight and good taste. Amazingly, she grinned at Citlali and let loose a nervous laugh, then took a massive gulp of her drink.

"So, what happened with the murder of crows?" Citlali asked, a little impressed Puppy knew a flock of crows was referred to as a murder.

Puppy hid behind her hand for a second. "The little fuckers actually attacked me, like it was their fucking baby! Once I finally got away from them, I fell in the stupid pond."

Citlali tried so hard not to laugh, but she could feel the amused smile burning her face. "That's not that bad."

Puppy's face fell into a deadpan. "And then came the geese."

"Oh no!" And there went the laugh. "At least you helped that poor child."

"Except the kid laughed when the geese attacked."

Citlali pouted for Puppy. "But you did a good deed."

"Yeah, and no good deed goes unpunished." She gulped down her soda. "I got sick from the pond and got scolded by both parents and my grandma for the next few days. I felt like such a dumbass."

Citlali shook her head. "You shouldn't feel that way. You did a good thing. It's all too rare for people to go out of their way to do something nice. That's special."

Puppy puffed out her cheeks, which looked a little red again. "Whatever. I swear all I do is get in trouble for trying to help." She went into another twisted tale about her bad luck. Citlali couldn't help listening. Puppy was a softie, a good Samaritan. It surprised her.

Citlali smiled at the end of the tale. "Wow, you do have all sorts of adventures."

Puppy regarded her as if she was insane. "Adventures? I broke my leg!"

"You saved a woman from being hit by a car. I would say what you see as bad luck is actually good luck for others. They're lucky you're around. You're a guardian angel."

Puppy frowned, eyes focused on her now empty soda glass. "You work here, right?"

Citlali blinked at the change of pace. "I do."

"Shouldn't you be working then? You'll get in trouble sitting here chatting with me all night."

Wow, she really has no idea what goes on here. "I'll be fine. You won't get me in trouble."

Puppy grunted, tapping her empty glass. "Have you worked here long?"

"About a year. Do you want another drink? Some food?"

Puppy squirmed and radiated that nervous energy again. Citlali waved Sonya back over. This time, Puppy didn't spare her a glance beyond making eye contact as she ordered more cola and a gourmet burger with the works. Sonya tried to explain the size of the burger to Puppy, who put her hand up.

"I get that it's big, but I'm really hungry. Please bring me one with the works and then right after you bring that one, have them make me another one," Puppy said.

Sonya's brow furrowed. "Are you sure?"

Puppy laughed a little, glancing at Citlali. "I haven't eaten all day."

"Well, we have one of the finest kitchens in the city. Maybe you'd like to sample some of our new Cajun dishes," Citlali replied.

Puppy paused for a moment, as if that was tempting. "No, no, no. I like judging restaurants by their burgers."

Citlali smiled. "Then next time?"

Puppy grunted and Sonya left.

Citlali wasn't put off. Puppy intrigued her. *I wonder if I could get her to tell me her name.* "You know, you never introduced yourself."

"How did you get this job?" Puppy asked.

Citlali wasn't put off by the blatant dodge either. "My father recommended me."

"Your father works here?"

Citlali laughed. "No. He's familiar with the owner, who was complaining about never finding a good manager. Businessmen make up a good portion of our clientele. He came by when I put together my first show."

"Show?" Puppy's voice quieted, and she glanced at the stage where the performers still moaned and writhed. Her eyes snapped back to Citlali. "You put together that show?"

"Yes." Citlali watched for a reaction, but Puppy seemed intent on not looking at the stage more than anything else. Funny enough, the show was fairly tame. Some employees wanted to show off their talents by acting out positions from the *Kama Sutra*. So far, they did a decent job. She and Daphne would probably let them do it again. "My father was impressed with the creativity."

Most people didn't understand why her father would come see her shows or condone her working somewhere like The New Moon. His parenting was often questioned.

Puppy's brow furrowed. "Porn is creative, like the art on the walls."

Surprisingly, there wasn't any judgment in her statement.

"Interesting." Citlali rested her chin in her hand. "Most people would focus on my father coming to see a sex show I put together."

Puppy shrugged. "Not like you were in it, right? 'Cause that would be weird."

Citlali chuckled. *How strange.* "I was not in it."

"No offense, but your dad's weird. He got you a job at a sex club."

Ah, there was the judgment.

"To be fair, I'm the manager and I make very good money. Besides, he raised me to embrace all things sensual. He's happy I'm comfortable with sex rather than seeing it as something sinful."

"That's good." Puppy nodded. "Sex shouldn't be considered sinful. I just feel like some things are private."

Another surprising turn. "I think seeing certain things might inspire people into trying something. It could spice up a relationship or make someone see that a fantasy isn't as outrageous as it seems."

Puppy tapped her glass again. "I guess. Seems like talking to your partner could get the same effect."

Citlali tilted her head and was about to say something, but Sonya swooped back in with another soda and a beast of a hamburger. She wasn't sure how a tiny being like Puppy would finish it, but she was done by the time Sonya was back with the second burger. Somehow, the woman ate that one as well with delight in her eyes, then washed it down with more soda than Citlali would recommend. She glanced at her wrist the second she was done.

"Shit!" Puppy's eyes went wide.

"Is everything all right?" Citlali asked.

"I gotta get home. I've got a paper due and I have to meet up with my parents tomorrow morning. This morning. I wasn't supposed to be out past midnight." Puppy climbed to her feet.

Citlali smiled. "I'm glad you decided to spend your time with me. I do hope you'll come back. Maybe even give me your name."

Puppy smiled and pulled out her wallet. She dropped several bills on the table and took her leave with a mumbled farewell. Citlali chuckled as she eyed the money. Puppy left Sonya a nice tip, even though she only had two hamburgers.

"She left in a hurry," Daphne said, sliding into the empty chair.

Citlali nodded. "She had matters to tend to, but she'll be back."

Curiosity would bring Puppy back. And if not, the food would.

***

As soon as Tala got home, she sighed. Her shoulders dropped and her body deflated, finally draining of tension that had wound up every inch of her. It helped that her belly was full and, for once, not with those stupid butterflies. Despite not wanting to go to the place, she actually had a good time speaking with Citlali. She wasn't used to such a striking woman taking an interest in her and actually listening to her boring stories. She stopped at her bedroom, hand stilling on the door.

Fuck. *I didn't check on Kyra!*

Chapter Three

BARELY AN HOUR AFTER getting in from her failed mission to The New Moon, Tala sat on her sectional sofa, laptop beside her, ready to write her paper. The ticking sound of her wall clock made her face twitch. Her phone went off, and the sound made her want to scream. *Raina.* She knew that before she even looked. She didn't need this right now, but she couldn't leave Raina hanging. Unfortunately, this wasn't the type of conversation they could have over text.

"Hey, Raina," Tala said, glancing out of the window to see it was still quite dark. Well, that was good. Hopefully, the conversation wouldn't take long so she could get this paper out of the way. She just wanted to go to sleep, and it was harder to do when the birds were out being annoying and chipper.

"Good, you're still up. You went to the club?" Raina asked.

"Yeah."

There was a beat of silence. "And?"

Taking a deep breath through her nose, Tala scratched her forehead for a decent answer. Her cheeks burned, and she was thankful no one was around to see her blush. The hot musk of sex clung to her skin, even though she had showered the moment she came in. But the night wasn't a total loss—the delicious burger still haunted her tongue. *Should've taken one for the road.*

"Tala!" Raina sounded impatient.

"Uh..." Tala wasn't sure what to say. Even though she spent the whole time there talking with the manager, Citlali, she had seen more than enough of the place to dub it light years beyond a "gentlemen's club." Raina wouldn't want to hear that, even if Kyra was working in the kitchen. Hell, Tala hadn't even seen the kitchen yet, so she didn't know what went down in there. How else would she describe The New Moon? "The hamburger was really good, like Kyra said."

"Dude, you can't judge a place like that."

"It's a good way to judge a restaurant," she insisted, laughing. It hadn't failed her yet. Good burger meant good beef.

"Fine. How was Kyra?" Raina asked.

Tala held in a wince. "Uh...I couldn't find the kitchen." *Geez, you suck so hard at lying!* Still, she would rather tell a bad lie than admit to being distracted by an intriguing club worker. *She said she was the manager, but she looked better than almost all of the ladies there.* Her curvy figure worked for Tala, and the manager smelled like fresh berries and jasmine. It took a lot of effort not to lean in and fill her lungs with Citlali's scent.

"How the hell could you not find the kitchen? You're like seventy-five percent stomach and nose. Did you just stuff your face?"

"It's definitely a high quality restaurant." At least she wasn't lying there.

"Okay, fine, you are starvation personified. What was the rest of the place like? Kyra doesn't need to be around anything unsavory." Raina sounded a little panicked.

Tala rubbed the back of her neck, trying to think of something to say to ease Raina's nerves. "Oh..." *Yeah, that's not going to cut it.* Her stomach fluttered. *Don't be nervous.*

Raina huffed. "Did you even go in? You probably chickened out at the door and made up that crap about the food."

"I did go in!" Despite her anxiety, she went to that damn place for Kyra. *And then promptly forgot all about Kyra thanks to an alluring scent and some attention.* "The staff mentioned trying the new Cajun stuff, which has to be Kyra. When I ordered, the waitress made sure I knew the kitchen was the best in the city. Kyra's smart. We have to trust her to make good career choices. And I'm sure when Kyra interviewed, the place wasn't doing business, so she didn't see it being a gentlemen's club." She didn't want Raina to think Kyra lied or misled her to keep the job.

Raina grunted. "But is she around a bunch of bullshit she doesn't need to be around?"

"Probably no more than the usual kitchen bullshit." From the stories Kyra told, kitchens had way more drama than Tala would've ever expected. She hoped pharmacies didn't end up being that way. She wasn't built for drama. "I trust Kyra and you usually do, too."

Kyra and Raina were one of those gross couples who talked about everything and could swap phones for days and never see one untoward thing. Probably wouldn't even realize they had the wrong phones.

"I do trust her, but you know how she'll suffer with a decision just to avoid people seeing she's wrong. I don't want that to happen."

Tala groaned. She didn't want that to happen either. Kyra would suffer in silence if she was in a bad situation, as she'd perceive it as the consequences of her poor decisions. That was no way to live, especially when there were people who'd be there for her when she was ready to go make another, better decision.

"You're right. I'll go back." As soon as Tala offered to go back, her stomach twisted. Her throat went dry. "I mean, the place is definitely raunchier than Kyra thought."

Raina sighed. "I hope this doesn't actually screw up her resume."

Tala shook her head, even though Raina couldn't see. "I think it's probably the restaurant she thinks it is. I mean, my burger almost cost twenty bucks."

"And you had two."

"Worth it." She spent over fifty dollars on food and drinks and left almost that for a tip. She felt bad for gawking at the waitress, even though that was the point of barely wearing anything. Still, objectifying someone wasn't cool.

Raina sighed. "I really appreciate this, Tala."

"I know. We both worry about her." She would never forgive herself if something happened to her little sister.

"Thanks, though."

"No problem." They disconnected the call, and Tala dropped her phone down next to her. Her throat tightened, making it hard to breathe.

Citlali flashed through her mind. Somehow, thinking of going back to The New Moon and seeing Citlali made her feel calm. Those deep brown eyes, like thick honey, had drawn her in and set her at ease enough to make it through the night. She groaned. *It's not like she was really being your friend. She was working. Go there, check on your sister, and never look back.* That was enough to set her resolve.

✷✷✷

It always took four in the morning forever to come. Citlali fell into the nearest armchair, sinking into the plush cushions, and sighed. Daphne sat down next to her. The building was quiet, empty. Citlali let loose a yawn she had been holding in for far too long. She wanted to kick her shoes off, but that was something to do at home, not on the freshly mopped floor.

"The *Kama Sutra* show was good filler." Daphne took off her glasses to rub her eyes.

"Agreed. We'll add it to the rotation," Citlali replied. It was bland for a grand show, but for a regular night it would work as background. Perhaps spark a newbie into trying something different after seeing the positions weren't completely impossible.

Daphne gave her a grin. "You spent quite a bit of time with the puppy woman."

Citlali shrugged. "Part of the job is making sure our patrons are comfortable."

"She definitely looked like she needed handholding. Why was she here alone when she was so obviously uncomfortable?"

Citlali shook her head. "She didn't say. She was a little weird."

Daphne snorted. "No kidding."

"No, I mean beyond the deer-in-headlights look. I told her about how my father got me this job and it didn't gross her out. She didn't go into a judgmental speech or comment on it being disgusting."

"That is strange. I'd have pegged her as a prude."

Citlali leaned back in her chair. "I don't think she was a prude. She was definitely shy. It was cute."

Daphne chuckled. "Just your type."

"She was adorable. I wanted to put her in my pocket." Citlali grinned. "And the suit didn't hurt."

"Which is why you held her hand for the night."

Citlali scoffed. "If it wasn't me, it would've been you. We might not see her here in the show hall, but she seemed appreciative of the food."

"Did she have the jambalaya? I had some, and it was like heaven in my mouth. Did we hire the girl that makes it?"

"We didn't, but we can tell people we did." Citlali held up her fist and Daphne leaned over to tap hers against Citlali's.

Daphne settled back in her chair. "Whether you're joking or not, I'm totally doing that."

Citlali nodded. She wasn't joking. They needed everyone to know the head chef was an idiot, even if he occasionally made the right decision. Even a broken clock was right twice a day, meanwhile they worked their asses off and everyone just expected miracles pulled from those asses all the time. "Are you ready to go? It's been a long night."

"It always is. I feel like we're forgetting something. Staff meeting?"

"Tomorrow before we open." While the restaurant was open from noon, the showroom did not open until nine at night. "We checked all the rooms. Cleaning staff's here. We should be good."

Daphne nodded. "It's time to go."

Citlali rolled her neck then climbed to her feet. They exited The New Moon to be bathed in the oranges and yellows of the coming morning. Joggers headed toward the boardwalk, but aside from them, the streets were quiet. The New Moon parking lot was empty. They strolled to their matching cars.

"One day when we hit it rich, maybe we'll buy different cars," Daphne teased.

"I blame you. You're the one who corrupted me," Citlali replied.

Daphne was two years older. Growing up, Daphne influenced everything about Citlali, and it was clear in how she was as an adult. While they liked different colors and styles, they both wore suits. They wore similar makeup, even though their complexions were different. It used to frustrate Citlali to no end that she couldn't do her hair like Daphne's, but she tried anyway. And failed some more. Now she accepted and loved her straight black hair.

"Text when you get home."

"You text."

Daphne scoffed. "I'm home before you. Obey your elders."

Citlali laughed. They hopped in their small sedans—powder blue for her and yellow for Daphne—and went on their way. The ride home took a little less than twenty minutes, and she enjoyed every moment of the smooth drive. She even got to listen to mellow neo soul. It was a nice switch from the heavy music at The New Moon.

Parking her car in front of her modern apartment building, she stretched, eyeing the many boutiques that lined the streets. Her trendy neighborhood never failed to make her happy. It inspired her to be trendy as well.

Entering the top floor apartment, the calming scent of lemongrass greeted her. She stepped out of her shoes and sighed, feet tingling and thankful to be free. Meandering through her apartment, she passed the kitchen and hall closet, and then went by the bathroom door to her bedroom. She glanced at her queen-sized bed, every part of her longing to sink into its lush covers.

"I'll be right back," she said, heading to the bathroom instead.

Citlali took a long, hot shower and tossed herself into her bed. As she drifted off to sleep, odd, pale eyes floated through her mind.

***

Tala was incredulous that she was at The New Moon for the second time in one week, but here she was. *This better be good for Kyra's career or I'm never speaking to her again.* But then again, she'd be the one to suffer if she never spoke to Kyra again. At the least, she'd starve to death and, at most, she'd go insane from loneliness. It wasn't like she had other friends, or a desire to have other friends. *Damn, I hope Kyra's all right in there.*

Tala's nerves trembled and her stomach crunched in on itself. *No, none of that. You got this. For Kyra.* She took a deep breath and marched to the front door. She paused, only for the bouncer to nod her in. *Great, they remember me at the crazy sex club.* That didn't sit well with her, but she made sure every ounce of her screamed "back the fuck up!" She had a lot of practice at that, pushing her anxiety down under a mask of gruff confidence.

Even though the lobby was busy, no one came close to her. Even the lobby seemed like a show—people milling about, eating their meals, and enjoying drink like they didn't know that behind the double doors performers had sex for an audience. *Did that woman put this show together, too?* She shook the thought away. She was here for Kyra, so she needed to find the kitchen. Unfortunately, the kitchen was through the sex hall, at the back of the building from what Kyra said.

"Hi." The same guy manning the desk from before smiled. He might as well have been a hotel concierge rather than the literal gatekeeper for live porn. After showing her ID, he waved her in. "Your outfit looks even more amazing today. Total badass." He made an "okay" sign with his long fingers.

Tala arched her eyebrow. *Is he making fun of me?* She dressed herself tonight and had on black leather pants, a light blue short-sleeve shirt, and her leather jacket.

"Thank you," she replied, trying to keep her confidence high.

As soon as she made her way through the wooden double doors, the bass hummed through her. She focused on the music to block the moaning and screaming of the show, but nothing could block the overwhelming scent. The thick musk went straight for her nose and clawed its way to her brain. Not even the cigar smoke could cover it up. For the first time in her life, she wished that she was in a regular strip club. *It's really that bad where I'm having weird thoughts like that?* There was too much sensory information.

Under the music, she could still hear the moaning of the performers. It assaulted her mind, combining with the heady smell of sex, ruining her thoughts. To save her peace of mind, she tried again to concentrate on the other din, like the discussions around her. So much sex talk. Her face burned as all sorts of sordid bits reached her ears. The conversations even set her on edge.

Focus. You're here for Kyra. Taking a breath, Tala decided that following her nose would probably be best, needing to fight down the show's invasion of her nasal cavity. She wandered as far away from the stage as she could to get away from the tang of sex and arousal, and finally she got what she needed. Steak. Spices. Chocolate. *Food.* She dipped and dodged through the crowd and then caught sight of obsidian hair.

"You're back!" Citlali smiled as she slid in front of Tala. Her honey brown eyes sparkled, like she was actually happy to see Tala.

No, don't be fooled by the pretty face. This is her job and she probably just wants to make sure you tip her this time. The dazzling smile made her want to reconsider, but while she was a lot of things, stupid wasn't among them.

"I'm so glad you decided to grace us with your presence again." Citlali clasped her hands together in front of her mouth. Her eyes glinted. She was dressed in a red suit with a black shirt and pink tie. For a split second, the crazy thought of touching silky hair went through Tala's head.

"Yeah." Tala fought the urge to back up. She never consciously gave ground if she could help it, especially when she was sure she was being teased. Well, the tone suggested taunting, but didn't quite match the look in those beautiful eyes. *Beautiful, really? You're about to lose your shit over a little bit of attention? Pathetic.* She should want to sink into the floor right now from all this attention, but curiously, she didn't mind so much from Citlali.

Citlali pouted. A hint of disappointment flashed in her eyes. "You don't seem happy to see me tonight. I suppose we won't be able to continue our conversation."

Tala rubbed the back of her neck, not sure what to do with that disappointment. Citlali seemed to want her company, and it seemed like it was for more than a tip. *This just gets weirder and weirder.* "I have something I need to do."

Yeah, do it and then get the hell out of here before any of these smells become tattooed on my brain. She'd have to wash her hair for days from the smoke alone.

Citlali's dark brows wrinkled. "Something to do?"

Tala winced. *Probably shouldn't have said that.* She wasn't the best liar, and if she got hit with enough questions she'd spill the whole mission. Citlali probably wouldn't let her wander into the kitchen. Feeling trapped, she rubbed her sweaty palms against her pants. Citlali reached out and took Tala's hand with both of hers. It took all of Tala's self-control not to flee the scene and never come back. *I'll have to move across the country after this. Probably change my name, too.*

"What do you need?" Citlali asked in a patient voice, like she cared, like she might help.

Tala took a deep breath, hoping it'd settle her. *Don't try to lie. You'll just make it worse.* "I'm supposed to check on my friend."

Citlali blinked. "You have a friend who works here? I suppose that explains your attitude."

That sounded like an insult, but Citlali's thoughtful expression didn't imply that. "What do you mean?"

"Oh, just that you're not judgmental about the situation. Who's your friend?" Citlali scanned the area. Her eyes drifted toward the stage, but wisely shook that away. Tala would never, ever go someplace knowing a friend would end up fucked in front of an audience. Some things were just private.

Citlali didn't seem put off by Tala's admission, so might as well keep going. "She works in the kitchen. Kyra Mogollon."

Citlali's eyes widened. "The new girl who does Cajun food. It's quite popular in the lobby. That might have to do with spices." She tapped her chin as if she had never considered it until now. "Around here, people tend to want to avoid extra spicy foods, but they still order her dishes."

Hell yeah. Tala preened. "She cooks really well, doesn't she?"

Citlali arched an eyebrow. "Is she your girlfriend? Oh, what name did she write down?"

Tala grunted. "Not mine. She's got a girlfriend named Raina."

Citlali thought about it for a moment and then nodded. "Ah, that does sound familiar."

It seemed odd that Citlali would remember that about a new staff member. *What the hell does a manager do exactly?* "You interviewed her?" Seemed like the best time to ask.

A hint of mischief sparkled on her lips. "Maybe I'll tell you and even take you to her if you tell me something in exchange."

Tala scrunched her face up. *It's not like I'm someone of any kind of importance.* "What do you want to know?"

Citlali smiled. "Your name would be a nice start."

Tala chuckled. "Wow, you're reaching."

"Well, it seemed to be a closely guarded secret." Citlali winked.

"I'm Tala." She held out her hand, hoping the extra politeness would get her a little closer to her goal.

"Tala. Lovely name." Citlali went silent for a moment, like she was appreciating the information. "All right, let's go see your friend."

Tala's mouth fell open. "It's that easy?" *It can't be.* She spent too much time agonizing over having to do this, imagining all the ways it could go wrong, imagining all the ways someone would try to stop her. Her hackles went up. If it was that easy, something bad had to be coming. She learned that lesson often in her young life. *This is what happens when you let a pretty face distract you. You're about to be pranked or something.*

Citlali shrugged. "She's a chef and you're not her significant other. There's not much of a problem, unless you plan to start drama." Citlali looked her up and down. "And you don't seem like the drama type."

"Nope," Tala replied. "Hate drama."

Citlali beamed, pressing her hands together. "Perfect."

She allowed Citlali to tug her through the crowd to a small corridor, then passed a man standing guard. Once in the hall, the crispy, warm scent of freshly baked bread hit Tala. At the end of the hall, they came to two swinging doors and were almost mowed down by a barely dressed waitress. She offered a quick, mumbled apology, more at Citlali, not that Tala cared. Citlali waved the server off and everyone continued on their way.

The swinging doors opened to a bustling kitchen. A beehive of activity covered in white and stainless steel. Tala gawked at the meals being put together. Steak and pork, fish stew, the wafting of roasted vegetables as a chef opened a nearby oven. *Well, this is heaven. Can she just leave me here?* Tala would pay good money to just stand here whenever she felt overwhelmed with life.

Even though it seemed like chaos, the kitchen was clean, tidy, and everything had its place. Hell, there was a chef making bread. *Handmade bread. That explains why the burger bun was so good. And a fully clothed chef!* Everyone in here was fully clothed, in fact, and Tala felt another knot loosen in her chest.

Tala did her best to avoid drooling. *That would not be cool.* And the woman standing next to her wouldn't be impressed, either.

She had little problem spotting Kyra, busy stirring a large pot. Her white chef's jacket had a few orange-red stains on the side, and a burn mark decorated her pants, but she was there, fully clothed, in her element, and probably happy as hell.

Perfect! Now time to go. Tala stepped back and almost tripped over Citlali.

"Sorry," Tala said.

"Do you want to speak with her?" Citlali asked.

"No, no, no. She's happy. And professional. Plus, I don't want her to know I was checking on her. She'd be super pissed." Her stomach folded over itself as she thought about Kyra yelling at her for doing this. Then she'd get yelled at for feeding into Raina's paranoia.

"Very well." Citlali led her back into the corridor. "It's sweet that you were worried about her."

Tala frowned. "She won't think it's sweet. She'll literally bite my head off if she finds out. I mean, how would you feel if your friend came to check up on you?"

"She did." Citlali chuckled. "I helped get her a job here."

Tala did a double-take. "Wait, what?"

"Yes." They emerged from the corridor. "We've known each other for my entire life, so this was very much in her wheelhouse."

Tala smiled. "I've known Kyra her entire life. She's basically my sister and, yeah, this is in her wheelhouse, too."

"Perhaps you'd like to try her food as prepared in our kitchen."

Tala was set to decline. She really didn't want to be there longer than necessary, but her stomach growled. Her metabolism never ceased to get her in trouble. *I burn way too much energy for someone who doesn't move around a lot. It's almost a curse, which is what regular people would think.* That was enough for her to hesitate and give Citlali an opening.

"I'm sure you've had Kyra's cooking many times, but not made in our kitchen with the finest ingredients," Citlali continued, giving her an encouraging smile.

That was true enough, so Tala found herself following Citlali to a table like a faithful puppy, wondering if her stomach was about to get her into trouble once again.

Chapter Four

CITLALI SAT ACROSS FROM Tala at one of the small tables in the back. The moans from the show and the cigar smoke were both less pungent here. The way Tala jumped into her butter steak bits with mixed rice, peppers, black beans, and asparagus told Citlali the way to her heart was through her stomach. The woman would most certainly visit the restaurant section, and that was enough for her. A customer was a customer no matter what part of the establishment they patronized. *Although, I won't see her again if she goes to the restaurant section.* A sinking feeling shot through her.

"Kyra must use you for all of her experiments, huh?" Citlali said, shaking herself out of the strange feeling.

Tala smiled, flushed with her cheeks stuffed with rice. It would probably help business greatly if she could put Tala's face on a poster as an ad proclaiming the wonders of The New Moon's kitchen.

"Yeah, I've always been her lab rat, but it pays off," Tala replied with a light in her eyes. Citlali was captivated by the twinkle there, like sunlight glinting through thick frost. Tala continued, "There's also the good feeling of helping my friend achieve her dream. She's always wanted to be a chef." Tala chased her statement with a big gulp of cola.

Citlali nodded. "I'm glad we snagged her before some lesser place wasted her talent."

"You never did say if you interviewed her."

"No, I didn't have that pleasure, but I'm familiar with our entire staff."

Tala was quiet for a moment, studying her, trying to size her up. She took a deep breath. "Is it really good for her to be working in a sex club, though?"

Not wanting to offend Tala, Citlali held in a chuckle. "We are so much more than a sex club. Yes, sex is a part of it, but it gives a unique flavor to the place. I promise you, everything here is top notch, and it's recognized all over the world. After us, she'll be able to go anywhere and it'll be a respected credit on her resume."

"And what about you?" Tala asked, twisting her fork so the asparagus and peppers mingled together. "Can you go anywhere you want?"

Citlali leaned against the table. "If all goes to plan, I won't need to worry about being hired. I'm hoping to open some place similar to this." She and Daphne still had to calculate a complete business plan, but they liked most of the things they did at The New Moon. They just needed to sit down and hammer out all the details. She couldn't wait.

Tala tilted her head, like a confused puppy. "You're going to turn into the competition? Some thanks."

Citlali chuckled. "If my mother taught me anything it'd that there are no friends in business. Besides, I've always felt like being on the boardwalk and casinos gives the place a bit of seediness, even if it's at the more expensive end of the boardwalk."

Tala scoffed. "Just because the hookers over here charge more doesn't make this the good end of the boardwalk."

That was unexpected. Citlali settled back into her seat. "Ouch. Do you have something against sex workers?"

"Sorry." Tala sighed. "I don't mean to sound like an ass. I don't have a problem with sex workers. I just think sex should be done privately, like smoking." She looked around, face falling into a deadpan. The joke landed awkwardly, but she was cute.

"I'm going to assume you don't smoke." Unlike half of her patrons.

Tala frowned. "It smells and gets everywhere and harms others who aren't doing it."

Citlali nodded. "All valid. So, what do you do?" She glanced at the empty plate in front of Tala. "Beyond eating."

Tala rested her elbow on the table and leaned into her hand. "Sorry. Guess I was hungrier than I thought."

Citlali waved over a server to take the plate and ordered another serving for Tala, as well as another soda. Tala lit up. Citlali fought down a smile. *Good thing this is work, or someone might think you're on a date.* Tala wouldn't be that someone; Citlali had a feeling the woman was quite oblivious to certain things. "So, you were saying what you do."

Tala blew out a breath and glanced away. Small talk probably killed her. Citlali would change the subject if she was silent long enough. Their conversation had gotten awkward, and she didn't want to make this experience any more uncomfortable for Tala.

"Right now, I'm just a college student. I'm studying to be a compound pharmacist," Tala replied.

Citlali blinked. She'd been expecting a lot of answers, but that wasn't one. Hell, that wasn't in the top one hundred from a person wearing leather pants like she'd been poured into them. It was rare, but she didn't know what to say. "I was not expecting that."

Tala smirked. "I'm sure that's how people feel when you tell them you manage a sex club."

Citlali laughed. "It doesn't come up as often as you'd think. My mother, business genius that she is, isn't sure it's the best business model."

Tala looked around. "Looks pretty packed to me."

Citlali shrugged. There was a sizable crowd there. Tonight's show was a tier above filler. It wasn't something they advertised or had to book people weeks in advance for, but people would check the website to find out when it was being done again and show up to see it a second time, or at least tell their friends about this show.

"Yes, but we've made some changes since coming aboard, and she's always too busy to come back." Citlali waved it off. "I'm well supported otherwise."

"It's good to have support."

"Like what you're doing for Kyra?"

Tala scratched her cheek. "Sneaking in here to check on her isn't really support. Hell, my first time in here wasn't really supportive either, even though she wanted me to see the place."

"Maybe she wanted your approval. Have you given it?"

Tala shrugged. "I've taken to downplaying what happens here to her girlfriend. Does that count?"

"You're not against Kyra, which I'm sure helps. You're not trying to shame her for working here."

Tala nodded. "I guess." Another helping of steak tips was brought before her. She gave it a fleeting glance, then looked at Citlali, shifting in her seat.

People probably made Tala feel self-conscious about how much she ate, even though it shouldn't be a problem. Tala had the body of a sprinter. *Bet she's got stamina, too.*

Citlali tried to put the dirty thoughts out of her mind. "Please, eat. And tell me more about being a compound pharmacist."

"I feel bad that you're not eating, too."

That would definitely be more of a date, which Citlali usually wouldn't mind. She wasn't really hungry, and she didn't have to play into a fantasy to get Tala's attention. *I doubt many of her fantasies have to do with sitting in a sex club.*

"I'm not terribly hungry. Usually when I eat while I'm on duty, it's to play into a fantasy. Is that what you'd want?" Citlali replied.

"Not really. Still, it just wouldn't feel as weird." Tala hunched over some.

"Maybe I shouldn't have ordered you another helping?"

"No, no, no!" Tala held up her hands. "I appreciate that actually. I'm hungry."

"Then don't let my lack of food stop you. If it makes you feel any better, I could go for a drink." She did a lot of talking through the night, so water and juice were always appreciated.

Tala nodded and Citlali wasted no time getting a virgin piña colada. With her drink in front of her, Citlali motioned to Tala's plate again, and she eventually picked up her fork and began eating. Their conversation turned to her schooling, and how she needed to prepare for her finals.

"I do not miss those days," Citlali said.

Tala scratched the bridge of her nose and glanced away for a second. "It's annoying, but I kinda like it."

And Citlali believed that.

Tala's face brightened as she talked about school and how busy she was, her passion obvious. It was like talking to an artist, or a doctor. *Beautiful.*

***

Tala hadn't expected to spend the whole night out. It wasn't the best use of her time, considering she had class in the morning and another paper due, but she didn't regret it. Looking back, she had a good time chatting with Citlali. She sighed as she stepped into her apartment. She didn't even bother to turn the lights on. It wasn't like she needed them.

She could actually taste the difference working in The New Moon had on Kyra's cooking. There was an underlying spice in everything that gave it extra life. If a couple of weeks could do that, what could a year do? *Looks like I'll be lying to Raina for a while.*

She hated that it was such a big deal, but the second she told Raina there was sex in the club, Raina would get worried. But Kyra wasn't taking her clothes off, and that shouldn't be a problem if they discussed it beforehand. Kyra didn't seem to be around anything unsavory. *Why are you trying to make sense of it? You have work to do.*

She peeled herself out of her leather pants, and would've loved to brag to Kyra that she dressed herself and looked pretty good. After hopping in the shower, she tossed herself into her messy, full-sized bed. The firm mattress was a godsend. She fell face-first into a fluffy pillow covered in wonderful satin. Her eyes drifted shut.

Class was in the afternoon, but she still would only get a few hours of sleep. Papers wouldn't write themselves, after all. And then the phone rang.

Damn it, Raina.

She groaned. "Yes, Raina?"

"Well?" She huffed into the phone, like she'd been made to wait. "Was she okay?"

Tala shifted onto her side. "I get that you're worried, but you're still being damn rude."

Raina had the good sense to yelp. "Sorry about that. Um...was she okay?"

Better than me, falling for stupid tricks. Citlali outright told her that she dealt in fantasy and Tala still found herself thinking about the woman. *But she was helpful, and thanks to her I can honestly answer this question.* "Kyra's happy. She's tucked away in the kitchen. I think this'll be good for her."

"Good for her? It's a strip club!"

Tala yawned and then rubbed her eyes. "It treats sex as entertainment, but it's not the same. Other than that, it seems to be what Kyra said it is."

"How does it treat sex as entertainment and not be a strip club?"

"I guess it's more like performance art meets porn. It's not gross or anything. There's nudity and sex, but for a show. It doesn't have a strip club's culture." *I can't even believe I said this phrase out loud.*

Raina was quiet for a long moment. "Did they get to your antisocial ass? You're practically endorsing them."

Tala growled into the phone as her blood boiled. "I'm not antisocial. There's just not a bunch of people I want to be around for long periods of time." It was fine. She was fine. *There's nothing wrong with wanting to be left alone.*

"But those people's asses are fine."

Tala wanted to snap at Raina, but with her actual teeth. Hard to do over the phone. "You're being an ass and a prime example of why I don't like to be around a bunch of people." Fuck people and their ungrateful asses. While she didn't have anything against Raina, she tolerated her presence for Kyra more often than not. "Remind me to never do you a favor."

"Sorry!" Raina sighed. "Sorry. I really appreciate you checking on Kyra. I'm happy you're there for her."

"I'm happy you're there for her, too." It wasn't a lie. Kyra deserved all the love and support, but destiny liked squatting on people. It could be worse, but she didn't want to go down that road. "Look, she's fine. I promise. And I gotta go. I've got class in a few hours."

"Okay. Thank you again."

Tala made a noise of acceptance and disconnected the call. She buried her head in her pillow, closing her eyes. As she faded from consciousness, a pair of honey eyes drifted across her mind. *She bewitched me. How bothersome.*

***

A few weeks had gone by, and Citlali glanced at the doors as one opened. Her heart jumped, but quickly deflated as she saw it was only a club regular. She fought down disappointment, but not fast enough.

"Waiting for your date, huh?" Daphne asked, pulling her into a dance with a teasing grin. Somehow, her dark lipstick made it even more taunting.

Damn. Citlali rolled her eyes and stepped out of Daphne's grasp. "She's not a date. Just a customer."

"A customer you were on a date with the last time she was here. It's nothing to be ashamed of." Daphne walked around her, circling like a predator. An old dance of theirs. "After all, to quote you, wasn't she smart and looking after her friend, and her ass looked good enough to eat in those leather pants?"

She had said all of that. She wished Daphne didn't throw it back in her face like that. *What's the matter with me? Tala's a customer, nothing more. Why would I bother talking about her enough for Daphne to remember? Well, beyond the fact that her ass looked absolutely delicious in those pants.*

With a chuckle, Daphne slapped her shoulder. "Relax, Li. You said she was complaining about papers and finals and things. That's probably why your little puppy hasn't returned. I get that you like her and all, but stop watching the door."

Citlali groaned. "Could you please just stop talking?"

"I could, but I don't want to. This is how people feel talking to you, just so you know."

Citlali had no doubt about that. There were times when she was purposely annoying, like Daphne was right now. It was terrible to be on the teasing end, though.

"At least you have good taste. That hair is awesome, but isn't she too young for you?" Daphne nudged her with a pointy, naked elbow.

Citlali stepped away from Daphne. "Stop acting like I'm ancient."

Daphne grinned. "Is it an act? You're one digit off from your late twenties while she could possibly still be a teenager."

"You're in your late twenties and I've seen you in action."

Daphne laughed even more. "They come onto me because of my youthful appearance."

Citlali curled her lip and turned away from Daphne. She was in no mood for this, and might even need to check herself the next time she brought such nonsense to someone. She turned her attention back to the door, even though it would only bring more teasing. *What the hell am I doing?*

And then the door opened and her heart jumped. Tala stepped inside, looking as gorgeous as she did the other two times she visited the club.

Tala had on a red plaid long vest, but it only had two buttons, one across her breasts and another below. It gave a good view of a muscled abdomen. Citlali would lick honey off of that slit of golden brown skin. Suspenders hung from her waist, highlighting her brown pants and red Oxford shoes. And then Tala smiled at her, small and cute. It didn't go with the outfit, but it worked with Tala's demeanor. Tala gave her a shy wave.

"Hey, Citlali," Tala said as Citlali approached her.

Citlali managed to contain herself, even though she couldn't believe what she was seeing. *Is she here for me?* "Tala, I didn't expect to see you back."

Tala shrugged. "I got grades back today and I wanted to treat myself."

Treat herself with food, not with me, Citlali told herself. *But maybe, just maybe, Tala liked the company.*

"Well, I am delighted to see you again. What sort of treat did you have in mind?" Citlali gave a playful smirk.

Tala went stiff for a second. "Just dinner. Usually Kyra makes me something to celebrate the end of the madness, but she worked tonight."

"She could've taken tonight off to celebrate with you," Citlali replied lightly.

Tala shook her head. "I told her no. She's new. She shouldn't be taking days for me. Besides, I could come here and have a meal made by her just as easy as at home."

"That's thoughtful of you."

"I guess. I didn't think it was a big deal."

Citlali nodded and led Tala to a table most people wouldn't want. There were two lush plants near it that almost blocked the whole stage. If Tala positioned herself right, she wouldn't have to see any of the show. She pulled out the chair for Tala.

"Thanks, but you didn't have to." Tala sat down.

Citlali smiled. "You deserve it if you survived the semester. I'll send a server your way."

Tala hunched over, her expression dropping. "Aren't you staying to eat?"

Citlali had to swallow. All of her attention was meant to bring customers back, but they came back for the shows and the flirting. *But Tala wants me around to just stay and eat?*

"I can sit with you." Citlali eased into the chair across from Tala.

Tala put both hands up. "You don't have to! I'm just used to sharing this time with someone."

A ping radiated in Citlali's chest. Perhaps Tala wanted a friend after trying to look out for Kyra's best interest. And Tala deemed her worthy enough to take Kyra's place. Tala hadn't seemed to buy into the magic of The New Moon. She looked at Citlali and saw a person. Citlali looked at Tala as not just a customer, but perhaps an acquaintance.

"It's fine." Citlali smiled. "Is everyone else working?"

Tala shrugged. "I don't really have an 'everyone,' but yeah, they're all busy today." Her pout was heartbreaking, like that of someone who wished that someone else would make time for her, even if she insisted they didn't have to.

Citlali couldn't imagine no one being able to make it out to celebrate with Tala. "Well, no one should celebrate alone. I'll eat with you. Do you want the steak bites again or a hamburger?"

Tala blinked. "You remembered." It wasn't a question. It was amazement.

Citlali giggled. "It's actually a little hard to forget, you ate much more than I'd expect from someone of your height."

Tala glanced away and gnawed the inside of her cheek. "I have a high metabolism."

"Well, let's get you fed and watered. Do you drink to celebrate the end of the term?"

"Just beer."

"Oh, we have amazing craft beers." Citlali went into sales pitch mode. She couldn't help it. She loved helping people find items they would like in the club. Tala didn't seem to mind, nodding the whole time.

Citlali ordered beers, wanting to show solidarity in the celebration, and food for herself and Tala. "So, school's over?"

"Yup." Tala stretched her arms out across the table, flashing her a grin. "I finally get to play video games and maybe work on my motorcycle."

Because of course she had a motorcycle. *Is this a test? Dump the world's cutest lesbian in front of me and see how professional I can remain?*

"What's your workload like?" Citlali asked.

"Mostly papers. I like reading, and I do want to be a pharmacist, so it's not that hard," Tala replied, gaze cutting to the side as a group of patrons hooted with laughter. She shifted in her chair. Maybe it was crowds that bothered her. The woman was a mystery Citlali wanted to figure out.

Their drinks and food came, and Tala sipped her beer. She made a sound like a squeal. "It's so good!"

"I'm glad you like it." Citlali sipped her own drink, the beer tart just like she liked it.

"Do you get to taste all of the stuff here to know what to recommend?"

"It's not as fun as it sounds."

"Work puts a sense of duty on things that lessens the fun factor."

Citlali couldn't believe the insight. "True. So, you were saying about your classes..."

Tala launched into her class list, and Citlali listened as she enjoyed her creamy shrimp and pasta. She was used to hearing about people's careers. It was part of her job, but Tala spoke differently. She wasn't jaded or arrogant. Tala was a breath of fresh air.

"I never would've thought there'd be someone so interested in pharmaceutical work," Citlali said. She had never heard of a compound pharmacist until Tala, but the more Tala spoke on it, the more it made sense. Everyone couldn't take the same thing all the time, not food, not drink, so why wouldn't drugs need to be specially made for some people?

Tala looked down for a moment, cheeks growing darker. "I'm sorry. I've been talking all this time, haven't I?"

Citlali laughed. "I'm fine with listening. You seem like you really want to help people and you want to do good. Your enthusiasm has me hooked."

Tala gave a little shrug. "Well, yeah. I like the idea of making medicines for people who can't take the mass-produced ones, but really, I just like puzzles."

Citlali nodded. "And here I thought you only liked video games."

"Oh, I play strategy games, puzzle games, and when I'm not doing that, I tinker with my bike. I used to do that when I had a pedal bike."

"So, you've been at it since you were little?"

A half-smile ticked onto Tala's round face. "Yup. I think I get it from both parents. What about you? I remember you saying your dad came here to see your show and your mom's a businesswoman."

Citlali smiled. "You remembered."

Tala grinned and it stayed that time, her eyes sparkling.

And then in a flash everything about Tala shifted, transformed. The smile became a snarl. The sparkle turned to fire. Her eyes darkened. She looked...dangerous.

Citlali's heart raced. Her chest tightened. Why had Tala changed so drastically?

"Citlali!" a much too familiar voice called out, and it was then Citlali realized Tala's glare was beyond her, not at her. Citlali turned to see Ruby Quills grinning at her. Citlali held in a groan. *I really don't need this right now.* She never needed Ruby.

Chapter Five

TALA COULDN'T CONTROL HER scowl as she watched the newcomer approach. Citlali rose, standing before a clearly younger woman dressed in a short, crimson dress. She had curves in all the right places with auburn red hair done to cover part of her face in an alluring manner. Batting her cat-like cerulean eyes like a pro, the woman went in for an embrace, which Citlali gave. Tala growled, but the newcomer didn't seem to notice her. *Why the hell am I so angry?*

A scent of rose water wafted from the redhead, but something lingered underneath that. It burned like the worst spice. Like sulfur stuck to her tongue. *She smells like fire, danger and evil.* Tala wanted to drag Citlali away.

"Ruby." Citlali's voice was soft, along with her smile, but the expression didn't reach her eyes. A professional mask.

"I'm so glad to see you, Citlali." Ruby pressed herself against Citlali, shoving her balloon breasts against Citlali's side. Citlali winced imperceptibly.

Mine! Tala had to take a breath to remain calm, but it felt like barbed wire had tightened around her lungs. *Cool off.* It wasn't her place to say or do anything. Citlali was working. Still, Tala's blood rushed in her ears, her heart pumping harder than it should for someone sitting in a chair.

"Lali, you have to come sit with me. We'll catch up." Ruby nuzzled Citlali.

"Ruby, I'm currently with someone." Citlali's face twitched, but her smile remained. She glanced at Tala and gave her a true grin. Her eyes twinkled. The expression made Tala's stomach flip, but it didn't cut through the razor's edge brought on by Ruby.

Ruby seemed to notice Tala for the first time, dismissing her with a roll of her eyes. "Lali is all mine whenever I come here. We're gonna go to one of the private rooms." She giggled, an obvious cross between a ditz and a schemer, and pushed herself even closer.

Tala understood the implications, and she wasn't going to let anyone—customer or not—take Citlali from her. *Mine!* She was more than ready to tear Ruby's arms off of her to get her away from Citlali.

Tala couldn't comprehend her all-consuming rage. It was like her fury committed scorched Earth on every good feeling she had working for her just a moment ago. *Why do I want to rip this stranger limb from limb?* Her blood boiled, burning every inch of her. Her bones roared with savagery and her muscles ached with indignation, like her body was about to tear into itself. Her eyes remained locked on Ruby and she could practically feel them bleeding with outrage.

Instincts howled inside her, calling forth the beast within. She clutched the table, barely feeling her nails cutting grooves into the polished wood. She wanted to fling the furniture across the room, but shot to her feet instead.

Ruby laughed, probably because she almost towered over Tala's five foot tall frame. It didn't matter. Not many were taller than she was when she laid them out on the floor, and she had done that to plenty of people who wanted to antagonize or underestimate her. She'd have no problem doing it to someone who tried to take what was hers. *What is wrong with you? Citlali isn't yours. You're her job, just like Ruby is her job.*

Tala took a breath. Her body went from volcanic to flat. Deflated like her frame was shorter, but it didn't last long, fire still lapping at her nerves. "I gotta go!" She bolted, going for the nearest exit, not caring about the neon fire exit sign above the door.

"Tala, wait!" She heard Citlali's cry over the fire alarm, but didn't stop. She needed to get out of there before she did something stupid. Warm air slapped her face when she burst out into the street.

Tala could barely breathe. Her blood buzzed and felt like it might fire out into the atmosphere through her skin. She kept walking, streets populated with happy college students making plans for summer now that they were free. She felt chained, gripped, and crushed by a strange powerful force inside of her. *The hell is this kind of reaction?* She'd been jealous before, sure, but this...this rage was something else. Whatever this intense reaction was, it was ready to explode outward. Sweat soaked her body and she actively fought down the urge to gnash her teeth.

"Holy shit! I almost completely lost it. And for what? A stranger claiming a woman I'm not even involved with? The fuck is wrong with me!" Tala bit her lip, felt hot blood drip down her chin. She wiped it away. The sharp pain should've calmed her, but anxiety gnawed holes in her belly. She ducked into an alley and away from prying eyes, doing her best to breathe. "It's okay. You're okay. It's okay."

She slammed her back into the wall. Her heart raced. Her chest tightened, like there were boulders on her torso. No matter how much air she managed to get in, it didn't feel like enough. She rubbed her hands against her pants. Her clothes stuck to her skin.

Tala stared at her hands, veins bulging and nails sharp. There was no chance she'd calm down enough to stop this. "I need to get out of here."

Pushing off the wall, she ran to her bike. She had to twist and turn more than she liked, forgetful of where she parked. Focusing was too difficult. She damn near fell over her motorcycle once she found it. Once she mounted her bike, her new goal was staying upright until she got home. Somehow, she managed.

She ran at top speed to her apartment, taking the stairs rather than waiting for the elevator, and once inside, yanked out of her clothes. The fabric ripped. Throwing herself into an ice cold shower, she pressed against the cold tiles, willing herself to calm. Forcing herself to be calm. The anger subsided. *You're such an idiot. Everybody's right about you.*

***

Citlali didn't even see Tala when she rushed after her. The night was unforgiving, too many people crowded the streets. *What the hell are you doing? You have an heiress customer you left to chase after someone who only came for the food.* Deep in her heart, she knew that wasn't true. Tala was sharing a moment with her and now it was gone.

But she couldn't do anything about it.

With a sigh, Citlali went back inside to find Daphne assuring everyone the high-pitched noise screaming from the fire exit wasn't something to worry about.

"Someone just went out of the wrong exit. Carry on!" Daphne said over the loudspeaker. The alarm stopped, and gradually everyone went back to their business. The music hummed, just loud enough for people to be able to claim they couldn't hear someone several feet away.

"Citlali!" Ruby appeared at her side, both arms wrapping around her arm.

Citlali bit back some choice words, slipping away from Ruby's grip. "I've told you about clinging."

"But I want to cling to you!" Ruby grinned and put herself into Citlali's space. Their arms touched. "You'll like it. I promise."

Citlali's shoulders dropped a bit before she caught it. It was her job to keep the customers happy, even if the customer was a spoiled brat who didn't understand the concept of "no." *Actually, that's a lot of our customers.* "Let me get you a table."

"And have a drink with me!"

"You know I can't drink on the job." Hopefully, Ruby wouldn't notice her half drained beer glass from her table with Tala. "There are so many servers who delight in seeing you. Come." Citlali began walking away, but Daphne suddenly blocked her path.

"Thank goodness I found you." Daphne wiped her brow. "Chef is having a meltdown and you know I'm not dealing with that guy!"

Citlali laughed. *This woman is a gift from God!* She owed Daphne big time, and always did when she rescued Citlali from Ruby. "I'll go. Will you take care of Ruby? Treat her well." She patted Ruby on the shoulder. For almost any other customer, she'd have given more physical contact to push the idea they were special. She wouldn't dare with Ruby.

"I'll take the best care of one of our favorites." Daphne fell to Ruby's side.

Citlali rushed in the direction of the kitchen. After all, she needed to pretend to go put out a fire. She passed the table she and Tala had occupied. It hadn't been cleared yet. She wouldn't have thought anything of it, but then she noticed deep grooves by Tala's plate. Arching an eyebrow, she took a closer look.

Four deep scratch marks ran down the wood on either side of Tala's plate. She ran a finger along the grove closest to her, the shortest of those four. *Did Tala do this?* She couldn't figure out how Tala could have. *Did she have a screwdriver?* While she could imagine Tala carrying a weapon, she couldn't imagine Tala defacing property. *But do I really know her?*

Tala had come here to celebrate ending the semester and wanted company. Tala had chosen her to spend that moment with and Ruby came to spoil it, as she spoiled many things. *Does this mean anything?* She wasn't sure.

She shook that away and moved on to keep looking busy. While she trusted Daphne would keep Ruby from her, she didn't want to give the redhead an opening. Ruby was willing to pour out money like it was water, but she didn't understand there was a high level of fantasy here. She also seemed to believe her money could get her anything, including things that weren't for sale.

Citlali heard a shout and went to save one of their dancers from a grabby patron.

Tai, a young danger, struggled out of the patron's lap and spun, quickly smoothing her sparkly pink dress. "You have no right to do that," she shouted.

Citlali swooped in between Tai and the man. He stood eye to eye with Citlali, even in her heels, but she held her ground.

"Doctor Miller, I'm sure Tai didn't mean to offend you," Citlali said quietly, knowing full well that telling someone 'no' shouldn't offend anyone.

"She's lucky I'm willing to pay for a private dance," the doctor replied, straightening his black tie and lifting his chin.

No one was allowed to take privileges with any staff in the club, and they needed to know that. "I'm sure you understand that every single employee in this building, every person in here, has a right to their own body. She's decided hers is on a 'look-don't-touch' basis, as many dancers and servers are." She gave him a hard look. "You know the rules."

He scowled. "I pay a lot of money—" She couldn't let him finish. She hated the "I paid for it" speech.

Citlali held up a hand. "Doctor, you pay for the show, food, and drinks. You can pay other dancers who are open to it for a private dance, but if they say no, you can't buy them against their will. That's called slavery."

He narrowed his blue eyes, pointing at Tai. "I just want her."

His words made her blood boil. "The show is art, the dancers are art, and the service staff don't mind being eye candy. Anything beyond looking requires consent. Take your money to a strip club or the internet. It's not welcomed here anymore." She waved over a bouncer. The doctor was removed before he could sputter anything else. Citlali turned her attention to the doctor's small party, a man and two women. "I'm sorry to have interrupted your evening."

The older brunette woman held up her hand. "It's fine. He had too much to drink. Even we couldn't settle him down."

Citlali appreciated their candor. "Your next round of drinks are on the house should you decide to stay."

"Of course we're staying." The brunette woman smiled.

Citlali nodded. "Very good." She turned to Tai, touching her elbow to direct her away from the table. They went to a corner. "Are you all right? Do you need the rest of the night off?"

Tai's eyes went wide. "Are you firing me?"

Citlali reeled back. *Is that what the staff thinks of me?* She had never fired anyone over being harassed. "Of course not! You have every right to say no to a private dance. I hope no one's made you think otherwise. I certainly hope I've never done anything to make you think otherwise."

Tai shook her head. "No, no, no. You're great. Thank you for having my back over there."

"Always." Citlali squeezed Tai's arm. "Now, I have to circulate. Are you sure you're all right? Do you want to go home?"

Tai took a deep breath. "I'm fine."

"Good. I'll set up another server for that table."

Tai sighed. "Thank you, but I think I'll be okay over there now that he's gone."

Citlali nodded and stalked away. She then had to go save Bobby from a drunken patron who was trying to blow him as he cleared a table. Weariness crept into her bones. *It's going to be one of these nights.* An hour and three fires later, she let her guard down, and Ruby was at her side again.

"Ruby, I'm working," Citlali said, trying to ease her limb out of Ruby's iron grip.

Ruby pressed herself close, breasts against Citlali's arm. Citlali had never been more turned off by tits in her life. Ruby pouted, matted red lips poked out. "But you've made time for everyone except me."

"I'm working." Sometimes, she was certain Ruby had a disconnect with reality. She saw Citlali interacting with people and seemed to think she was spending quality time with them. Quality time meant to be spent with her.

Ruby's face dropped even more. "Then have breakfast with me once the night is over. We could eat, stroll the boardwalk, and then get a nice room down at *the Mer*."

Citlali held in a groan. "I'm not a fan of *the Mer*."

It was an expensive hotel where people bragged about their wealth without saying a word, and she wasn't interested. More so, she needed Ruby to understand she couldn't be bought. Money didn't impress her.

Ruby batted her eyes. "It really is ordinary, isn't it? The one in Paris is so much better. We should go experience that one together. Well, that and all of Paris. It would be magical."

"I have work. Excuse me." Citlali rushed off to put out another figurative fire. Daphne intercepted Ruby so she couldn't follow. What an irksome night.

***

Tala sat in her beanbag chair in front of her television, game controller in her hand, but she couldn't focus on the game, couldn't even bother to look at the screen, staring at the blank white wall behind it instead. Her stomach folded, gaze dropping to her hands. Something was off. Her hands seemed like someone else's. She flung the controller away. The remote shattered against the wall, but she didn't flinch.

"It's like you've got no damn control now," she muttered. It was like she might vibrate out of her skin. Snatching her phone up, she dialed the only person she trusted to give her counsel.

A groan came through the speaker. "Hello?"

"Hi, Mama." Tala sounded embarrassed to her own ears, so she could only imagine how she sounded to her mother.

"Tala, are you all right?" The sound of her shifting, sheets rustling about, came through the line.

"Nothing's wrong, Ma." The last thing she wanted was for her mother to rush to her over this. Well, she didn't really want her mother to rush to her point blank.

"Tala." Her mother's voice took on a stern edge. "It's three in the morning. What's wrong?"

"I'm just a little off balance." She took a breath. *Just tell her. She could help.* "I almost lost control in a room full of people."

Her mother made a noise like a squeal and a grunt mixed together. "Oh. And?"

Tala gnawed her bottom lip. "Because of a girl."

A girl who probably didn't even like her. Her throat burned, and she wished she could just vanish. *You're such an Idiot, like they always said.*

"Ah," her mother said.

"Look at my pup landing girls!" her father's voice filtered over the line now.

Tala went stiff. "Ma, why the hell is Dad there?" He shouldn't be there.

"Do you really want to know?" her mother asked.

Tala curled her lip. "Nope."

Her mother chuckled. "I thought as much. Now, Rocky, shut up."

"What? I should be able to advise my daughter when she picks up pretty girls," her father complained.

"Dad, you've never given me good advice on girls," Tala said.

Ever since he noticed she was attracted to women, he was nothing but terrible words on how to lay ladies. How he managed to get her mother, possibly the smartest woman Tala ever met, was the greatest mystery of her life.

"Hold on." More shuffling noises, then silence. "Okay, I'm in the living room, and he's not because he doesn't want to risk waking your grandmother."

Tala groaned, rubbing her face. Grandma would tear him apart for his trespass. "He shouldn't be in the house in the first place."

"That's neither here nor there. Now, the good news is you didn't lose it. You have control. Holding back that first time is always the hardest. It was unexpected and you were emotional, but you reined it in before anything happened. Or is that not what you're worried over?"

Tala sighed and rubbed her face with one hand. "I'm not sure. My emotions were all over the place, and I felt like I wanted to claim her, but I barely know her!" It was like she had no idea who she was anymore. She rubbed her eye with the heel of her hand. "I'm just not sure what happened, Mama. Was I jealous because another girl was claiming her? Do I see her as property or something like that?"

She was accustomed to the rest of the world not understanding her, but Tala generally knew what she wanted in life. With Citlali, things were different. She wasn't really attracted to people in this way. Usually, she just wanted to be left alone.

"Of course you don't see her as property, sweetheart. That's not who you are. Have you talked enough to work it out on your own?"

Tala blew out a breath, tried to relax. The tightness in her stomach eased. No, she didn't think she owned Citlali, but there was a bond forming, or one already there. *Can't be there, not this fast. I don't bond like that.* She was weird, after all.

"Yeah, Mama. I'll work it out." She was capable of sorting this madness out, and if not, her mother would be there for her. Hell, her father, too, with all of his bad advice. At least she was old enough now to realize to do the opposite of what her father said. His heart was in the right place, but he didn't realize they weren't the same.

"Always the lone wolf, huh, sweetheart?"

"Ma!" Her mother said it with fondness, but it still tore a hole in her heart. Her mental illness was the biggest insult growing up. Her mother tried to help her reclaim it, but it would never endear itself to her.

Her mother chuckled. "Maybe that'll change, though."

The hope in her mother's voice pinged in her chest. Her mother deserved a bit of normalcy in her life after getting stuck with her and her father. *Or maybe you're looking too deep into this and Mama is teasing you like she likes to do.* It was probably the latter.

"Ma!" Tala groaned. "Can you just go back to sleep?"

"I look forward to meeting her. I'm sure your father does, too."

"And why the hell is Dad there? You should know better, Ma." She should've made a video call, so her mother could see her reprimanding face.

"While I appreciate the scolding from my extremely undersexed child, I think I'll make my own adult decisions."

Tala felt like her face would burn off from her blush. "Goodbye, Ma."

"I do hope she's a nice girl."

Tala slumped back onto her beanbag chair. "We're not even friends."

"Then why did you lose control?" She could hear the damn smirk on her mother's face.

"Because I'm an idiot and she was practically being molested!" That made sense. Ruby was all but dry humping Citlali, and Citlali didn't seem too into it. She wanted to protect Citlali from a predator.

"It sounds like you want to be friends and more."

Tala grunted. "Goodbye, Ma."

"Have a good night, sweetheart."

"You, too, Ma. And tell Dad goodnight and tell him to not be a jerk and make you breakfast in the morning or else I'll make him regret it."

Her mother laughed. "You do give better advice than he does. I'll be sure to pass that along. Love you."

"Love you, too." They disconnected the call.

Tala sank into the beanbag, feeling even more unsettled than before. It sucked to think there was a savage inside of her that wanted to possess Citlali. She had wanted to believe a hero was inside of her, one that wanted to protect Citlali. Her mother seemed to think there was something more than even that. *More than friends?* She scoffed. *Yeah, right.* Citlali only saw her as a customer and nothing more.

"Just enjoy having some time with the games before summer starts, and I've got more work to worry about." She got her spare controller and went back to what usually brought her joy. Her heart wasn't in it.

She wanted to sink into herself, but fought down that feeling. There were times when she wondered which parent she inherited this gnawing sensation from, but she didn't have time for that. It wouldn't help to know, anyway.

***

Citlali found herself watching the doors for the main hall. When Daphne called her on it, she didn't even bother to deny it. She was waiting for Tala. She hadn't seen her since the incident with Ruby and that had been over a week ago. She was tempted to go ask Kyra about her friend, but that would start too much trouble for both of them. *Besides, what if Tala doesn't want to hear from me?* She didn't want to risk upsetting Tala more so than she already was.

Citlali wasn't sure where the strange desire to see Tala came from. She wanted to apologize for Ruby, but truth be told, Citlali had enjoyed Tala's company and then Ruby had ruined that. Now Citlali might never see Tala again, and her heart ached over that.

She placed two fingers to her shirt, right over her heart, and massaged the area. *Why do I feel this way?* The thought of not seeing Tala actually pained her. Bothered her in more ways than one.

"I don't understand why she's so under my skin," Citlali whispered. "She doesn't care about the show, but she keeps showing up here. Which is odd."

Daphne chuckled. "She's coming here for you, obviously."

Citlali had played with that idea, but couldn't turn it over in her mind. Tala wasn't one to give into the fantasy, not like Ruby. *Is that what fascinates me?* Tala understood what this place was and wasn't into it, yet she kept coming back. *For me.*

"You always bewitch the strangest people," Daphne said.

Citlali arched an eyebrow. "Unlike you, who bewitches everyone."

"Which means I've failed you." Daphne put her hand to her forehead and pretended to faint. She then danced away, grinning.

Sighing, Citlali moved to get some work done. It was foolish to think Tala came to the club for her. Daphne swooped back in, draping herself over Citlali's shoulders.

"Are you trying to drive me insane?" Citlali asked, shrugging her off.

Daphne linked her hands behind her back. "Do you think more people come here for the food or our shows? I know some people think of the show as live porn, but some people also think serving hamburgers is low brow."

"Is there a point?" Citlali glowered at her. "We have work to do."

Daphne snickered. "Well, a customer requested a table that made it hard to see the show. Weird, eh?"

Citlali perked up, turning to see the table.

And there was Tala, sitting hunched over, like she wasn't sure she was doing the right thing. She looked cute. *Such a puppy.*

"Go get her." Daphne slapped her on the ass.

Citlali yelped, but it got her moving. She'd have to thank Daphne even more later.

Chapter Six

TALA FOLDED HER HANDS. *Why the hell did I do this?* Usually, it would never occur to her to subject herself to crowds and loud noises, but here she was, wanting a glimpse of a woman who probably thought she was weird.

"Is this seat taken?" Citlali asked.

Tala opened her mouth then closed it. *Just once, don't be awkward.* She motioned to the chair across from her. *Shit, that felt awkward.*

Citlali eased into the chair. "Good to see you again, Tala. More steak bites?"

Tala managed a breath, but damn her stomach. It was like her insides all wanted to fold into each other. Her heart probably couldn't beat any faster without bursting in her chest. *How long have I been sitting here looking at her? Answer her!*

Tala licked her lips. "I was thinking of something different this time."

Citlali laughed, and it was both music and daggers. Tala didn't know if she was being laughed at or not. It didn't seem that way, though, but now that her brain had melted into a puddle of confusion the world was on a tilt in a bad way.

"With the way you eat, you might bankrupt yourself eating here. How will you afford school books?" Citlali asked, the light in her eyes setting Tala at ease. She wasn't being taunted.

Tala grinned. "Books are damn expensive."

Citlali nodded. "I do not miss that."

"How long have you been out of school?"

"A few years. I was able to pick up my masters and bachelors in a five-year program that also allowed me to double major. How many more years do you have to go?"

Tala shrugged. "A few. I gotta get my doctorate and interning and junk like that. I applied for an internship and should hear about it soon enough."

Citlali smiled, warm and bright. "Do you have plans on working in a pharmacy, or running your own?"

"My own. I'm bad with people and would probably end up fired, anyway." Tala chuckled. *No! Don't say that or she'll think you're bad with her! Wait, what does that even mean? Shut up!* "Oh, do you want to eat?" *She works here, idiot! This isn't a date.* Tala could feel herself sweating through her black shirt.

Citlali held up a finger. "I'm going to have the kitchen make you something special. It's not on the menu, but I want it. I have to do my rounds first."

Tala's face burned with shame. "Of course!" *Why the hell did I think this was a good idea?*

Citlali put her hand on Tala's shoulder. It was a simple, soothing touch. "I really want to see you try this dish, so I'll be right back."

Tala blinked. *She wants to see me enjoy it?* Of course, her stomach flared up and her throat burned. It took everything in her not to fidget. Taking a breath, she counted slowly to ten in her head.

"I'll be here," Tala said.

"Good." Citlali stood there for a long moment before walking away.

Barely ten seconds later, a glass of cola was placed in front of her. The server smiled, but it only made Tala want to sink into the floor. She mumbled a thanks the waitress probably didn't hear. *You could've stayed home, played games, and pretended she didn't exist.* Instead, she took a chance, which caused a different kind of gnawing sensation in her stomach. Maybe it wasn't just Citlali's job. Besides, she should check on Citlali, in case that awful woman came back.

Her gaze fell right to the marks she left in the table. They had been filled and colored, but she could see the subtle difference between the original finish and the fresh paint. Before she could think anything else, food was eased in front of her, blocking her view. Tons of food. Her eyes went to the waitress.

The waitress smiled. "I'm not sure if Citlali warned you that it's spicy."

Tala shook her head. "It's fine. I can do spicy."

"Good. It's a Mexican stew`, but spiced like it was meant to melt your face. I don't know why they make it so hot. They do it to the Indian dishes here, too. We serve it with a side of plain yogurt."

Tala managed a smile. "Thanks for the warning."

The waitress nodded and left her with two steaming plates and a bowl of stew. There was a tall, creamy drink as well, which she couldn't smell any alcohol on. Everything else smelled like beef and spice and her mouth watered. Time to eat.

***

Citlali rubbed her eyes. *How the hell did I manage to sit down with her three times?* It was like she couldn't catch her breath tonight. Customers and staff alike were acting out, like no one had any common sense anymore. In between, she saw Tala sitting at her table, focused on her food. *Does she like it?* Hopefully, the place wouldn't literally burn down while she stole a couple of minutes.

"How are you enjoying it?" Citlali asked as she eased into the chair across from Tala.

"It's so good! How have I gone all my life not eating this before?" Tala's eyes actually sparkled and those odd bursts of color in her blue eyes looked like fireworks.

"I tired to get it added to the menu once. I had to bribe one of the cooks to introduce it to the head chef because he hates me and Daphne."

Tala reared back slightly. "Hates you? Why?" Bless her. She asked it like it was impossible.

Citlali shrugged. "He thinks this place is the food. We think this place is the shows." Tala might help her reconsider, though.

Tala pursed her lips. "Can't it be both?" She ate a bit more. "Why'd you go for these Mexican dishes?"

"My abuela used to make them. I think hers was better, and I wish you could try it, but she's passed." Citlali missed the woman every day.

"Do you make it?" Tala asked.

Citlali couldn't help being taken aback by that. "I do actually. Maybe I could..." She swallowed, brain catching up to her mouth, but she decided to press on. Sometimes, it was best to go with impulses. "Make it for you sometime?"

Tala's face, a warm russet already, burned a bright red. "I'd like that."

Citlali's heart leaped. "I'm going to work a little more, all right?"

Tala nibbled on her bottom lip, and it would've been sexy if only she meant it that way. Instead, it displayed her nervousness in a way she probably didn't mean to broadcast. "I don't want to take time from your job."

"It's all right. I'm not usually this busy." *Liar.*

Citlali went back to work. Every now and then, she glanced over to see Tala still there, scrunched up in her seat. At one point, she arranged for dessert to be brought to Tala. At another, she looked over to see the chair empty. Tala was gone. Citlali's insides dropped. *Well, what do you expect? You don't have time for her, and she's not an asshole who demands to be noticed.* She wouldn't want Tala to wait for her.

The night pressed on, and they locked up. As they stepped into the parking lot, Citlali stopped. Tala stood by the gate, hands in her pockets, shy smile tugging at her lips. Daphne patted Citlali on the shoulder.

"Go get that girl before I do, because she is damn fine. And please make sure you tell her I dig the braid mohawk," Daphne said.

She didn't have to tell Citlali twice. "See you tomorrow." Citlali approached Tala with her most practiced sexy walk. She had never been so self-conscious about her swagger before, but from the blush creeping up Tala's face, Citlali had to nail it.

"Sorry if this is creepy," Tala said with a shrug.

Citlali shook her head. "It's all right. You haven't been out here all night, have you?"

"No. I asked when you guys close up, so I went home and came back. I didn't want to keep bothering you at work."

"It's fine." *Liar.*

"So...I know it's late for you, but you wanna go for a walk on the boardwalk or something?" She scratched the back of her head.

"Sounds wonderful." From anyone else, it would've sounded boring. She had turned down offers like this before, but usually they came from patrons who didn't understand the word "no." Beyond that, she was touched Tala had considered what a hassle it was for her to try to spend time with Tala and handle her managerial duties at the same time.

Daphne drove up and honked. "Get it, ladies!" She cackled as she sped off.

Poor Tala's face flushed so dark, she was almost the same color as a brick. Citlali fought down a smile. *Adorable.* She was such a tiny thing dressed like a badass, but blushed at the drop of a hat.

"I'm sorry about Daphne. She's always a pain," Citlali said, taking her hand.

Tala glanced at her feet, but didn't pull away. "It's okay."

"Let's go to the boardwalk." If they managed to hold out for an hour, they could watch the sunrise together.

***

Tala was certain her heart would explode when Citlali held her hand. Usually, she didn't like when people touched her. With Citlali, it wasn't that bad. That meant she was comfortable with Citlali. How had that happened? *Stop wondering about stupid stuff and talk to the damn girl before she ditches you.*

"I know it's not everyone's ideal date to go on an early morning stroll in the dark after working all night," Tala said as she started toward the boardwalk.

"I don't mind. I wanted to spend time with you, and that's hard to do at work," Citlali replied.

A light brightened inside her as they walked up the ramp to the boardwalk. "I'm glad you want to spend time with me. I want that, too. So...the Mexican food was really spicy, but in the best of ways. You said your grandmother used to make it?"

Tala resisted the urge to focus on the passing lampposts on the boardwalk. The quiet waves of the early morning helped distract her. A few drunken idiots staggered around, and some had friends trying to wrangle them, but it wasn't out of the ordinary. *If you don't look at her, at least look ahead. You're interested in her and you need to let her know.*

"Yes, my abuela. She was the family chef until she had a couple of strokes. She used to cook for every major holiday, even ones she only did because of my dad."

That was a weird phrase. "What do you mean?"

"Oh, so my father is Chinese and my mother is Mexican. They met in college. They got paired together on a project and were just always together after that. They loved learning about each other's cultures, and my abuela always tried to fit in stuff from my dad's culture when she could. It was nice. I'm sorry, I've gotten off track."

Tala smiled as they passed several closed food stands. "No, please. Talk. I like listening. I'm much better at it." *Why did I say that? It was weird.*

Citlali squeezed her hand again. "Yeah, well, my father came here for a student exchange program. For him, so much was about trying to fit in, but my abuela liked making sure people were comfortable. The moment she learned about any Chinese holidays he celebrated, she cooked, even though we spent those holidays with his family, who emigrated by the time I was born. She'd probably still do it if she were alive, even though my parents separated."

Tala gasped. "What? No. It sounded like they had a cool love story going."

Citlali laughed, briefly overpowered by gull cries in the already hot morning. "I'm sure they still love each other since they haven't gotten a divorce, but they haven't lived together for about fifteen years. They both date, but it's never been serious."

It reminded Tala a little of her parents. "What happened?"

Citlali's face scrunched up. "I just don't think they offered the support they both needed. I also think my mother's more ambitious than my father, and he didn't know how to deal with it."

Tala wasn't quite sure what to say. Citlali didn't seem broken up about it and her parents seemed to be a source of pride. Sometimes, being apart was the best thing, but she still went with what she thought a "normal" person would say. "Oh, I'm sorry."

Citlali snorted and waved that off with her free hand. "Don't be. I've come to understand this was for the best. When I was younger, it bothered me, but the fighting stopped, the yelling stopped. I think they learned how to be better parents. I used to spend so many odd hours with my grandparents. I didn't know it at the time, but it was because my parents were fighting."

Tala nodded. It was good Citlali understood it worked out for the better. "Did they share custody?"

Citlali shook her head. "My father had primary custody, but he made sure I saw my mother and her family as often as possible. They worked it out that way. My mother wanted to focus on her career. When I was younger, I thought I ruined her life."

Tala gasped. "No!" Sometimes, she felt the same way about her mother.

Citlali glanced at her. There was such a spark in her eyes that it was easy to tell things were all right. "She squashed that as quickly as she could. She made sure I understood that what happened between them had nothing to do with me. It was their inability to work together. They both always made me understand marriage is hard and they couldn't rise to the occasion. They work well together now. I think it bothers them that they can't make a marriage work because they're both high achieving, like, to ridiculous levels."

Tala rubbed Citlali's knuckles with her thumb. "So, that's where you get it from."

"Yes. What about you?" Citlali asked, voice lilting, engaged.

"I'm not like either of my parents." Tala took a breath, her stomach flipping. *It's okay. Simple conversation. You can do this. She's not going to make fun of you and this isn't a trick. She talked about her parents, now you talk about yours. Where would I start? Fuck. I should've practiced this at home.* Panic closed her throat, and she took another breath. Started again. "They're really good with people and I'm, well, me. I'm usually happy with not having to interact with people. I'm bad at it."

Citlali nudged her shoulder. "You're doing fine now. Everyone has levels to how much they're willing to deal with people."

"You seem really good at it."

Citlali smiled. "I might be good at dealing with people, but I'm not dying for company outside of work."

Shit! Tala gawked at her. "Oh...um..." *You should've just let her go home.*

Citlali chuckled. "I am enjoying this company outside of work, Tala."

Tala blushed. "Noted." *How did she know I needed to hear that?* Citlali cared enough to try to figure her out. Not many made the effort.

"So, how about you tell me how you're similar to your parents?"

Tala squinted as she looked ahead of her. She needed something to help this make sense. Then it hit her. "You ever been to the arcade? It's right next to the fair." She pointed ahead of them. The fair was a decent walk away, but the motionless roller coaster and equally still Ferris wheel were in sight.

Citlali nodded. "I know where you're talking about."

"Me and my dad used to spend a lot of time at the arcade well into my teens. We played the racing games a lot."

"So, you get your love of gaming from him?"

"Yeah, he's a big kid. He's also a mechanic."

"And the reason you ride a motorcycle and tinker with your motorcycle."

He really was. "He always had bikes when I was growing up. He liked taking me to work and letting me tinker with stuff. I've always been into building stuff. Or making stuff." Tala rubbed her forehead. "I'm sorry if I'm not making any sense."

Citlali nudged her again, lightly. "You're doing fine. Take your time," she said, a gentleness to her voice that made Tala more confident.

"My mom's a doctor. She's all about fixing people. My dad's all about fixing cars. I was like that with everything. They bought me models, anatomy, cars, and stuff like that, and I'd focus all my attention on those until I was done."

"Do you still do models?"

"I haven't in a long time. Maybe I'll do models again once I'm done with school." It would be nice. She could focus on her anatomy models without someone laughing at her, like when she was little. All of the pups thinking she was weird for wanting to be by herself, all of the adults saying she was crazy, and it only made her want to be alone all the more. She would probably always hear the insults, echoing in the back of her mind, but she also knew every part of the hand, and she was okay with that.

Citlali nodded. "It might depend on how hard you're going to work. I only realized once I was done with school how much time I actually had. Which is to say, not much outside of work."

Tala's muscles clenched. Was Citlali saying time was precious and she was wasting it with Tala...or that her time was precious and she was gifting it to Tala? *Would she dare once she gets to know me better?*

"What do you do with your spare time?" Tala asked to get out of her own head. She inhaled, hoping the salty sea air would somehow reboot her brain.

Citlali snickered. "Walk with cute girls on the boardwalk."

Cute girls. Other girls. Tala's throat burned, like she might throw up. *Why did I think this was a good idea?*

Citlali squeezed her hand. "Are you all right?"

"I should go!" She wasn't sure why she said that, but running sounded like the best idea.

Citlali stopped walking, but didn't let go of Tala's hand. "I thought we were enjoying ourselves."

Tala pressed her hand to her chest. "I am, but I don't want to waste your time."

Citlali arched an eyebrow. "You're not wasting my time. I like being with you. I thought my comment about walking with cute girls made that clear."

Tala couldn't stop her mouth from dropping open. "You meant me?"

"Of course I meant you!" Citlali eyed her, blatantly looking her up and down. "Do you not realize how cute you are?"

A blush burned her cheeks. "I'm...not."

"Oh, darling, you very much are. I'm enjoying my time with you, so don't think otherwise, and please relax. I like you."

Tala couldn't help standing up taller, and everything inside of her howled with pride. Citlali liked her! She was doing something right. But...now she had to keep it up. *She said relax. Don't wear yourself out trying so hard.*

"I was hoping we could stay out long enough to watch the sunrise. Is that all right?" Citlali asked.

This beautiful, intelligent woman wanted to spend time with her, was willing to put up with her weirdness. Accepted her, sort of.

"Can I buy you breakfast after?" Tala took a chance. She had never done this before.

"If I can get your phone number at some point." Citlali winked at her.

"Okay." She squeaked, like a mouse. *Damn, she makes you a mouse. Be stronger. You're strong.*

Citlali's eyes sparkled and Tala relaxed. She could do this.

Chapter Seven

CITLALI FELT LIKE SHE floated into her apartment. Delirious from a good morning, beautiful scenery, delicious food, and a lovely companion. She had asked Tala's permission to kiss her at the end. Just thinking about Tala's blush put a smile on Citlali's face. It was almost as wonderful as the gentle peck they shared.

"Oh!" That reminded her. She pulled out her phone. She'd bet her right arm Tala was a texter. **I made it home,** Citlali texted. Tala had wanted to know if she got home all right. It was sweet.

Tala's response was almost immediate. **I'm glad!**

Citlali smiled and kicked out of her shoes. If her feet could sigh with happiness, they would. Those shoes were amazing, but people weren't meant to be on their feet for twenty hours. **Now, I'm going to take a hot shower and fall into bed.**

Me, too.

I'll text you later. She'd have to take the initiative for communication. Tala seemed to think she was a bother every single time she opened her mouth. People were missing out on a wealth of knowledge and probably a good friend, but then again, lots of people were assholes, and Tala shouldn't have to put up with that.

Citlali went to take a hot shower, and collapsed in her bed wearing nothing but a long t-shirt. Tala was cute, so she decided to be cute herself. She positioned herself against her pillows and flipped her hair, looking at herself using her phone. *It'll have to do without makeup, but I feel like she'll appreciate the natural look*. She took a few shots, not exposing any skin beyond her shoulder. She blew a kiss in one selfie and then winked in the other. While Tala seemed all right with sex in the abstract, Citlali wasn't sure about how much she liked it personalized.

She sent those off and put her phone down on the nightstand on its charger. Exhaustion pulled at her. Morning light poured into her room—bathing the space in gentle pinks and yellows—and she should pull the curtains closed, but she just wanted to sleep. Crawling under her sheets, she closed her eyes. Her phone buzzed. *Tala?* Her whole body sagged. It was Daphne. She was tempted to ignore the call, but her friend would just keep calling. Incessantly. She answered the video call.

Daphne's smiling face appeared. "Aw, no! You're clothed and alone."

"Of course! I'm not going to answer a call from you if I'm otherwise occupied in bed, you perv."

Daphne laughed. "You say that now, but one day, you'll have such boring sex, answering a call from me will be a million times better."

Citlali snorted and propped herself up on her elbow, turning on the light by her bed stand. "Those were high school and undergrad problems."

She didn't want to think about those days. At least she got to learn what she liked. Hopefully, her former partners had that chance as well.

"I can imagine." Daphne winked. "So, how was your date?"

Citlali didn't even bother to hide her smile. "I enjoyed it. It was so simple. We talked as we walked on the boardwalk, watched the sky change color as the sun rose, and she treated me to breakfast." Tala had insisted on paying because she ate so much. Of course, she had blushed when she had offered. Citlali had all but melted. *I've got a weakness with her already.*

"Sounds sweet, yet you're going to bed alone."

"I think she's at least a 'three dates' type of girl." That didn't bother Citlali.

"Is she worth it?"

"I think so. She's cute and sweet. She didn't think my parents were weird for being separated for fifteen years, but still married. Which is impressive, actually." She was used to being on the receiving end of strange looks whenever that information came up and out.

Daphne gave her a knowing look. "Well, I wish you luck. I'm sure you'll have to put some work in."

"I don't mind." Citlali looked forward to finding out what made Tala tick. What she found out so far was enough to keep her digging, because things didn't seem to go together. Someone who dressed like a badass and carried herself like one while also being frightfully bashful.

"See you tonight."

"See you later." She disconnected the call right before she yawned. She opened her thread with Tala and wrote something to go with the pictures. **Don't overthink the pics. Reply however you feel or tell me not to do stuff like this, but please reply.**

With that said, she was about to put the phone down, but dots popped up. An incoming message.

You're beautiful. More dots. **I don't take good pictures.**

It was nice Tala texted in full sentences, since most of the time Citlali did the same.

It's okay. Citlali smiled. **I'll take enough pics for both of us. Time to sleep.** She took a selfie of her blowing another kiss. **Goodnight.**

Have a good sleep.

Text when you wake up. I'll get back to you when I can.

Okay. And she sent a kissy face emoji. *Damn, she's adorable. I don't stand a chance.*

***

Tala didn't believe she had the courage to send that kissy face emoji, but the world didn't end. She was surprised at her boldness with the way butterflies had filled her chest after she got home. The pictures Citlali sent weren't risqué by far, but she didn't know how to react until Citlali sent her that reassuring text. Sleep took her soon after their conversation.

When she woke up, the sun was in her face from the window, drawing a miserable moan. She had forgotten to draw the blinds. Whatever. She reached for her phone, wanting to get in touch with Citlali again. *But wouldn't that be lame? You just talked to her five hours ago.* She didn't want to mess things up.

She heard a noise, like someone setting a pan down on the stove. Leaping out of bed, she moved to the door, opened it. "Kyra! What are you doing here?"

Kyra moved about the kitchen like she owned it. She basically did. Almost everything in it was hers, except the bowls. Kyra grinned. She seemed light and carefree, dressed in Raina's sweats and Tala's college t-shirt. One Tala only bought because she knew Kyra would steal it.

"It's been a while. You must've been starving," Kyra replied as she went back to preparing a meaty stew. Beef, from the smell of it. Spices hung in the air, teasing her senses.

Tala grunted, pulling up a chair to the counter that separated the kitchen from the living room. "I've just been eating out more."

"Oh, wow." Her golden eyes went wide. "Do you still have money left?"

"Yes!" She was good enough with her finances that she saved enough to treat herself every now and then, but over the past month, she had been so loose with her money there wouldn't be much treating herself in the future.

Kyra gave her an amused smirk. "So, it's been all ramen then."

"No!" It would've been that if Kyra disappeared for a month and she didn't feel like going outside.

"Come on, Tala. You eat enough for three people. You either have no money now or you have a sugar mama."

Tala sucked her teeth. "Or I spend wisely. Mom takes that into consideration." She got an allowance from her mother to make sure she didn't have to worry about money while she was in school, and her father paid her tuition. "What are you making?"

"Beef stew, so you can save some for tomorrow." Kyra clapped her hands, staring around the kitchen. "I've actually learned how to make it better, and I brought more supplies." She motioned to a tote bag on the counter and moved over to it.

Tala left Kyra to do her cooking and dropped onto the couch. She grabbed her laptop, wanting to check to see if her grades were up and hoping to hear word on an internship. It should've been a sure thing considering her grades were always stellar, but the pharmacist in charge didn't like her much.

Shaking her head, Tala decided not to worry about it. Things were going pretty good, so she didn't want to mess up the nice vibes. Shutting the laptop, she went to get her phone instead. She swallowed as she opened the message thread, scrolling up for the pictures. Her stomach lurched and a blush burned her face.

She really sent me pictures of her in bed. No girl had ever done such a thing. Women didn't usually go out of their way to entice her, mostly because of how shy she was. They tended to think she was prudish. Tala wouldn't have thought she'd like something like the pictures, because she didn't think pictures would do anything for her. She'd much rather have someone in person, scent being sexier than visuals to her, but she liked the pictures a lot. *I want more.*

Should I send a picture? She tapped her chin in thought. She didn't typically take pictures, especially of herself. Citlali didn't ask for pictures, either, didn't pressure her to change. It was a wonderful change of pace.

"Hello!"

Tala jumped. "I'm sorry." *I forgot Kyra was here!*

Kyra tilted her head. "You okay?"

Tala shrugged. "Yeah, just checking my messages. What happened?"

"I was asking you if you wanted to watch some of our show while I'm here." It had been quite a while since they had just lounged around together.

Tala chuckled. "Raina must be working."

Kyra made an offended sort of yowl. "Don't start! I'm here. Can we please watch the show?"

Grinning, Tala set up the medical drama show, then settled on the couch again, legs tucked underneath herself. *What can I do that's like the pictures, but not pictures?* She wasn't sure there was such a response. *There's gotta be something.*

A few minutes later, Kyra joined her on the couch with a pan of beef nachos with the works. Tala's stomach growled and Kyra laughed. Tala wasn't self-conscious about it. Kyra knew how she was and knew why.

"The way you eat, you'd think you were an alpha or something." Kyra snickered.

"If only there was such a thing. I might've been able to get everyone to leave me alone sooner," Tala replied.

"If it makes you feel any better, you were an alpha to me until I was a teenager."

Tala scoffed. "I'm still an alpha to you."

"You want root beer, or something else?" Kyra asked with a chuckle.

"Root beer's good." Tala inhaled the nachos, enjoying the smell, and then her mouth was full. Thick, warm spices burst over her tongue, and she moaned. "Dude, these are better than ever!" A thought flashed through her mind and she snapped a picture. Citlali knew she was all about food, so she'd reinforce that. It could be funny.

Kyra fetched their drinks. She placed them on the coffee table, on coasters because they weren't complete savages, before she flopped down on the sofa again. "Guy at work traded recipes with me. I gave him my stuffed peppers and he did beef nachos. I improved it, of course."

"As you do. You are the best little sister I could've found on the side of the road!" Tala grinned.

Kyra punched her hard in the shoulder. "Shut up or I'll never make anything for you ever again. My work friends have tons of recipes you've never even heard of."

Such a valid threat. "How do you like work?" Tala asked. They might finish the food before they got to the show, but she needed to catch up with Kyra. It was important to hear from Kyra's own lips how amazing The New Moon was.

Kyra's entire face lit up and she sat up straighter. "I love it! I've learned so much in a month! Almost all of my coworkers are awesome."

Tala frowned, facing Kyra now instead of the nachos. "Almost? You need me to go up there?" Nobody was going to trouble Kyra if she had anything to say about it. Not now. Not ever.

Kyra rubbed her thigh. "Calm down. I'm not a tiny cub anymore that needs you to fight my battles. I've worked in enough kitchens to know there'll always be assholes. I like it." She looked Tala in the eye. "I really like it."

Tala nodded. "I'm glad."

Kyra sat back and had a nacho before Tala's greedy ass ate the entire platter. "Thanks."

Tala arched an eyebrow. "For what?"

Kyra bumped her with her shoulder. "I know there's more to The New Moon than just being a great restaurant. Thanks for not telling Raina. She'd worry."

"I know she would. She's a good one." Raina wouldn't ask Kyra to quit, but she'd drive herself crazy over the idea that Kyra ruined her career by accident. "But you deserve to work somewhere that's the best."

Kyra grinned. "You agree with me?"

"You're a talented chef." Tala looked Kyra dead in the eye. She needed Kyra to know she meant every word. "You deserve the best. If I didn't think that place was the real deal in restaurants, I'd tell you. I still can't believe some place like that is such a good restaurant. I mean, how?"

Kyra shrugged. "I think it was a sex place at first, and then the owner hired a couple of good chefs and word got around. Did you see the show when you came?"

Tala turned her nose up. "It was gross."

"Like live porn?"

Tala thought about it. "Not that bad. It was artsy, but it's still gross. Rutting shouldn't be a show."

Kyra chuckled, but didn't argue. They watched their show and finished the nachos. After an episode, Kyra got up and plated a meal for them, then brought those to the coffee table. Stew on one side, rice with black beans on the other, split in half like two hemispheres. Kyra then brought over buttered bread. Tala leaned down to breathe it all in.

"Let me put everything in the fridge and then we'll get back to it," Kyra said.

Tala nodded and snapped another picture of her meal. She sent it. **I'm jealous of whoever's feeding you.**

The quick response sent a jolt through her system. A winking emoji followed the words.

She quickly typed a reply. **You don't want to have to pay to feed this beast.** As soon as she hit send, her stomach sank. *Well, shit.* Her words weren't really a joke. She was going to ruin this one way or another. A text message seemed like the appropriate way to destroy her world.

I knew the job was dangerous when I took it, came the response.

It was meant to be funny, she knew that, but her throat tightened. Kyra sat back down before she could respond.

***

Citlali smiled as she looked at the food pictures Tala sent. Even without saying, she got that was Tala's response to her pictures. It was funny. And while it might seem weird, she figured this was Tala's way of inviting her into her world.

Invitation accepted.

She spent her day running errands and texting with Tala. Tala seemed to have an average day, watching a show with Kyra, playing video games, and lamenting that her grades weren't in. Citlali gathered her laundry, went grocery shopping, and tried to put together a plan for a new show at work. Tala responded to all of it, making sure hardly a minute went by.

Would you like to go out? Citlali was getting ready for work, thinking of her time with Tala. She could use some soothing downtime after.

Wen? The typo showed Tala's eagerness, and Citlali's heart leapt over being so wanted.

I really want to see her now, but it wouldn't be fair to ask her to come out so late...or early depending on how you look at it. **I'm off on Tuesday. We can see each other at a "normal" time.**

Sounds good.

Citlali walked into work, and within minutes, Ruby attached herself to Citlali's side. *I guess my day was going too well.* Ruby pressed the length of her body into Citlali and she could barely hold in a shudder.

Thankfully, her lime-green sleeve protected her from the violent assault of unwanted flesh against hers.

"Lali." Ruby purred the irksome pet name. "Have a drink with me." She tried to tug Citlali in the direction of her table.

Citlali held her ground. "I am at work."

Ruby had the nerve to purse her lips and arch a dark red eyebrow. "And?"

Take a breath. "I can't drink at work. That's one of the basic principles of work, unless you taste wine for a living." Ruby had probably never done a day's work in her life.

Ruby frowned. "You always say that. Sit with me anyway. I brought friends!"

Citlali held in a groan. *Clever girl.* She couldn't ignore Ruby now, not with a table of potential return investments. Time to suck this up and put on her business smile. They walked to Ruby's table.

"Hello, everyone," she made her voice bright. The four friends grinned back. Two men, two women, all dressed for a typical night out. They didn't look like they would be any trouble, but she had plenty of harmless-looking patrons who turned out to be a nightmare. "Ruby tells me you're her friends. How could I make your time with us special?"

One of the men, wearing a fedora rather stylishly, pointed to the stage. "How is that legal? Like, doesn't it count as indecent exposure or something?"

Citlali glanced at the center floor, where two performers went through some rather basic BDSM moves. "Performance art." She felt it was classified appropriately, but the group of four snickered like children.

"We should remember that if we ever decide to have a go in public," the woman seated next to Fedora said.

"So, does everyone here perform?" He wiggled his eyebrows and there were more snickers.

Citlali smile faltered. *I don't have the patience for this right now.* "I don't know what Ruby told you, but this isn't a brothel. The show is the show. Much of the staff will dance at your table without being asked. Some will dance close if you do ask. Even less will give you a dance in our private rooms."

"Oh, yeah? How much for that performance?" Fedora asked, apparently the official spokesman of the group.

Citlali kept the grin on her face, but it was forced. "A room is anywhere from two hundred to five hundred dollars. A dance is usually a hundred, plus tip, and generally lasts twenty minutes."

Ruby pressed herself against Citlali. "We could be in one of those five hundred dollar rooms immediately. The gift baskets are amazing."

Citlali stepped away slightly. "Thank you." She, Daphne, and a couple of other managers put together the gift baskets, more for promotions than anything else. Most of the items weren't actually that expensive, just soap, candles, sleeping masks, and the like. She continued, "I, and all other managers and bouncers are forbidden from going to the private rooms. We have to be on the floor at all times."

Ruby's shoulders fell slightly.

"Since it's your first visit, please allow me to send over complimentary wine or Champagne along with a friendly platter as your server takes you orders." She motioned to Alisha, who came over with a practiced smile. At least she'd trust Alisha to keep it professional, but also stand up for herself if this crew got out of hand.

"Will she dance for us?" Fedora asked, raking his gaze up and down Alisha's body.

Citlali glanced at Alisha. "If she's so inclined, and it's not free." Alisha's gaze told them she wasn't so inclined, but Citlali continued as if she hadn't noticed. "Let me get your Champagne."

She made her escape, except Ruby followed her to the bar. Citlali ignored her, flagging down Bobby, the barkeep. "I need you to send over a welcome wagon to table fifteen."

"Gotcha." Bobby winked, and then did finger guns. She couldn't help but laugh.

With that out of the way, Citlali did the usual rounds. Or tried to, as Ruby followed her. She paused. *Why me?* "Ruby, don't you want to help your friends have the best experience they can while at The New Moon? I have to do my job."

She scowled. "Was it your job to go strolling along the boardwalk and out for pancakes with that blushing virgin?"

Citlali's body went cold, but somehow she managed to maintain her cool. *Is Ruby stalking me?* She doubted it. Coworkers had probably gossiped about it or something. Still, Ruby gathering intelligence on her was disconcerting. *I might be underestimating her.*

"Who I choose to spend my time with, what I spend my time doing, and why I spend my time doing it is none of your concern," Citlali said.

Ruby's eyes flared. "You're my girl."

What the hell? Citlali stepped back, putting space between herself and Ruby. This was definitely worse than she'd ever guessed. The woman was making it sound like they had a relationship of some kind. Outside of work. Citlali wanted none of that.

Citlali looked Ruby dead in the eye. "I am not your girl. Now, I have work to do."

She walked away, and for once Ruby didn't follow. She fumed at the bar for several minutes, had a couple of drinks, and then tried to get back at Citlali. She and her friends tried to call Citlali over for every little petty problem—from spilled drinks to too loud music to too few napkins—but they didn't count on Daphne, who handled each and every line they came up with. At the end of the night, Daphne was clearly exhausted.

"We have to ban that little bitch," Daphne said, taking her glasses off. She rubbed her eyes and didn't bother putting the glasses back on.

"If only it was our call," Citlali replied. "I'd do it this second if I could."

Daphne sighed. "Well, Raul's going to have to do something, or she's going to have you tied up in her damn basement."

Citlali scoffed. "The only way she'd get me is over my dead body."

While they might joke about it, she'd definitely have her guard up from now on.

Chapter Eight

CITLALI BREATHED DEEP, THE sweet spring air filling her, and squeezed Tala's hand. So far, their date—their walk—was going well. It was a nice, warm day with summer closing in. Tala was dressed casually, and while her checkered navy sweatpants weren't as sexy as her leather pants, Citlali liked seeing her relaxed. Citlali had gone in a similar direction, putting on a pink sundress covered in different colored roses.

"I'm happy you decided to come out with me," Citlali said. It needed to be said.

Tala gave her a small smile. "I'm happy you asked."

"Feel free to ask me out any time you want."

Tala rubbed the back of her neck. "I'd love to, but I never go anywhere. I stay on my couch all day."

It seemed like a big deal for Tala to be out then, and Citlali was flattered that she chose to spend any spare time with her. Citlali made an exaggerated gasp. "Tala, are you inviting me to your house for our third date?"

As expected, Tala blushed to the roots of her dark hair. "I didn't mean it that way!"

Citlali smirked and bumped Tala with her shoulder. "I wouldn't mind if you did." She'd slept with people she knew in less time and liked a lot less, but how would Tala feel about it?

Tala focused ahead of them. "I don't want to disappoint you."

"I doubt you would." She meant that.

Tala glanced at her. "Can I think about it?"

"Of course. No pressure. I like spending time with you." She did. Maybe Tala needed a certain level of intimacy before sex. There was still more to discover about each other before getting to their bodies. She could wait.

"How has work been?"

Beyond drama with Ruby, it had been normal. "The usual. You know, you don't have to stay away. You can come in and enjoy the food."

Tala's brow furrowed. "I can? But it's your job, and aren't we…"

Girlfriends. A burst of joy burned in Citlali's chest. That's what Tala was trying to say, she was sure of it. Citlali tilted her head. "Are we?"

Tala swallowed. "I…um…like you."

"But?" It didn't sound like there was a "but" coming, but Tala needed to know that she had that option.

Tala shook her head. "No but. I like you."

Citlali gave her hand a squeeze. "I like you, too."

Tala licked her lips. "So…are we?" Her voice trembled.

Citlali grinned and decided to have mercy on Tala. "I'd like that."

Tala stood up taller. "Good." There was a beat of silence. "So, I should be on the list now, right? I can't go in The New Moon."

Citlali chuckled. It was almost like she liked having an excuse. "Not really, no."

Tala suddenly looked troubled, blue eyes squinting as she went through a problem. "Wait, can I go to the restaurant part?"

Adorable. "I'm afraid not. You can place orders with me and wait in the parking lot for it." Tala brightened. She had never met someone who loved food as much as Tala, and it was too damn cute. *I'm so gone on this woman* "Good thing I asked you out to get crepes."

"I love crepes!" Now, her voice was a chirp.

Citlali gave her hand another squeeze. "I figured."

"You think I just eat all the time, don't you?" Tala blew out a breath.

"Makes it easy to plan dates." Citlali wrinkled her nose at Tala, which didn't help pick up her demeanor.

Tala pouted. "I'm not that greedy."

"I like how you enjoy food, but since you're about more than food, you'll be fine with walking around a museum with me." That was really what the date was about. She liked quiet walks, typically around museums, and their city had dozens to offer. *Will Tala be able to weather this storm with me?* It would certainly make things harder if Tala couldn't.

Tala pursed her lips for a long moment. They looked very kissable, shining thanks to lip-gloss. "Is it a sex museum?"

Citlali nodded. "It's a historical museum. It just happens the event I want to attend for is about sex. They're doing a few new exhibits, including underwear through the ages. Does that bother you?"

Tala shrugged. "I wouldn't go on my own, but if that's what you want to do. You work too much, though."

Citlali laughed. "Maybe I'm doing this because I like historical sex stuff."

Tala scoffed. She was right. Citlali wanted to see if she could incorporate anything into The New Moon.

"Would you be more excited if it was a different museum?" Citlali asked. Maybe on another date, they could go to the modern art museum.

"Historical stuff is always interesting. For me anyway." Tala scratched the side of her head, braids already fuzzy. "I feel like I'm not making any sense."

"You're fine. You don't have to be so self-conscious about what you're saying. You like learning things, so history is fun. I'm glad. I enjoy spending the day at a museum if I can get the time."

Tala nodded. "Then we should do it again...as fun, not work related reconnaissance. I don't mind doing this with you. You should know, I'm not grossed out with sex in general, okay?"

Citlali pulled her a little closer. "What I like is that you don't assume I'm promiscuous or easy because I put together shows centered around sex." She had several people pursue her thinking she'd sleep with just about anyone.

"Well, one, I wouldn't care if you liked having sex and had it with a bunch of people, but I wouldn't assume you like having sex with different partners just because you put on sex shows. I like to eat. Doesn't mean I like to or even can cook. You know what I mean?" Tala looked at her, eyes wide.

Citlali melted. Despite loving what she did, there were times where people made it seem wrong. Tala didn't. The job didn't make her who she was.

"Will you let me pay for the crepes?" Citlali asked.

Tala smiled. "Never."

They got crepes before the museum. Tala only got one, which was surprising, but then they walked to the museum hand in hand. *Did she only get one so we could keep holding hands?*

While Tala didn't seem put off by the museum, she didn't seem engaged either. She stood behind Citlali, hunched over, as if trying to look smaller. Maybe this was a mistake. *Maybe she said what she thought I wanted to hear. Or maybe she thought she'd be able to deal with this, but she's clearly not interested.*

"We can leave whenever you want," Citlali said as she put the trash from her crepe in a garbage can. Tala had finished hers soon after they entered the place.

Tala shook her head. "I don't want to be in your way."

Oh. Tala lived inside her head, inside a shell. She would put up with stuff because she could check out of it, especially if she thought being seen would make her seem like a nuisance.

Citlali gave Tala's hand a squeeze. "I appreciate that. You can tell me if you're uncomfortable."

Tala waved that off. "The museum's okay. It's kind like your shows."

Citlali arched an eyebrow. "Hmm?"

"One of the reasons you do your shows is you want to help people be comfortable with their kinks. This lets people know they're not alone in their likes or desires. Sometimes, it's important for people to know they're not weird." Tala shrugged, even though that was rather insightful.

Citlali grinned. "Or maybe they are weird, but that's not always a bad thing. I'm weird."

Tala scoffed. "You're not weird."

"Thank you, but I manage a sex club." While she didn't like to be judged by her job, she knew it wasn't something most people aspired to.

Tala conceded that point with a shrug. They continued on, and Citlali noticed Tala was reading the things on the displays. *Not lost in her head then. Good.* She worried over nothing.

"Did you get any ideas?" Tala asked as they left the museum a couple of hours later.

The warmth of Tala's large hand seemed to cradle hers. The security there hummed through her. "Maybe getting a few displays and maybe doing some lingerie modeling. I might be able to scout some boutiques and see if they want to give it a try. Nothing truly inspirational like I had hoped."

The lingerie thing could work with the proper advertising, but they couldn't do it several nights in a row.

"Sorry. This place is kinda cool, though."

Citlali resisted the urge to throw her shoulders back a little. She got Tala out of the house and to enjoy a sex exhibit. "Glad you liked it."

"Yeah. It made me think about intimacy through the ages, and also how opinions change about things over time. I mean, could you imagine sharing a bed with your whole family and your parents might be..." Tala made a face, sticking out her tongue and flaring her nostrils.

"No, I don't want to imagine either." Citlali shook her head. She wanted to spend more time with Tala and since Tala wasn't moving to leave, it was safe to assume she wanted the same thing. "I don't live too far from here. Want to go watch a movie at my apartment?" Her breath caught as she asked, but it was worth a shot.

Tala gnawed at her bottom lip. "Okay, lead the way."

Riding on Tala's motorcycle, Citlali gave all the directions while happily clinging to Tala's broad back. Wind whipped through her hair and stung her cheeks, but she didn't care. Each turn allowed her to clutch Tala even tighter. The way the motorcycle vibrated between them caused some rather dirty thoughts to drift through Citlali's mind. *No, no, no, save those for when she goes home. We're going to do whatever she's comfortable with.*

Citlali released a slow breath when Tala turned the bike off. She thought it was discreet, but the way Tala locked eyes with her let her know she was wrong. She smiled, hoping it was reassuring. Tala grinned. She grabbed Tala by the hand as soon as they dismounted the bike.

They made their way to Citlali's apartment, grabbing some Persian food on the way. Tala insisted on paying because her order was almost three times as expensive as Citlali's. Citlali had a feeling she'd never pay for a meal again whenever she was with Tala.

"Wow, you could fit my whole apartment in here," Tala said as they stepped inside Citlali's apartment. Tala took off her sneakers without needing to be told.

"Do you have a studio?" Citlali asked as she removed her shoes.

"No. I purposely got a tiny apartment to make sure a bunch of people never show up."

"How much is a bunch?" she asked, walking to the kitchen and grabbing some place mats and plates.

"More than two."

"I don't like to entertain many, but I will have more than two over." She put the mats down on her long, rectangular coffee table.

Tala curled her lip "Nope. Then it gets too loud and there's too much going on."

Citlali studied Tala for a second. "Drains your energy?"

Tala blinked, like she didn't expect that. "Yeah."

"I know the feeling. There are times when being around people drains me, too."

"Really? But you seem so social."

"I am, but that doesn't mean I don't get tired of being around people after a while. Now, let's eat while it's warm. Any particular movie you want to see?" Citlali grabbed the remote as she sat down on the couch. A relieved sigh escaped her. While the day was great, they'd been on their feet for most of it and it was nice to sit down.

Tala sat next to her. "No, you can pick."

Citlali put on one of her favorite movies, a rom-com. It would serve her well to find out if Tala shared her tastes. She opened the containers, spooning some rice dish onto the plate. Tala didn't say anything about it, just graciously accepting the plate. Citlali also got them some wine.

"I hope you like this," Citlali said as she put the glass down next to Tala.

"Most wine just tastes like modified grape juice to me anyway," Tala replied.

Citlali laughed. "I don't think that's what any wine maker is going for."

"I'll do my best never to tell them."

They settled next to each other on the sofa, legs touching. They ate and sipped their wine. At some point during the movie, Citlali's legs ended up in Tala's lap, and Tala massaged her calves. Her touch felt so good, firm but not painful, just enough to get the knots out. Citlali moved closer and tucked into Tala's shoulder.

"That feels really good," Citlali said.

Tala smiled. "You're on your feet a lot."

"You're sweet."

Tala ducked her head as a blush stained her cheeks. Citlali couldn't help herself, dipping down to Tala's level and kissing her. Tala kissed her back. The kiss was hot. Tala's lips pressed against hers like magic, and the caress of her tongue was sweet. *How is she not taken?*

Citlali straddled Tala's lap. Even though she had a good six or seven inches on Tala, Tala supported her weight with no problem. She longed to press their bodies together, but she didn't want to move too fast. Leaning down, she cupped Tala's face as Tala stared at her with dark, hungry eyes. The color bursts in her eyes popped with energy. *God, I hope she devours me.*

"Is this all right?" Citlali asked, body begging for more.

Tala nodded, panting. She put her hands on Citlali bare thighs, and the skin contact, even if it was just her hands, set Citlali's blood on fire.

The blaze burst higher when Tala gave her thighs a squeeze. "This okay?"

Citlali kissed Tala in response. Kissing became an experience, exciting and new. Each one sent tingles through Citlali's body. Small, wondrous breathy noises came from Tala, and Tala was able to pull moans from Citlali in response.

The way Tala stroked her thighs only added to fire building between them, and Citlali couldn't help grinding against Tala. She tugged Citlali closer with an ease she wouldn't expect from someone's Tala's size. Pleasure surged through her like a wave. Citlali moaned. She rocked even harder against Tala as heat built between them.

"I want you." Citlali tugged at Tala's shirt, needing it off immediately.

But then, Tala pulled away.

It was like a punishment, and Citlali whimpered.

"I gotta go!" Tala moved Citlali with an effortlessness that shouldn't have been possible, then leaped off of the couch.

"Tala, wait!" Citlali tried to get up just as quickly, but her legs gave out.

"It's not you! This was awesome. Gotta go!" Tala was out the door by the time Citlali got up.

"What the hell just happened?" Citlali wasn't sure if she should scream, cry, or break something. Screaming seemed the least destructive and most therapeutic, so she let out a single low scream that was almost a groan.

***

Tala winced as Citlali's groan blasted her ears. *Idiot! Idiot! Idiot!* But she did the right thing. She couldn't sleep with Citlali, not when she felt like she might tear out of her skin. Citlali's sweet taste was tattooed on her brain. The feel of Citlali grinding against her was the stuff of dreams. She'd never be the same again.

It was good that she had a long ride home. She had over a half-hour to get herself together, but it wasn't enough. Even the cold shower didn't help. Her body burned for Citlali, but she had probably just confused the hell out of her for running out. *Idiot*.

Throwing herself onto the couch, she glanced at her phone. Her heart jumped. A message from Citlali brightened her screen. *She's breaking up with me.* She opened the thread.

I'm sorry for making you uncomfortable.

Tala's breath hitched. Citlali was apologizing to her, even though she was the one who ran. Her thumbs hovered over the keypad. She wasn't sure how to explain what happened. And she found herself hitting the FaceTime button because some things needed to be said out loud. *She's probably not going to pick up because you ran out on her without saying anything like a crazy person.*

"You're calling me!" Citlali's face appeared on her screen, a small smile on her lips. Her face was flushed, like she was still frustrated with Tala abandoning her an hour ago.

Tala ducked her head. She should've been relieved Citlali picked up, but her chest felt like it was wrapped in barbed wire. "Yeah, I owe you an explanation."

"No, you really don't. I pushed you, made you uncomfortable."

"But that's not what happened!" Tala couldn't bear the thought of Citlali blaming herself. "It wasn't you. It was really nice, kissing on the couch. Everything about it was nice and you felt so good."

Citlali grew serious. "But you're not ready for that step, right?"

Sighing, Tala shook her head. "There's still so much you don't know about me. It wouldn't be right or fair. I just..." She rubbed her forehead as if she were trying to wipe away a hard spot. "I don't want to scare you."

Citlali smiled. "I don't think you'd hurt me on purpose."

"Because you think I'm this sweet, shy nerd, but I'm really an awkward idiot. Who else would run away from a beautiful woman who wanted to make out with them?"

"I'd go with an awkward, shy sweetheart, and I really don't mind. I understand if you want us to get to know each other better."

If only it was that easy. No matter what, this was probably going to end badly. She'd hurt Citlali eventually. She should just walk away now before it got worse. Citlali could get a normal girlfriend and live a happy life.

"Citlali..." Tala started, but the words refused to come out. *You're such a selfish ass for this.* It should've been easy to cut ties with Citlali—she hardly knew the woman. She didn't bond with people like this. She didn't like people in this manner. This should be so easy, yet it was so difficult, she couldn't even manage it. She didn't have the strength.

"I'll try to tone it down with you, but you're so hot." Citlali winked.

Tala could feel her face flare up. "I'm not!"

There was a lilting chuckle from Citlali. "You really are."

Tala almost wanted to cry, and her throat tightened. *You can't do this to her.* It wasn't fair to burden Citlali with someone like her. Citlali deserved the best. "What if I told you that you could find someone better?"

Those honey-colored eyes sparkled. "I'd call you a liar, but tell me if this is too much for you. I want to get to know you better, but I don't want you to be uncomfortable. I didn't mean to get so carried away that you'd run away."

"I was into it. I'm into you."

"Oh?" Citlali smiled as she spoke, but she still sounded a little surprised.

Tala sighed. Citlali tried to understand her, tried to speak her language, tried to fit her puzzle rather than make Tala fit in everyone else's puzzle. Tala sniffled. "I really like you. I like the way you make me feel."

Concern filled Citlali's expression. "That shouldn't make you sad."

"Not a lot of people make me feel like I'm okay. You do that." And Tala wanted that, wanted to keep this feeling. She wanted to be selfish.

"I want to keep doing that if you let me."

A lump formed in Tala's throat. Citlali wanted to take care of her. It was so tempting. *No, you can't do this to her.* Do the right thing.

"I don't want to burden you," Tala said.

"You're not a burden, and I'd love to help you realize that." Citlali's gentle gaze held only kindness and affection. "I like you, Tala. I don't know you like the back of my hand, but I want a chance to do so. Will you give me that? Give me the chance and let me decide?"

Tala's resolve crumbled. "I want you to take that chance."

"I'll do so happily."

Tala's stomach wrung itself in and out like a wet rag. *Take the chance. You've been taking the chance with her and she hasn't let you down. Go for it!* But Citlali didn't really know what she was asking for. What Tala really was. Still, the selfish part of her wanted to give Citlali the chance. And that part of her had already won. "Wanna watch a movie together?" Mentally, she winced. *You really are stupid.* A movie was what had gotten them into this mess.

"If we have the same streaming services that could work. You pick this time. I want to see what you like."

Tala grinned. "Okay." *She gets me.*

And maybe that was what made this decision to pursue her even worse.

Chapter Nine

LEANING BACK IN HER beanbag chair, Tala stared at her email. The internship rejection stared back at her. Her stomach balled into a knot, but surprisingly, she wasn't disappointed. A part of her had hoped she'd get it, but a larger part—the anxious, downtrodden, sad part—saw it coming.

"You okay over there?" Kyra asked from the kitchen. Curry chicken permeated the whole apartment. Kyra was so talented. She would definitely go places. Tala wasn't so sure about herself, though.

"Yeah, fine." Tala closed the laptop and picked up her phone. Opening her thread with Citlali, she typed out her news. **I didn't get the internship**. Citlali was probably asleep now, but when she saw it, she might be able to help Tala get over the odd gnawing sensation that started deep in her bones.

Kyra snorted. "That's obviously not true."

Tala tossed her head back, sprawled out on the beanbag. "You suck."

Kyra snorted again. "You used to do that to me all the time and then cheer me up."

"That was different."

Kyra scoffed. "Why? Because you're older than me? It's only by four months."

"I'm expected to take care of you." They both knew that, understood it, and agreed with it. As weird as Tala was, she took her responsibility seriously. Nothing could or would harm or upset Kyra while Tala lived and breathed.

"Because your mom told you to." The teasing smile was so obvious in her voice.

Tala curled her lip and growled, which was only half effective since Kyra couldn't see her baring her teeth. "See if I ever stand up for you again."

Kyra waved the spoon at her, winking. "And yet you will."

Tala didn't have a comeback for that. She glanced at her phone. No response.

"You wanna talk about it?" Kyra asked as she put their plates down on the coffee table.

"Let's just watch the show." Tala didn't want to do anything to bring Kyra's mood down.

Kyra gave her a little whine. "Tell me."

Tala shoulders slumped. "I didn't get the internship."

Kyra frowned. "What? How could you not get it? You've been a freaking straight A student since kindergarten! You graduated undergrad summa cum laude." She growled, a low rumbling sound coming from deep within her chest.

Tala waved it off. "Calm down. You know as well as I that I wasn't getting it."

Kyra glared at her like she was lying. "You were a shoo-in! Who else could Raff pick?"

Tala shook her head. "It doesn't say who he picked. He hasn't been a fan of mine since I punched Lowell's dumb ass in the balls."

"Ten years ago! And Lowell was in the wrong."

Tala scoffed. "We both know nobody cares it was his fault. He was just trying to help the weird kid socialize, obviously." She shuddered, the flash of memory coming back to her. The overwhelming scent of sweat and wild, the pressure as the jackass tried to mount her. He was lucky she didn't rip his throat out.

Kyra flopped back down and put both of her hands on Tala's forearm. "You're not weird, and he had no right. You're entitled to feel the way you feel. How do you feel?"

Taking a deep breath, Tala scratched her head. "Not sure. I'll email my advisor tomorrow, once I get a better handle on things."

Kyra sighed. "This sucks. I was gonna bake you a huge cake."

"Triple chocolate?"

"You know it. I guess I'll save it. You'll eventually get an internship. You're really smart, even if you don't look it." Kyra grinned.

Tala laughed. "Hey!" She shoved Kyra, who fell to the floor in a heap.

"Don't push me. You could break me, you know?" Kyra chuckled as she sat up and rubbed her arm. Tala winced. It was something Tala was scolded over her entire life. Kyra liked her being rough when they were younger, though, so she could prove she was tough.

Tala held out a hand. "You okay?"

"I am, you freaking ox." Kyra pushed Tala's hand away, still smiling. "That really sucks you didn't get the internship. I was really hoping you would." She hugged Tala.

Tala ran a hand over her braids. "It's okay. I don't think I'd have been very happy working for Raff, anyway."

"Probably not, but I wanted to celebrate you being one step closer to your career. You've been there for me. This was my chance to be there for you."

Tala looked at Kyra like she had eight heads. "You're an idiot, you know that? You're always here for me and I'm happy you're around. You're the best little sister I could ask for."

Kyra hugged her tighter. "I know. Now, let's eat. Actually, wait, I have something that will cheer you up."

Tala arched an eyebrow. "Really?"

Kyra nodded. "It was supposed to just be something nice for us, but it'll work as a pick-me-up right now." Pulling away, she got up to bring them something to drink. "So, I don't know if you know this, but they sell sorrel at my job, and the lady who makes it hooked me up." She had two tall glasses filled to the brim with the dark red drink.

"Your job just gets cooler and cooler." *The New Moon is a good job.* Tala met Citlali. Kyra learned a bunch of new recipes and how to make her old stuff with better ingredients. And now they had a source for sorrel.

"I agree." Kyra raised her glass and smiled. "Every single time I have this in a wine glass I think of Rocky 'sneaking' us some sorrel, making us think it was wine."

Tala nodded. "And little did we know, Mama got it from a coworker at the hospital just for us whenever she knew they'd be drinking wine for whatever reason."

"She always wanted us to feel included."

Tala sniffed the sorrel. "She came by it honestly."

"Damn straight." Kyra took a sip.

"Damn that's good," Tala said as she looked at her glass. The perfect balance of sugar and ginger and herbs.

"It really is." Kyra gulped it down.

"This definitely cheered me up." Tala finished her own glass before she started in on the food.

They enjoyed their meal and drink. They watched a few episodes of their show. It was nice, like old times. Tala treasured these moments. *This is just what I needed.*

Kyra eventually left to go be with Raina, and Tala was alone with her thoughts. She really didn't want to work for Raff. He was a mean son of a bitch on a good day, and she had never caught him on a good day. Groaning, she knew she'd have to tell her mom. *After all the work she did to pull strings with Raff, too.* There's no way a tool like Raff put on his big boy pants and called her, after all. *Well, at least I already had a lifetime of disappointing my mother to cushion this crap.*

Before she gathered her strength to call, her phone went off. Citlali! **I'm sorry you didn't get the internship. Can I call you? If not, what do you need right now?**

The question eased the knot in her stomach. **Please call. Well, not right now. Have to tell my mom**. She took a deep breath and went to the text thread with her mom, deciding a text was just easier. **I didn't get the internship**. If her mother wanted more details, she could call. She barely had time to blink before her phone came to life. Her mother. She put it on speaker. "Yeah, Ma?"

"Who else could that son of a bitch have given it to?" Her mother's voice was way too loud for her to be at work.

"Ma, where are you?"

"I ran into the parking lot! I should go kick his ass while I'm out here."

"It's okay, Ma."

"No," her mother snapped. "We're supposed to look out for each other, and that massive jackass has the nerve to do this. I don't like him much, but that didn't stop me from cutting that growth out of his throat. You're also the most qualified, so this shouldn't have even been a favor. What else does he want?"

"Beyond an apology, possibly grandchildren." She was pretty sure in the scuffle she'd popped one of Lowell's testicles. But he did have two, so...

"Then he should've told his little mutt not to try to mount people who want to be left alone."

Tala smiled, shaking her head. Her mother was so supportive of her. "Thanks, Ma." *I wish I was better for her.*

Her mother sucked in a breath. "I'm sorry about this. I know other pharmacists."

"It's okay, Ma. Let me just use my advisor. She's been taking good care of me."

"But I want to help you. We're in the last years where you might need me."

"Ma! I'm always going to need you," Tala replied. She wasn't one of those pups who thought she'd outgrow her parents. Whenever she had to make a decision, she sought their counsel, even though her father was often wrong.

Her mother blew out a breath. "I know, but school things were our thing."

That was true enough. She remembered learning to read with her mother. Their nighttime stories, curled up in the bed, tucked under the covers, reading with different character voices. Simple math at the dinner table that grew more complex. History that didn't sound like enough, so her mother helped her hunt for books to fill in the pieces. Sciences that led to nature hikes and museum visits. Sometimes it seemed like her mother was with her every waking moment, even though she had a full time job.

"We have other things," Tala said.

Thanks to her mother being so interested in her as a child, she grew interested in things her mother liked. It was always comforting that her family got along so well.

"I know." She groaned. "Speaking of other things, whatever happened with your girl?"

Tala's cheeks burned. *Thank goodness this isn't a video call.* "We've gone out a few times."

"Good. Is she treating you well?"

"So far." Tala had always hoarded her time and space, but now, she wouldn't mind spending all day with Citlali. Not once while they were out did she think about going home. She never felt drained. *Is this how regular people feel when they hang out with girlfriends? Friends? Relatives? Anybody?* It was a new and wonderful feeling.

Her mother made a pleased noise. "And are you treating her well?"

Tala gnawed on the corner of her mouth. "I'm trying, but she's probably going to get bored with me."

"Tala!" The gentle reprimand was clear in her mom's voice. "Stop being hard on yourself. She won't get bored. Never think that. Do you think she cares about you?"

Tala thought about how she had run out of Citlali's apartment not too long ago, and how Citlali liked her enough to put up with her, to call her, text her, request her presence. Her stomach twisted, and her nerves buzzed. *She'll get fed up with you. They always do. No, don't think like that. She's already accepted more about you than any other girlfriend.*

"I think she does." She had to say it out loud before she let her anxiety take over. "She does nice things for me and she doesn't push me."

"Good. You go at your own pace, but I want to meet her."

Tala groaned. "Ma!" She wasn't sure how that would go down, but no matter what she'd be embarrassed.

"This is the best you've made a girlfriend sound without stammering or lying, so of course I want to meet her."

"Ma." Tala groaned. She was saved by a text. Citlali wanted to know if it was all right to call. "Ma, I gotta go."

"Girlfriend calling?"

"Ma!"

Her mother laughed. "Love you, paw print."

"Love you, too." She disconnected the call and texted Citlali to call. She FaceTimed instead. A rush of excitement coursed through Tala. "Hi."

"Hey, I'm sorry about the internship," Citlali said, her tone soft.

"Don't be. I didn't want to work with that douche. I should've had a plan B." She'd go see her advisor and see what was out there. It would've been a more educational experience for her to work with Raff, but something was better than nothing. Not to mention, her peace of mind and self-worth were priceless. Raff would've made it his mission to tear her down.

Citlali took a deep breath. "I want to hold you and watch a corny movie with you and make you dinner."

Tala whimpered. All of that sounded nice. "Can you?" Tala frowned. "No wait, I don't want you to go out of your way for me. I know you're at work. You should sleep after and not worry about me."

"You go out of your way for me all of the time."

Tala's brow furrowed. "Not really."

Citlali smirked. "Oh, come on. You came to a sex club to see me. You waited for hours in a parking lot for me. You went to a sex exhibit with me."

Tala twisted her mouth up. "Well, I like you."

"And I like you. Let me do things for you."

Tala sighed. Her anxiety rose up like bile in her throat. "I'm sorry. I'm not used to letting people do stuff for me."

"I want you to get used to it with me. I want to do things for you."

Tala scrunched up her nose. *Let her in.* "I could meet you at The New Moon. We could go to your place since it's closer."

"I'll see you after work then."

Tala smiled. "I look forward to it."

"Me, too."

They hung up. Tala sighed and it felt like everything fell out of her, but in a good way.

***

Citlali smiled as she tucked her phone into her pocket. She wasn't surprised when Daphne intercepted her. It was like she could sense embarrassing moments. Citlali had ducked behind a plant in the hall that led to the private rooms to make that call.

"That smile says you just got off of the phone with a cute girl," Daphne said.

"Yeah, *my* cute girl." Citlali smirked as she made her way back to the show area with Daphne hot on her heels.

Daphne snickered. "There you go, trying to be more mature than I taught you. Who has time for a steady girlfriend?" Daphne blew a raspberry.

"I do, and I'm enjoying her, thank you very much."

"The sex must be nice."

"I don't kiss and tell." Citlali blew a kiss at Daphne.

Daphne grinned. "Good. Let's get to work."

They went their separate ways. Tala texted her a little after midnight. **I'm so bored, so I'm coming down to the boardwalk now. I'll figure out what to do with myself until you get off work.** The text made Citlali smile before she even realized it. *Why does she make me so happy?* It didn't matter.

Come to the club first. Citlali could treat her for being so sweet. **I'll meet you in the parking lot.** She'd bring out a piece of chocolate lava cake for Tala. It would definitely help lift Tala's spirits.

I should order her some dinner as well. As much as she'd love to cook for Tala, she'd be too tired to do it after work. If she could get Tala to stay at her apartment, she'd be able to make breakfast for the two of them. She looked forward to that.

***

Tala pulled up to The New Moon, stopping her motorcycle in the club parking lot. She got off of the bike and took out her phone to let

Citlali know she was there. Before she got a chance, the stomp-stomp-stomp of spiked heels coming toward her drew her gaze. A young woman marched toward her. The redhead. The young lady that hung on Citlali's arm the night she fled The New Moon.

Tala's blood immediately flared and her hackles went up. The urge to claw the woman's face off coursed through her. She took a calming breath as the woman stood before her, smirking. It took all of Tala's self control not to growl. *She wouldn't understand anyway.*

"Still sniffing around after Lali? You shouldn't bother," the woman said towering over Tala. Her gaze was hard, boiling with hatred. Underneath her expensive perfume, there was a sour scent.

"I'm sorry?" Tala arched an eyebrow. *The hell is going on?*

The woman snarled, and the sound made Tala's nerves twitch. A challenge. *No, she doesn't know what she's doing. Stay calm.*

"Lali's mine. She doesn't want anything to do with trash like you." The woman motioned to Tala with a wild swipe of her hand.

"What?" That comment pushed Tala off balance. Was the redhead in a relationship with Citlali? She doubted it since Citlali hadn't even mentioned her. *Something is wrong here.*

"Taking her on the boardwalk and for pancakes is childish," the woman practically spat at her.

Tala frowned. *Is she stalking Citlali?* If that was the case, the redhead better watch her own back. She clearly didn't know who she was dealing with. Tala would defend Citlali at the drop of a hat and tear a person in half if Citlali requested it. "How do you know about that?"

"I know she's just being nice because she wants you to spend money at the club." Her eyes narrowed, but were on fire. "You mean nothing."

Tala clenched her fists, a little surprised her anxiety didn't latch onto those words and use them to beat her like a bad dog. Instead, annoyance flared up inside her at this woman going out of her way to try to make Tala feel insecure, but she wasn't as insecure about her and Citlali's relationship that a literal stranger could shake her. Citlali had taken everything she'd freaked out about and made her feel okay.

"Look, I'm not sure what you want," Tala said slowly. This woman was a customer of The New Moon, and she didn't want to do anything to mess with Citlali's job.

The woman tried to shove her, but Tala barely moved. The woman didn't seem to notice, eyeing Tala down. *If only she knew I could pick my teeth with her juicy bones.*

"You just stay away from Lali! She's mine," the woman said before storming away.

Confusion filled Tala at the exchange. *What the hell was that?* Who knew, but she did know that she had to watch her back, and Citlali's. She texted Citlali. **I'm here.**

Chapter Ten

CITLALI MARCHED INTO THE parking lot, greeted by the hot air of the summer with the cool breeze from the beach not too far away, to deliver the chocolate cake to Tala. Tala stood at the edge of the lot, face scrunched up. *Something's wrong.*

"Babe, what happened?" Citlali asked. She put her free hand on Tala's shoulder, her soft t-shirt bunching a little.

Tala squinted. "I just had a weird encounter."

"Someone propositioned you?" It sometimes happened. People seemed to think that because sexual things happened in the club, sex workers had to hang out around the building. They occasionally did, but the staff chased them off.

Tala gawked at her. "No."

Citlali laughed and took Tala's hand. "Then what happened?"

Tala glanced around then pointed to nothing. "That redheaded woman. She warned me away from you."

Citlali blinked. "She what?" *Who the hell knows we're involved?* Well, beyond Daphne. Her friend might have talked about Citlali being with Tala, but no one should know what Tala looked like enough to approach her.

Tala scuffed her boot on the pavement. "She wanted me to know you're only giving me attention to get me to spend money at the club. She knew about our first date."

Citlali shook her head. "The whole club might know about the date. My friend Daphne teased me about being romanced by you and perhaps someone overheard." But even that was stretching things. As much as Daphne teased, she didn't give away specifics about Citlali's dates where people might hear.

Tala's eyes went wide, like a teacher called on her and she didn't know the answer to the question. "I..."

Citlali gave Tala's hand a squeeze. "She wasn't being mean. She thinks we're cute. She liked that you waited for me to get off of work, because that showed that you're serious about me."

"I'm sure people in the club ask you out all the time."

Citlali could hear the underlying sorrow in the drop in Tala's voice. "I never say yes. You're the only one, I promise."

"Okay, but you should be careful. The woman...She felt almost feral to me. Dangerous."

Feral? Why would a bouncer let someone like that hang around here? Citlali frowned. "What did she look like?"

Tala glanced to the side. "She was the woman who interrupted celebrating my last day of school."

"Ruby." The thought of her made Citlali want to punch something. *What made Ruby harass Tala?* It was a little off-putting that Ruby knew Tala, but she had been dealing with Ruby for almost a year now and she hadn't done anything dangerous. Yes, she kept a close eye on her, but it was more because she popped up at the worst damned times, wanting to be under Citlali. Overzealous and irksome, sure, but dangerous seemed a bit much.

Tala tilted her head. "Sorry?"

"That's Ruby." Citlali waved her off. "She's just annoying. She likes me."

"She wants to possess you. She told me to back off."

Citlali arched an eyebrow. Tala was definitely taking things far with Ruby. *Maybe it's good she's on the list and can't come into The New Moon.* It seemed like Tala couldn't handle people who were a little pushy in their affections for Citlali.

"Babe, she's just a spoiled brat who's used to getting her way. Many of the customers are like that. Are they all dangerous?" Citlali asked.

Tala blew out a breath. "Of course not. It was just the look in her eyes."

Citlali fought down a scowl. *Why won't she let this go?* "I've handled her long enough to know what I'm doing. I can take care of myself."

"I'm not saying you can't." Tala put up both hands. "I'm just..." She started pacing, back and forth, back and forth, like a caged animal. Then she stopped and groaned. "Never mind."

Citlali sighed. She didn't want to take this the wrong way, even though it felt like Tala was trying to tell her what she could and couldn't handle, but Tala was the one who had to deal with being harassed. Tala had every right to be on edge, so maybe she wasn't expressing herself the way she meant to.

Citlali reached out, rubbing Tala's shoulder with the hope of soothing her, keeping her voice calm. "Look, I've been doing this for a year. I know how to take care of myself. You don't have to worry. I'm sorry she bothered you."

"That's not it." Tala sighed, her broad shoulders dropping, but Citlali was at a loss on what to do. She wasn't some helpless damsel. Maybe this was something more than Ruby, and maybe Tala was frustrated and just not dealing with it the right way.

"Are you okay?" Citlali asked, sliding her hand down Tala's arm and giving Tala's fingers a squeeze.

Tala shrugged. "I'm worried about you."

"You don't have to be. I have everything under control."

Tala glanced away. "Okay."

"Are you still coming over?" It didn't take much to send Tala running back to the safety of her home. Hopefully, this little disagreement and trouble in the parking lot wasn't it.

"Do you still want me to?" Tala asked.

"Yes. Nothing here was a rejection of you, okay?" Citlali could handle reassuring Tala since Tala's behavior came from a good place. "I understand you care. I'm happy you do. I appreciate it."

Yeah, so don't be annoyed with her just because she cared. She's not doing this to control you or out of jealousy. She's just caring. Thinking about it like that made Citlali's annoyance turn into a puddle of mush.

Tala was silent, probably processing. She gave Tala a peck on the lips, made sure she had a grip on the chocolate cake, and then went back inside to work. Hopefully, Tala would still be out there in a few hours.

Inside, Citlali was far from surprised when Ruby attached herself to Citlali's arm. Citlali fought down a sigh. *What made Tala think she's dangerous and feral?*

"I'm working," Citlali said as she eased her arm out of Ruby's grip.

"I know, but we could do something when you're done with work," Ruby replied with a smile, latching again onto Citlali's arm.

Citlali shook her head. "I have way too much to do. I just want to go home and sleep."

Ruby gave Citlali's arm a tight squeeze. "You should tell that to the bitch sniffing after you in the parking lot."

Anger sparked within Citlali, and it took everything in her to not curse Ruby out. *How dare this little spoiled brat call Tala a bitch when she's the one who can't take a hint?* She released a low breath, calming herself down. She wasn't sure if she'd be able to put up with Ruby badmouthing her girlfriend.

"You should concern yourself with yourself. Have you been seated?" Citlali glanced around for relief. Daphne hurried over.

"I gave Ruby one of our best tables since she's one of our best customers." Daphne looped her arm around Ruby's free arm and gave her a gentle tug away.

Citlali felt the yank as Ruby refused to let her go, but on the second pull, Citlali slipped from Ruby's grasp.

"You'll come sit with me, Lali." A request, but it also sounded like a statement.

Daphne chimed in. "Of course! I'll bring her over after I get you settled in."

As long as she wasn't left alone with Ruby, it was okay, and Ruby tended to spend more money trying to impress Citlali. A little while later when Daphne and Citlali sat at Ruby's table, Citlali knew tonight would be no different.

Ruby immediately called for the most expensive bottle of wine, wanting Citlali to take a drink with her. She refused, of course, and Daphne backing her up fell on deaf ears as well. Ruby also ordered the most expensive dessert and Citlali would happily eat that, if only it wouldn't encourage Ruby further.

"Ruby, you're always so generous," Daphne said.

Ruby nodded. "I take care of people I like." She winked at Citlali as she sipped her wine. "I take even better care of those who take care of me, especially girlfriends."

Citlali ignored the blatant overtures and took a sip of her water.

Daphne smirked, eyeing the space. "Oh no, it looks like there's trouble between Liz and Takashi. That's all you."

Citlali's expression fell, even though Daphne was giving her an out. The out was a real crisis, and Liz was the type of patron to throw a drink on someone before voluntarily leaving. She groaned and went to handle the situation.

As soon as she walked over, she got slapped with a full glass of cold wine. Chardonnay, from the smell. It immediately stung her eyes. She sputtered for a moment and blinked the wine out of her eyes just in time to catch Liz's wrist mid-slap.

Liz gasped. "I'm sorry, Citlali. I was aiming for this little bitch!" Liz glared at Takashi. Hard to believe he was her favorite.

"You're just upset because this bitch told you no," Takashi replied with unnecessary finger wagging and a rude expression. It was like he didn't care about making tips.

"I'm trying to improve your life!"

Citlali rubbed her eyes, having heard this dumbass argument more times than anyone should in a year. "Liz, time to go."

"Why the hell does the little bitch never get thrown out? He started it," Liz replied.

"I work here!"

Citlali held up a hand over Takashi's face. "I've got this. You know the rules, Liz. You both have choices, but your decision was to break the rules, so you have to leave."

In her usual fashion, Liz curled her lip, but she left on her own, a body guard right behind her. Citlali nodded for two bouncers to follow them and make sure Liz was gone for the night. Citlali turned to Takashi.

"You good?" Citlali asked, knowing the answer to that. One day, he was going to catch Liz at a bad moment, and things wouldn't end well.

Takashi waved it off. "She had too much to drink, celebrating a big business deal. She offered to buy me with her bonus."

She shook her head. "One of these days, they'll figure out we're not for sale."

Takashi scoffed. "We don't do good jobs at saying that. Liz paid my tuition this year."

"Please tell me you mean through tips and not an actual gift of paying your tuition." They always warned employees to be careful about accepting gifts.

His eyes went wide. "Tips. God, could you imagine if she actually paid my tuition? But Rico paid my rent and that wasn't in tips." He wiggled his eyebrows.

She shook a finger at him. "Be careful."

Everyone got presents from patrons, but many of their customers didn't understand "gifting" and could easily think they were now entitled to their favorites, which was why Liz got in trouble so often.

Thankfully, the night was over. Citlali walked outside, hoping to see Tala, and there she was, waiting by her bike. *She actually waited.* Citlali resisted the urge to throw herself in Tala's arms since there were other New Moon employees around. She waved. Tala nodded back and got on her bike. Citlali went to her car and they left The New Moon behind in their dust.

***

Tala sat on Citlali's couch, not sure what else to do. She thought they went to Citlali's house for her, but it turned out Citlali needed the comfort so much more. She looked worn down and smelled like alcohol. She had on different clothes from earlier in the night, explaining she got in between a dispute at the wrong time and caught a drink with her face. She went for a shower immediately.

Tala wasn't comfortable enough exploring the kitchen to have food waiting for Citlali. She hadn't even picked up food while she was waiting, not sure what would help smooth things over between them. The best she could do was candy she picked up at one of the casino shops. She put the box of chocolates on the table as an offering.

Citlali returned, dressed in a cream camisole and black yoga pants. The aroma of rose water and jasmine surrounded her. She sat down with a sigh and Tala wanted to nuzzle her to offer some comfort. She restrained, though, not knowing if that's what Citlali wanted.

"Um…I got you some candy." Tala opened the box, revealing numerous chocolates in a bed of plastic. Her gaze gravitated toward the dark chocolate ball with almonds. "I didn't know what you liked, so I just went with assorted chocolates."

It was a big box—almost as big as a shoe box—and the casino definitely got the better of her on the price, but it would be nice to see which ones Citlali liked.

"Looks good." Citlali leaned forward and selected a square, light-colored one. "I'm a huge fan of chocolate covered peanuts if you really want to know, though."

Tala smiled. "I'll remember. Any other candy?"

"I love licorice, red or black. Caramel popcorn is my go-to comfort food."

Caramel popcorn. Tala noted that. "I'll definitely remember. Want to talk about what happened?"

Citlali rubbed her eyes. "Just the usual nonsense. I'm a little tired. Would you mind holding me while I lie down?"

Tala swallowed, her heart picking up the pace. Doing that would make it so much harder to keep from nuzzling Citlali. It would be weird to not do it. Weirder still was that closeness and nuzzling wasn't something Tala tended to want, not even with girlfriends. Yet she wanted it with Citlali.

"I'm sorry." Citlali drifted back a little. "I've made you uncomfortable."

"No!" Tala replied.

Citlali blinked. "Are you sure?"

"I want you to feel better." The truth fell from her lips.

"Can we lie in my bed? I don't know if we'll fit on the couch."

Tala could only gape as Citlali stood. She followed Citlali to the bedroom. The bedroom smelled like jasmine lotion. *So good.* The room was bigger and neater than hers. A large television decorated the wall, right above a long dresser. A desk tucked in the corner, next to a window. An abstract painting stared down at her from above the queen-sized bed. The paint gave her an off feeling, like she should leave, but it was probably weird to think the blobs of paint told her that, so Tala tried to ignore it.

Citlali turned down the bed and slid in. Tala shrugged her leather jacket off and took a breath before lying down on cool, satin sheets. *Damn! This feels good.* The sheets were enough for this to be worth it, but then it got better. Citlali pressed herself against Tala, who wasted no time wrapping her arms around Citlali. Tala couldn't help the deep inhale, taking in the perfect scent of Citlali, and she buried her nose in Citlali's long, damp hair.

"I'm sorry about your internship," Citlali said, relaxing into Tala and stroking Tala's side.

The tickling sensation made her want to purr. "The chocolate cake made up for it. I'm sorry I upset you in the parking lot."

"You were looking out for me, which I appreciate. I know about Ruby. It sucks she knows I went out with you, but I don't think she's dangerous."

Tala shook her head. "I think you're underestimating her."

"Can we not?"

Tala sighed. Ruby was bad news. Staring into her eyes had been like staring into an abyss. She smelled of darkness. *Yeah, tell her that, so she can think you're crazy. Honestly, you should just tell her so she thinks you're crazy or a monster. Either way, she'll stop wanting anything to do with you and be rid of you. It's inevitable really.*

Tala swallowed. "Citlali..."

But Citlali's breath had evened and her body grew heavier. Her heartbeat was steady. She had fallen asleep.

It was just Tala and her thoughts now. Her demons.

What the hell do I think I'm doing in the first place? She was terrible at relationships. She didn't have a single ex who didn't hate her and didn't regret giving her the time of day. She wasted their time. They always said so. And now she was wasting Citlali's time, too.

In the past, her girlfriends swore she never liked them the right way. She didn't understand what that meant, but she was attached to Citlali. She hadn't felt that before, believing it never had a chance to develop. Citlali seemed to understand how she responded to things, and Tala appreciated that so much.

But Citlali also validated the many times Tala was told she was difficult. Citlali worked to understand her where others got aggravated and gave up, but how long was she going to put up with that? Sometimes, even Kyra got frustrated with her. When Kyra got vexed with her, it made her feel alone and wrong, like she was the only person in existence built like this.

It would be worse with Citlali. Kyra was sort of obligated to get along with her, try to understand her, and be there for her as her sister. Citlali offered those things voluntarily, and Tala worried that Citlali would eventually get fed up with it, like in the parking lot. Eventually she'd be told she was emotionally distant or socially inept. None of which would be a lie. *Yeah, you know where this is going.*

So it didn't make sense to get comfortable. She glanced down at Citlali, soft and smiling in her sleep. Yeah, this was too close. Wiggling, she planned to free the both of them, but each time she moved, Citlali burrowed in closer. She was stuck. *And fucked.*

***

Slowly waking up, Citlali sighed into solid warmth. *Tala.* She pressed herself closer. Tala smelled like the ocean, and Citlali felt blanketed in security and affection.

Reaching up to caress Tala's cheek, she kissed Tala's shoulder. Pushing herself up, she went for a kiss on the lips, but stopped as her eyes met Tala's. A coldness lingered there. A stillness.

"Should I brush my teeth first?" She wanted it to come out as a joke, but this was Tala. It was actually possible.

Tala gave her a small smile. It looked a little sad. "No, it's okay. But I have to go."

Good mood vanishing, Citlali sat up. "What? Why?"

"I emailed my advisor while you were asleep. She said I could come in this afternoon and we can figure out the internship."

"Oh. That's good." Okay, she could breathe a little easier now, but tension still lingered in the air. Something was off. "You can't do it over the phone? I could make us breakfast."

Tala shook her head. "I'd rather do it in person."

Sounded about right for a person who hated phone calls, but it felt like Tala wanted to escape, and Citlali wondered why. "Well, does it have to be right now?"

"I need to go home, shower, and put on some more appropriate advisor-meeting clothes."

All of that sounded reasonable, but it still seemed like an excuse. *Since when are you so insecure? She does all sorts of things for you. Let her go.* "Okay. Can I call you later?"

Tala nodded. "I'll text you if anything comes from this."

"Text me regardless."

Tala gave Citlali a kiss. At first, it seemed hesitant, but that faded quickly. Tala pulled her closer, until Citlali was draped entirely over her. Sparks of pleasure shot through Citlali. Tala's hands roamed her back, and Citlali chuckled into the kiss, gently guiding Tala's hand to her ass. Tala moaned and gave a squeeze that was harder than expected. Citlali winced and pulled away, breaking the kiss.

Tala's eyes went wide. "Shit, I'm sorry!" She eased Citlali off of her, then got to her feet. "I'm sorry. I gotta go!"

"Tala, wait." Citlali reached for her, but Tala was already out of reach.

"I'll text you!" Tala called behind her as she rushed out of the bedroom.

Citlali jumped out of bed, but by the time she hit the living room, Tala was already gone. Citlali couldn't figure out what just happened, but her heart fell into the void. She had pushed Tala again. Again, after they had sort of argued and Tala was already on edge. So stupid. She hoped Tala would text her later.

Chapter Eleven

CITLALI SIGHED, HUNCHED OVER her neat desk as she went through the month's books for The New Moon. Being in the back office wasn't so bad. It was quiet, the AC reached every corner, and she could play music she liked. Ruby had been coming to the club more often, and Citlali just didn't have time for it anymore.

Her phone chimed. A text from Tala. Ever since Tala had been in her bed, she felt like Tala was doing her best to present as normal, but there was a tension there. They had met up a couple of times since Tala slept over, and she seemed guarded. She thought more before she spoke, tone almost neutral, and she looked away more often. Citlali felt like it was her fault, more of the disagreement in the parking lot than Tala in her bed, but she couldn't apologize for acting like she did concerning Ruby. She explained how she felt, and she needed Tala to accept and understand that, but Tala still suffered in silence.

Citlali checked her phone. A picture of a bowl of instant noodles lit the screen, captioned, **I might actually die without Kyra. I forgot to go food shopping!**

Knowing her girl, yes, Tala might starve if she only had one bowl of ramen. **What happened?**

Kyra and her girlfriend Raina have an anniversary coming up, so she's been focused on that. I've only exchanged a few texts with her in the past week and a half.

She reminds you to shop? Citlali wasn't sure what to make of that. It was a bit odd that a grown woman needed reminding.

She invites me along with her or she does it for me.

Citlali frowned. Tala was too dependent on Kyra. Before the sleepover, she'd have thought this was cute and offered to go shopping with her, but now with the way she ran out so fast, she wasn't sure if Tala really wanted her company. Before she could figure out what to say, the door opened and Daphne stepped in.

"That girl is relentless," Daphne said.

"Ruby?" Citlali asked as she flipped her phone over. The last thing she needed, beyond Ruby continuing to visit, was for Daphne to see her texting with Tala. She couldn't deal with the teasing.

"Yes!" Daphne threw her hands up. "She's been here an hour and asked about you at least eight thousand times."

"Only eight thousand." Citlali rolled her eyes.

"Does she realize how rude it is to ask about a woman while sitting across from another?"

"I'm sure you're so insulted."

Daphne made a face. "She's creepy. She keeps asking about the girl stalking you, and she doesn't mean herself."

"She means Tala. And Tala thinks she's dangerous." She wanted Daphne to validate her opinion, that she wasn't wrong for telling Tala she was overreacting.

Daphne frowned and closed the door. "Wait, they've met?"

"Ruby confronted her in the parking lot about our first date that you told everyone about." Anger sparked within her and she glared at her friend.

Daphne put her hand to her chest, offended. "It wasn't just me there, and we talked about how cute you both were. Maybe you should listen to Tala."

Citlali scoffed. Not even Daphne. "I can take care of myself, and Ruby hasn't demonstrated any reason to worry."

"Beyond ignore any and every request you've made for her not to touch you and implying almost every time she opens her mouth that she wants to sleep with you?"

Citlali curled her lip. "That's tame."

Daphne arched an eyebrow and folded her arms. "You told Tala those things?"

"They're the truth."

Daphne shook her head. "You're good at picking up girls, but bad at being in a relationship with them."

Citlali glared at Daphne. "I am not bad at being in a relationship. I would dote on Tala if she let me." She'd give Tala the world if Tala allowed it.

Daphne snorted. "That doesn't mean you're good at relationships. That just means you're good at spoiling people. You can't just downplay Tala's interactions with a crazy girl stalking you."

"I didn't downplay anything. Ruby isn't dangerous."

Daphne shook her head. "To our knowledge, no, but you also basically told Tala she's wrong to worry about you. You have a girlfriend who doesn't give you shit for working in a sex club, and you're dismissive of her worries."

Citlali sucked her teeth. "And my feelings didn't count?"

"Your feelings? The ones where you were insulted by someone you like, who was worrying about you and made an observation about a person that was different from yours? Wow, haven't seen your mom's side in you in a while."

"To hell with you!" Citlali stared her down. Her experience was just as valid as Tala's observations. "And my mother is a great judge of character."

Daphne held up a finger. "But not always right. You're not always right, no matter how politely you put it. Think about it." Daphne ducked back out of the room.

Citlali sighed and dropped her pen. Had she downplayed Tala's feelings? She thought she did a good job explaining herself, but something was obviously bothering Tala. She picked up her phone. **We could go shopping this afternoon if you want**. They hadn't seen each other in a few days.

You sure?

Citlali sighed. That hit her deep now that she considered Tala was eating her feelings. Tala probably thought they were in a downward spiral, that Citlali was upset with her. Tala might even think they were about to break up. One disagreement wasn't the end of the world. Except to someone like Tala, especially considering how she bolted from the apartment. **Can I call you?**

Okay.

Citlali video called. She liked being able to see Tala. It helped her gauge Tala. She smiled. "Hey."

Tala glanced away, but looked back. "Hey."

"Are you okay?"

Tala shrugged. "I'm okay."

"Come on, babe. Talk to me." Citlali couldn't believe she had to beg, but she wanted to know what was up. "You've been off since you came up here before."

Take sighed. "I'm just sorry I upset you."

"And you've been dwelling on that?" While she was busy being upset that Tala questioned her judgment, Tala was beating herself up over expressing worry. *Am I really equipped to deal with Tala?* It felt draining right now. "Why?"

Tala shrugged. "Because I don't like making you upset and I did it twice in one night."

She couldn't let go of how fragile Tala was. "I don't want you to feel bad. I just need you to trust me." *Just can't help myself, huh?* All this anxiety was unnecessary.

Tala scratched the top of her head. "Yeah, I trust you. I'm sorry again." There was another short shrug.

Damn it, Tala was retreating into herself even more. "Tala, please understand."

Tala waved it off with way more waves than necessary. "I trust you. I won't say anything again."

"Tala—"

"I should go. You're working. Text you later."

Tala hung up before Citlali could say anything. *Damn.* Citlali blew out a breath. That didn't go as well as she had hoped. She wanted to blame Tala, but Daphne's words echoed in her mind. She shouldn't be upset with Tala for worrying over her.

It wasn't like Tala hurt her. Yes, it stung when Tala ran out on her, but that went back to the argument. Tala was worried, and suddenly Citlali was ready to reevaluate their entire relationship? Something was wrong there. *Maybe I don't like her as much as she likes me.* But the very idea made her stomach churn. She didn't want to lose Tala. She enjoyed being with her and wanted that feeling of waking up in her arms again.

"Damn it." Citlali put down her phone. She didn't like that she had to apologize, but she disliked the idea of Tala falling away from her even more.

To take her mind off of Tala, she got back to work. The math was a good distraction. She had to be careful or there'd be real consequences.

Eventually, Citlali had to do her real job, and she couldn't hide in the office all night. As soon as she finished with the books and stepped onto the club floor, Ruby was at her side. Ruby grinned, stars in her eyes. Citlali sighed, letting all of the air out of her. *Is this how a popped balloon feels?*

"Are you hiding from me now?" Ruby pouted.

"I'm working." It was something Tala understood, but also used as an escape. *Don't think about Tala right now. Focus on getting this leech off of you without insulting her too much.*

"I know." Ruby suddenly brightened. "But you get off soon. We could go for breakfast, or maybe later in the afternoon we could go get some lunch. It'll be perfect. I know the best places. Then we could go for a walk."

Citlali growled. "Look, I have a girlfriend."

Ruby's body tensed. "You have what?"

Fuck, why the hell did I say that? She wasn't supposed to reveal personal information. Citlali held up her hands. "Never mind. I have to go make sure we're ready for closing." That was a couple of hours away. *Damn it, that won't be enough to get rid of her.*

Citlali was too agitated. Too much was going on and her careful balancing act was off. *This is because of Tala.* It really was a good thing significant others weren't allowed in or she'd be even more of a mess.

Ruby wasn't so easily put off. She was there almost every time Citlali turned around. And, despite having been in the office for half the night, there were still enough crises to keep Citlali busy. Underneath all of that, she thought about Tala. She wanted Tala, wanted to be with her. *Can you handle Tala, though?*

By the time she got home, Citlali was ready to fall into bed, but Tala stood outside of her building. The pouty face was cute as always, but Citlali wasn't in the mood. She glowered at Tala.

"Uh...I wanted to say thanks for dinner. I don't usually do delivery," Tala said, stepping back. Instead of actually apologizing to Tala, she ordered her dinner and groceries, and apparently, the delivery made it.

But Citlali didn't care about that right now. "You're welcome. Look, I know you're going to apologize again and whatever, but I'm really tired."

Tala stiffened. "Oh, okay."

Citlali scowled. "No, no, no. Don't do that."

"What?"

"The sad, kicked puppy thing. Don't do that." She didn't want to deal with that right now. *And, maybe you can't deal with it point blank. It was cute for a while, but now I don't want to be bothered.* She didn't want to bother with the emotional juggling act that came with Tala. She didn't have the energy.

Tala took a step back. "Okay. Sorry I bothered you."

"Still doing it." Citlali moved to the building door as Tala continued backing away. She needed a hot shower to wash away all of this mess.

***

Tala's nose twitched as she made her way to her bike. No one wanted to deal with her. Nobody wanted her worry, not even her honestly. If only she could walk away from herself. So she, her stomach butterflies, and the intense feeling that she was about to vomit, mounted her motorcycle. Before she could pull out of the parking spot, a car blocked her. She sighed. *I don't need this.*

"Can you let me move?" Tala said as the back window rolled down in the town car. The sulfur scent hit her, and she snarled. Rage burned through her insecurity and anxiety, leaving her nothing but anger.

"What are you doing around here?" Ruby asked with a smirk.

"Why the hell are you here?" Tala hopped off her bike and stormed up to the car window, nerves itching, ready to tear out of her. She flexed, wanting to rip the door off of the car. *Calm down. You can't do anything crazy.*

"Stopping you from hurting Lali. Why are you stalking her?" Cerulean eyes stared daggers at Tala.

Tala couldn't believe her ears. "I'm stalking her?"

She was about to get right in Ruby's face, but the front passenger door opened. A man who had to be over a foot taller than Tala stepped out, brushing dust off of his black suit. Tala groaned. *What now?*

"I'm going to need you to step back," the guy said. He smelled of metal, oil, and a hint of gunpowder.

Tala looked up at him. He chuckled. Her jaw tensed. *No, no, no. Don't do it. You know the consequences. You really don't want to lose the little bit of things you have.* She forced herself to calm down.

"Just move the car. I'm trying to go home," Tala said.

"She doesn't want you. Leave her alone." Ruby spoke with a certainty that was jarring, especially considering what just happened.

Tala nodded. "You're right."

"And you're not her girlfriend."

"Probably not." Her throat burned.

"Good. Then leave her alone or I'll make you regret it." Ruby nodded to the big guy. He yanked down on his suit jacket, possibly to show off his size, but then got back in the car. They peeled off, Ruby's cackle echoing off the buildings.

In a huff, Tala watched the car disappear, and then turned to look at Citlali's building. She pulled out her phone, but Citlali didn't want to hear from her, especially about Ruby. After all, she was already annoyed. Tala put her phone away, hopped on her bike, and went home.

As soon as she opened her apartment door, Tala caught the lingering scent of fried chicken. The dinner she had a few hours ago. Dinner sent over by Citlali, like she cared about Tala's well being. But

Citlali also said she didn't want to see Tala now. Everything was confusing as fuck, and Tala wandered through her apartment in a daze trying to figure it out.

"Even if she doesn't want to be around you, shouldn't you tell her Ruby knows where she lives?" Tala asked the air.

She didn't want to upset Citlali again. She wasn't sure her stomach could take it. Maybe it would be all right to tell her in a few days. This was hard. And yes, the right thing generally was hard, but what was right in this instance?

She threw herself into her bed and tried to sleep. Her stomach twisted. Acid burned up her throat, and her heart wrung itself out with each beat. It was impossible to sleep with all of that going on.

When sleeping didn't work, she went to her video games, grabbing a soda and setting herself up on her beanbag. This was usually the best way to forget anything life threw at her, but this time the puzzles didn't help. Citlali might not know what sort of trouble Ruby might actually be. Or Citlali might know exactly what she was doing, like she said.

All day she wrestled with what to do. She very nearly asked her mother for advice, but she didn't want to be a burden. Especially when she knew her mother would be all sympathy when she didn't deserve it.

She could ask Kyra, but she didn't want Kyra to know she had been dating Kyra's boss. Kyra might get angry at her for doing something that could affect her work, or just not being honest. She groaned. *Did I do anything right?* No, she never did.

She needed advice. Good advice from someone who knew Citlali better than she did. *Well, her best friend works at The New Moon.* That settled it. She wanted to do right by Citlali, even if Citlali was done with her. *If only I had her friend's number and could talk to her.* Tala would have to make a trip for this, but Citlali was worth it.

Citlali was always worth it.

Tala rode to The New Moon as soon as it opened. The second she got off of her bike, her nerves felt like ants crawling all over her body. *Is this the right thing to do? Hell, will I even be able to get in?* She was Citlali's girlfriend, however briefly.

She might be on the list keeping her out, which might be for the best. She was probably overreacting. She should just go home. She went as far as mounting her bike and glanced across the parking lot.

Ruby's car pulled into a spot close to the entrance.

Ruby exited the vehicle along with four large men, including the one who tried to intimidate Tala yesterday. They were dressed in casual clothes, but something looked off. Ruby looked them all over and held up her index finger.

"Remember the plan. I'm getting what I want out of Citlali. No more excuses and no more playing nice. Any objections?" Ruby asked. None of the men said a word and Ruby nodded. "That's what I thought. You guys will get bonuses for this after I get my girl."

Heart lurching, Tala watched them go into the club and rushed over to the car. A tinge of oil and gunpowder lingered in the air. The New Moon didn't have metal detectors. Her instincts went haywire. Did they carry guns? The hell was this? She took a calming breath. *It's probably nothing.*

But it felt like everything.

Ruby sounded like she was about to possess Citlali in any way possible, including violence, and Tala couldn't stand the idea.

Citlali isn't something to possess. Her instincts scratched at her brain and said otherwise. *Citlali is yours, and you can't let that asshole take what's yours.* More than that, she couldn't let Ruby hurt Citlali. It didn't matter if Citlali was hers or not. Guns might be involved, and Ruby planned to force Citlali into whatever the hell it was she wanted. *But beyond that, she's trying to touch your mate. Can't have that.*

Before the word "mate" registered, everything inside of Tala got buried by a single thought: *Stop Ruby from hurting Citlali.*

***

Citlali didn't get a chance to duck out of sight when Ruby came in with her party. She yanked Citlali to an empty booth. A man who seemed to be with Ruby blocked them in as three other men sat opposite of them. Citlali's heart thudded. Something felt wrong here.

"Lali, you're going to have a drink with me," Ruby said. It wasn't an offer or a request. It was a command.

"I'm working," Citlali replied. She needed to get out of this situation. She tried to catch a bouncer's eye, but the man looming over her blocked her view.

"Yes, with me." Ruby stared her down. "You always push me away, but you have all the time for that tacky bitch."

Citlali shook her head. "Who are you talking about?"

"The bitch sniffing after you at your apartment." Ruby clutched her arm hard enough for it to hurt.

The words registered to Citlali's mind and got stuck there. "You've been to my apartment?" *What the hell? How?*

Ruby's eyes darkened, hardened. "We're going to a room, or my friends here are going to make sure you don't have work anymore."

Citlali glanced around. The man blocking them in stood and flashed a handgun tucked into his waistband. Her breath caught. Ruby yanked her out of the booth with a grin. Citlali had no choice but to follow her.

"Don't do anything stupid. They've all got guns, and they'd all happily shoot everyone in here for me," Ruby whispered in her ear. Citlali shuddered. "So, smile and take us to a room and no one has to get hurt."

Citlali grunted, but forced out a smile. She couldn't risk everyone's lives. She'd have to figure out something else to do. For now, she moved toward the private rooms. She would have to get them away from all of the patrons and alert a bouncer in the hall. Worst case scenario, she could use the emergency button in the room, but she didn't want to end up in a closed off area with armed men. With a glance over her shoulder, she tried to catch Daphne's eye, but the four men closed rank around her and all she saw was black suits and scowls.

***

Tala cursed as she marched to the entrance of The New Moon. The closer she got, the more she could smell Ruby. Her scent mixed with Citlali's. Underneath that, further in the establishment, she could smell sweat from Citlali's distress. That broke her into a run. Maybe she was already too late. Her muscles twitched. *No, you can't be too late.*

The bouncer tried to step in Tala's way when she got to the door, but no one could stop her as Citlali's fear scent invaded her nose and tore at her brain. A simple swipe of her hand and the bouncer went down in a heap. She'd have to apologize later.

Tala shot into the club as if her ass was on fire. She scanned the main hall. Seeing nothing, she sniffed the air, but paused as a person appeared by her side. Dressed in a purple suit, the woman stared at her with sharp, disapproving hazel eyes.

"If you're looking for Citlali, she went to one of the private rooms with Ruby," the woman said.

Tala took a chance. "Are you Daphne?"

"I am. And you're Tala. You shouldn't be in here."

"I know, but I saw Ruby in the parking lot with four guys who had bulges in their clothes." She couldn't think straight, could hardly think at all as she took in more of Citlali's scent and gun oil.

"Yeah." Daphne motioned around the club. "Sort of the point."

Tala frowned. "Not those kinds of bulges! Look…" She tried to think of something that wouldn't give her super fine-tuned senses away. No one else could smell the gunpowder or oil. "Ruby was talking about making Citlali hers."

Daphne's face gave a small tic, but she maintained a calm facade. Too bad she didn't know Tala could smell the shot of fear that went through her. "Ruby says things like that all the time. Are you sure about the bulges? Our bouncers are usually good at spotting those things. We'll get on it, but you have to get out of here."

Tala sucked her teeth. She dashed off before Daphne could say anything else. She heard Daphne call her name. She didn't care. She needed a scent to follow, but Citlali was all over the damn place. *Focus on Ruby.* That was easy enough. She locked onto that wretched aroma and cut through the crowd to a distant door that blended into the wall.

Opening it, Tala came to a corridor lined with doors. The crash of furniture from the end pounded in her ears, coming from the place where a lone man stood. The hallway was covered in Citlali's scent, drenched in her despair, mixing with Ruby's excitement. The mixture pulled Tala's face into a tight grimace, showing off her front teeth. Her teeth grew sharper by the second. Ruby was turned on at having abducted Citlali. Well, Tala wouldn't let it go any further than that. *Mate.* She shook that thought away. *Focus.*

"Hey, you're not supposed to be here," the man said, straightening his suit.

Tala growled as she stalked toward the man, muscles spasming, ready to burst out of her. She could hear her breathing echoing through the hall as she stood face to face with the man. More than that, she could hear Ruby snickering, smell Ruby's arousal. Citlali's aroma pushed into her skull. Nervous and scared, she was unknowingly calling out for Tala.

"Move," Tala said, her voice deep and scratchy. She was ready to come out of her skin for Citlali, but she didn't want to hurt anyone if possible. Perhaps it wouldn't be possible this time, not if Citlali's misery continued to fill her lungs.

"No one's supposed to be in here." The man touched his waist. "You might wanna take off if you know what's good for you."

Tala wiggled her nose. Metal and oil and fear mingled, trying to take over from Citlali's smell. It lashed her nerves. Citlali yelped. Tala's body tingled and her blood roared in her ears. Her rage awoke, out for blood.

His would do.

"Get the hell out of my way," she said, her voice little more than a growl.

"I can't—" She grabbed him by the shoulders, feeling some bones crunch under her fingers. Her nails extended into claws and tore through his jacket. Almost effortlessly, she flung him into the wall. He didn't move again.

"I've got you, Citlali," Tala said, her hand on the doorknob, her claws scratching the brass.

Chapter Twelve

"THIS IS A FIVE hundred dollar room? There's not even a bed!" Ruby kicked over a nearby chair.

The room was set up like a hotel suite living room. A couch sat opposite a television, a couple of armchairs tucked up to one wall, a desk and a table by the tinted window. The view of the boardwalk and ocean was stunning. It was meant to be comfortable, yes, but not *that* comfortable.

"Because we're not encouraging people to sleep with the dancers." Citlali leaned toward the lamp at the front of the room. A hidden button at the base was how she could signal for help. There had been a loud thump outside just moments before, and now a scratching noise was filling the room. The guards and Ruby seemed to ignore it, but the noise worried Citlali.

"Then the couch will have to do." Ruby shrugged. "Sit."

Citlali didn't move. One of the larger men picked her up and tossed her on the sofa. Citlali tried to get back up, only to be shoved once again. The man forced her head into the wall. Pain shot through her skull. She screamed. Dizzy from pain, the man forced her into the seat. He glared at her to keep her in place and she glared back, ready to jump up.

Before Citlali could move, Ruby cuddled up next to her. Ruby kissed Citlali's neck. Citlali hissed and tried to pull away, but Ruby pressed her entire body into Citlali, hand clutching Citlali's side. Her fingers dug into Citlali's blazer.

"We're going to have a good time. Much better than you had with that bitch," Ruby whispered.

Citlali flinched. It hurt to hear Tala being referred to as a bitch, especially after the way she had treated Tala. Tala had been right, and she had made Tala feel like an ass. *Look at where you are now. I have to get out of this mess.* Other panic buttons lay hidden throughout the room. She just needed to be able to hit one.

Ruby caressed Citlali's thigh, squeezing until it hurt. Citlali couldn't control the hiss that slipped past her lips. A crooked, demented grin appeared on Ruby's face, and Citlali knew the woman planned for pain.

Citlali shifted her weight on the couch, trying to reach the button just behind the headrest, but it would be too obvious. In the time it took help to get there, she'd probably end up dead.

"I brought so many presents." Ruby giggled. "I can't wait to tie you up. You like spankings?"

While Citlali didn't mind a good spanking, this wasn't how she planned to spend her night. She swallowed, trying to think of something, but her heartbeat filled her mind, pushing everything else away. "Shouldn't we have that drink first? This room has complimentary Champagne, and we could enjoy some fruit."

Ruby nodded. "Yes, it's taken us so long to get to this moment, so we should celebrate." She turned to one of the men. "Carl, pop the Champagne while I get started."

"I doubt I could do this with an audience." Citlali dipped her head, trying to buy some time.

Ruby scoffed. "You put together sex shows for a living." She leaned in, grabbing Citlali by the hair and yanking her head back. Citlali winced. Ruby was about to kiss her, but the scratching grew louder. "What the hell is that noise?"

The three men pulled out their guns. Ruby eased back, on alert. Citlali tensed. *Is that the club security? Do they know what was going on?* Citlali didn't see how they would, but she didn't care.

One moment the scratching grew louder, louder, louder still and then—

The door exploded open, bits of splintered wood blowing through the room.

Tala stepped inside. Her eyes glowed pure white, her face a grimace with her nostrils flared. She panted, showing off surprisingly sharp teeth, like a dog's teeth. Citlali leaned back from the odd sight, unsure if what she was seeing was even real. *How are Tala's eyes glowing?*

"It's the bitch," Ruby yelled.

"Get away from her," Tala replied, her voice a strange growl. *Is she taller?* Muscles rippled in her arms.

"She's mine!" Ruby grabbed Citlali and licked her cheek, like she was savoring an ice cream cone. Citlali didn't even have time to react before Ruby slammed her head against the wall. White-hot pain shuddered through her body, and the impact left her seeing stars.

"Let her go!" Tala broke into a howl.

Energy crackled throughout the room—like there was about to be a lightning storm—and seemed to center around Tala. Her body grew, bulky and tall. She tore out of her clothes, and black and copper hair rippled over her skin...or fur. It stood on end at the top of her head and raced down the center of her back, like her mohawk. Her face elongated until it was a muzzle, like a dog's. Or a wolf's. Her nails became claws and her feet morphed into paws. When she smiled, a mouthful of sharp teeth glittered.

Citlali couldn't believe what she was seeing. This had to be a dream, a nightmare. It couldn't be real. *Tala's a werewolf.* Citlali pressed a hand to her thrumming forehead. *I must've hit my head harder than I thought!* Tala couldn't be a werewolf. Werewolves weren't real. Tala wasn't a monster!

Ruby gasped and flinched, but regained her composure enough to make Citlali question if she was seeing right. "Kill that thing!" Ruby shouted.

Ruby's goons didn't need the order, already aiming their guns.

"No!" Citlali shoved Ruby away from her and managed to tackle one of the men. Shots rang through the room, echoing in Citlali's head, but she tried to grab his gun from him. He slapped her across the face with the weapon. Her teeth rattled, pain burning across her cheek. The world went blurry, and just as she thought it was coming back into focus, it went black.

***

Citlali groaned as she came back into consciousness. *What happened?* Gunfire echoed through her mind. She gasped and opened her eyes. "Ruby!"

Eyes scanning everywhere, she found herself alone in an unfamiliar room on a small sofa. Then, it flooded back to her—Tala carried her here. Tala saved her. Tala was a werewolf!

Her heart leaped, crashing against her ribs as she jumped up. She almost fell over, dizziness tilting her for a second. She turned in every direction, but didn't see anything beyond a neat, bare apartment. She checked herself out, finding everything intact. No missing limbs, no bullet wounds. Her head hurt, but that was expected.

"I have to get out of here." Citlali made a move for the door. Her hand was on the knob, and then a moan echoed through the place. She flinched at the sound and turned around, expecting to be face to face with a monster. There was nothing, though.

She was about to go when another groan ripped through the air. Her heart was about to explode, but nothing happened beyond more noise. It sounded like someone was hurt. *Tala!*

Tala had been the target of all the gunfire. Yes, Tala was a monster, but she came to Citlali's rescue and she was possibly hurt. But Tala was a werewolf. Dangerous. There was another groan, and it didn't sound dangerous.

"Tala could be hurt, and if it wasn't for her I could be dead," Citlali muttered to herself. It seemed like it needed to be said aloud. It gave her the resolve to do the right thing.

Following the noise, she moved through the tiny apartment and found Tala's bedroom. The door was open, and Tala was laid out in bed like a drowning victim washed ashore. Blood dripped down her motionless hands. Citlali's heart stopped.

"Don't be dead!" Citlali rushed over to the bed, finding Tala's eyes closed, but her chest rising and falling at regular intervals.

Tala wasn't dead; injured, bloody, and naked, though. Citlali couldn't leave her, not after what Tala risked. What kind of person would she be?

So instead of leaving like she probably should, she checked on Tala. She had a wound in her shoulder and one in her stomach. They didn't look as severe as bullet wounds, but they were bleeding. They needed tending to.

Citlali acted on autopilot, finding bandages and alcohol to clean Tala's injuries. Tala barely moved as Citlali worked on her. Citlali blinked back tears. This was her fault. *And I have the nerve to be scared of her. She was only in that mess because of me.* She didn't have a right to be afraid, to run out, to disappear. Tala hadn't done that to her.

***

Tala groaned as she opened her eyes. Her bedroom ceiling loomed over her head and her mattress had never felt so good on her back. The pillow under her head felt like a cloud. *Home.* She couldn't focus on anything beyond that. That and the pain. Everything hurt, like a million claws had been dragged down every muscle in her body. *Why does everything hurt?*

She swallowed, her throat dry like sandpaper. Every inch of her throbbed in time with her heartbeat. She tried to push herself up into a sitting position, but found herself to be entirely too heavy. *The hell?*

"Tala, are you up?" Citlali's voice came from somewhere to her left.

Tala forced herself to a sitting position. Pain tore through her. "Yeah," she answered through gritted teeth. *Why is Citlali here? Am I dreaming?* Not with all the agony. It was so bad she felt like she might vomit right there.

The door nudged open, and even the little squeak felt like it sawed through Tala with rusty, jagged teeth. Citlali came in with a tray in hand. She had on one of Tala's t-shirts and nothing more. A jolt went through her that had nothing to do with pain.

"You're here..." Tala couldn't understand why the hell Citlali would be here. "Why didn't you run?"

Citlali tilted her head. "Run where?"

"Away!" It would've been normal and very understandable for Citlali to get as far away from her as soon as possible, and considering the fact that she didn't even remember coming home, let alone falling asleep, Citlali had a chance to get away and didn't take it. That didn't make any sense.

Citlali looked at Tala as if she was out of her mind and then shook her head. *What the hell does that mean? What does any of this mean? How the hell can she be okay after she saw what I am?* While she tried to make sense of things, Citlali walked deeper into the room, like it was any other day.

"How's your shoulder?" Citlali asked as she put the tray down on the foot of the bed.

Tala arched an eyebrow. "My shoulder?"

She glanced at her shoulder. She'd been shot there. Several times. The memory of leaning on the barrel of the gun to take the shots came back, the pain radiating through her once more. *I had to make sure no one else in the room got hurt.* A white bandage covered the area. She didn't recall putting it on. *I got shot in the stomach, too.* She moved her blanket out of the way and discovered another bandage. *Citlali probably did it, trying to help.* She yanked off both bandages.

"Tala, wait!" Citlali gasped, putting her hands over her mouth.

"It's fine." The wounds had healed into smooth, unblemished skin. "I heal pretty quick. Are you okay?" Tala studied Citlali.

Citlali's sand-colored face had a maroon bruise under one eye, and her cheek had a bandage on it. A bruise decorated Citlali's temple as well. *You failed. How dare you even think you could claim her when you couldn't even protect her?*

"You took good care of me last night." Citlali moved the tray over Tala's lap and propped the tray up on short legs.

Tala looked at the food, a cup of apple cinnamon tea, toast, and a huge bowl of oatmeal. Probably the last thing she had to eat in the apartment. "Thanks for the food."

A blush colored the parts of Citlali's face that weren't busted up. "It's the least I could do."

"Oh...I'm a little fuzzy on the details from last night. I know I got emotional." *Or possessive? Why is she even here now? She could've left while I was knocked out.*

Citlali sat down on the foot of the bed. "Maybe you should eat. While it's warm." She rubbed Tala's leg. It was insane that she was touching Tala like everything was normal!

But Tala was starving, so she didn't argue. She bypassed the spoon and slurped the oatmeal out of the bowl. It was gone within seconds. She barely tasted the buttered toast and gulped the tea without taking a breath. Citlali watched her and she struggled not to squirm.

"It was good," Tala plucked at the bedding as her body settled. The pain dulled to a bearable level. "Thanks."

Citlali offered her a soft smile. "No problem. Sorry I couldn't make more. I know you have a high metabolism, and now I understand why." She opened her mouth, as if to say more, but quickly closed it.

Tala looked away for a second. "Yeah, it...takes a lot of energy." *To be me?* Her stomach dropped. There was no escaping where this was going. She sighed. "You don't have to stay."

Citlali rose off of the bed, and Tala's heart sank. Darkness laughed within her. *Did you think she'd stay? She dumped you before you even showed her what you really are.*

Surprisingly, Citlali climbed into bed next to her and embraced her. Tala couldn't breathe, was too scared to do so. The smallest movement from her might ruin the moment or wake her from this dream. There was no way this turned out well for her. Nothing ever turned out well for her. She lost sure-things, after all.

"I don't..." Tala shook her head. "Why are you still here?"

"Where else should I be?"

"Far away. Scared of me."

Citlali kissed her cheek before pulling away just enough to look into her eyes. "I'll never be scared of you."

Tala couldn't believe it. *This whole thing is a dream. You hit your head and you're hallucinating.* That was the only way to explain Citlali being there, cooking for her, and embracing her. In reality, Citlali should be running for the hills, shouldn't be here right now, and shouldn't want to see Tala ever again.

"I don't understand." It didn't make any sense! "How can you be so calm about this?"

"I've had a few hours to process this while you've been unconscious. I have questions, of course, but more than that, I've been worried about you. You could've died trying to save me from my own foolish ego."

Tala couldn't keep up with this, mind spinning. "Huh?"

Citlali took a breath. "You were right. I'm sorry I made you feel bad, and I'm sorry I didn't listen to your concerns. Thank you for coming after me."

Tala blinked. "Really?"

"I was stubborn, and I shouldn't have been angry with you for caring." Citlali caressed Tala's thigh over the blanket.

Tala couldn't believe that. Everyone always had cause to be angry with her. "I should've minded my business."

"No!" Citlali grabbed Tala's hand and held it with both of her own. "I am your business. We agreed we were girlfriends and the second you showed a bit of concern for me I got insulted that you didn't think I could take care of myself. It was like you threatened my independence and I couldn't take that. I knew the way I answered you would mess with your anxiety, but you still stood by me."

Tala's stomach turned over. "Well, I care about you."

Citlali smiled. She caressed Tala's hand with her thumb. "And I'm so happy you do, and thank you for saving me. Thank you for caring about me and trusting me enough to reveal this other side of you."

Tala swallowed. The simple touch from Citlali soothed her, but each stroke of her thumb rubbed her nerves raw. *Fucking anxiety.* Despite Citlali's words, Tala still expected to be pushed away, shunned, and outed to the world at any moment. "Uh, yeah, I..."

"I still like you, by the way."

Tala was pretty sure she misheard that. *Why the hell would she still like you?* "You do?"

"More so now that I see the lengths you'll go through for me, and now that I have my head out of my ass. I was so ready to take care of you, but I have to let you take care of me, too. We have to be there for each other." Citlali kissed her cheek. "I'm sorry. I want to make things up to you. I'm so sorry."

Tala wasn't sure what to say to that. In the silence, Citlali rested against her shoulder. She got to enjoy that for about a minute, which was longer than she expected. Then the anxiety took over.

"You don't have to stay because you're scared of me. I'm not going to hurt you. You can leave," Tala said. That was the only way this situation made sense. Citlali had seen her wolf form and was frightened, so she wanted to appease Tala to avoid having to deal with the wolf.

Citlali sat up to stare Tala in the eye, honey-colored eyes dead serious. "I'm not scared of you, and I'm going to be here to tell the truth when that nervous voice inside your head tells you the worst. You risked so much for me last night; your life, your secret, everything. That doesn't scare me, at least not in the way you'd think."

Tala frowned. "So how does it scare you?"

"It scares me because it lets me know how much you care about me. I feel like I don't deserve you. You're like an angel and I can't believe you picked me. I'm honored."

Tala's brow furrowed. She couldn't believe what she was hearing. "You don't have to stay because you feel obligated."

Citlali laughed and kissed her chin. "You're really trying to chase me away. I'm in this now, much deeper than before. I'm not going anywhere." Citlali placed a kiss on Tala's lips.

Tala leaned into it. The kiss was soft and sweet. It didn't feel like an obligation or fear. Tala's nerves settled. Citlali caressed her cheek. She wasn't afraid to touch Tala. She wasn't afraid of Tala. As the kiss broke, Citlali stared into her eyes, and Tala felt tears slide from her eyes. Citlali wiped them away.

Citlali sniffled as her own tears wet her eyes. "I'm so sorry. I never want to hurt you like that. I'll get better. And I'm sorry my stubbornness put us in such a horrible situation." She took a breath, and it sounded shattered. "I thought I got you killed."

Tala shook her head. "I'm pretty tough in my wolf form and heal easily regardless. It's just a good thing they didn't have silver bullets."

Citlali's eyes widened. "Do those really kill you?"

"Not in the sense the movies would have you believe. Werewolves are allergic to silver. Some more than others, but silver bullets are stupid anyway. Silver's too soft."

Citlali chuckled, kissing Tala's cheek. "Good to know. I've got so many questions, but they'll keep until you're better. Thank you for saving me. I'm sorry you got hurt doing it."

"While I didn't do it for the kisses, I don't mind them." That earned her yet another kiss. "I think...I think I'd always save you. I'd do anything to keep you safe." It felt dangerous to admit, but she didn't think too hard on it. She wouldn't give her anxiety the chance.

The apartment door opened, and an important fact finally registered in Tala's brain. *I'm naked.* Of course she was naked. There was no way she had enough brain power to put on clothes after last night.

"Tala, get your ass out here now!" A slam of the door punctuated Kyra's booming voice.

Tala jumped out of the bed and grabbed a t-shirt from her drawer. She barely had it on by the time she stepped out of the bedroom. Kyra was there to greet her with a glare.

"How could you fuck up this bad?" Kyra stomped her foot.

Tala winced. "I've done a lot in the last few hours. Narrow down this fuck up please." She pressed her hands together. It could be the obvious, or making the obvious part of a larger thing.

"Why the hell were you involved in a shoot-out at the goddamn New Moon?" Kyra gnashed her teeth at Tala, who, even though she was in the wrong, didn't flinch.

"It's a long story," Tala replied.

Kyra took a step forward. "A long story? A long story your parents will hear about and then the pack will hear about! How could you be so reckless and stupid?" She pushed Tala.

Tumbling back a little, Tala winced. It had been stupid and reckless. She hadn't thought it out, only needing to save Citlali, but she had put so many more people in danger in that building, Kyra included. *Stupid.* They really had no idea what Ruby had planned.

"Hey!" Citlali stormed out of the bedroom. "She saved me. Ruby might've raped me and probably would've killed me had Tala not been there."

Kyra blinked and stepped back. "Citlali? What are you doing here?"

"A patron forced me into a private room. She had men with guns and they were obviously more than ready to use them. Tala took them on to save me." Citlali grabbed Tala's hand. Tala, for the first time, squeezed back.

Kyra looked between them, golden eyes confused. "Daphne was looking for you, and the police will probably want to talk to you."

"The police?" Citlali arched an eyebrow.

"Yes, they came up. There were gunshots, and they found five wounded customers in the back."

"Five armed assailants," Citlali said.

Kyra focused on Tala. "More importantly, one of them was ranting about a girl turned into a monster and attacked them like a wild animal."

Tala shrugged. "What was I supposed to do?"

Because, yeah, this was going to get her in trouble, but what was she supposed to do? *Let Ruby have her way with Citlali?* Her nature wouldn't allow that.

"Keep a low profile!" Kyra's face turned red.

Tala's stomach twisted. That was what they were supposed to do. It was drilled into their heads from when they were pups. Always keep a low profile. *And you screwed that up, too.* Now, who knew what might happen. She had an idea of what was to come. Banishment. Then a lifetime of embarrassment and shunning for Kyra, for her mother. She swallowed down all of her discomfort.

"I'm sorry," Tala said. She wished there was more she could say.

"You can't 'I'm sorry' your way out of this." Kyra made a fist and her eyes burned white, erupting in a way that put the sun to shame.

Citlali stepped forward. "Could you please stop screaming at her? You've been her friend long enough to know she's shutting down."

Wow, Citlali really did know her well.

Kyra opened her mouth like she was about to unleash another tirade, but then she sighed, and her body slumped. "Just...why would you do this?"

Tala gave a rather pathetic shrug. "Would you just let people hurt Raina?"

Kyra winced. "It's different. I love Raina."

Tala frowned. "Maybe I love her." The voice inside of her head scoffed. *You don't even know how to love. That's why Kyra's skeptical. You hate people and people hate you.*

Kyra shook her head. "No offense, but how long have you even known her?" Kyra stared down her boss. "What did you do to her?"

Citlali narrowed her gaze and folded her arms. "Excuse me?"

Kyra put her finger right in Citlali's face. "What did you do to her? I know it's your job to charm people. Do you know what you could cost her?" Kyra ripped their hands apart. They both gasped.

"Kyra, it's fine," Tala said. *I don't think I've ever seen her this upset. She's scared.*

"It's not fine!" Kyra's voice cracked. Tears shimmered in her eyes, then finally streamed down her cheeks. "They're going to kick you out." She dropped her head into her hands and wept.

Tala let out a long breath. For once, the thing that should've given her anxiety didn't. She hadn't thought about her pack when she acted, and now that the consequences were in front of her, she didn't care. The pack couldn't take away the people that mattered to her.

What did bother her was Kyra having a breakdown over it. She didn't like stressing Kyra out. She gathered Kyra into a tight embrace, rubbing her back as Kyra cried on her.

"Kyra, are you going to stop talking to me if they kick me out? Stop hanging out with me? Stop being my little sister?" Tala asked. She needed Kyra to realize this wouldn't affect them as much as she feared it would.

The questions shocked Kyra enough for her to stop crying "Of course not." She laughed and sniffled. "You'd starve to death without me."

Tala smiled. "Then, it'll be fine. I don't care about them. I care about you. I care about my parents. I care about Citlali." She put her arm around Citlali's waist.

Kyra took a breath and stepped back for room to wipe her face with both hands. "I just...I hate that they're going to use you doing something good and hurt you with it."

"They can't hurt me. I have you. It's okay." Tala meant that from the bottom of her heart. "They never accepted me, not fully. But I've always had you and that's enough."

Kyra hugged Tala. "I'm sorry I came at you like that. I'm actually happy for you, Tala." Kyra then gave Citlali a hard look. "You better take care of Tala. She's the best person I know."

Citlali nodded. "I'll treasure her."

Kyra drew in a deep breath. "Okay, fine. I'll leave you guys to sort yourselves out. I'll text you later, Tala."

Tala was tempted to walk Kyra out, but she didn't want to leave Citlali's side at the moment. Kyra let herself out and the sound of the door closing dropped everything inside of Tala. She collapsed onto the couch. Citlali followed her down. Tala sighed in relief and reveled in the quiet. Citlali held her close. Her jasmine and alcohol scent helped keep Tala calm.

***

Citlali pulled Tala to her chest. Tala was heavier than she expected, which she supposed made sense. Tala nuzzled her, hair from her braids scratching Citlali's skin. She rubbed her nose in Citlali's neck.

"I like the way you smell," Tala whispered.

"Is smell a big thing for you?"

Tala nodded. "Yeah. Does it bother you?"

"No. Like I said, I have questions."

"Ask away. If you don't mind, I'm going to stay here for a while."

Citlali rubbed her shoulder, amazed that her bullet wounds had healed so fast. "I'm glad you like how I smell. Smell all you want."

"I thought you'd smell like gunpowder because of last night, but you smell like my crappy soap. You took a shower?"

"After I managed to cover you in bed. I'm glad you made it that far." She moved a few braids. "Is it tiring to change?"

"Not really. I just had adrenaline going and the gunshots. For the most part, it's like flexing any other body part."

One that transforms a person into a wolf! Amazing. Citlali shook her head. "You were born like this?"

"Yeah, all werewolves are. And no, you can't become one if you get bitten by a werewolf."

Citlali smirked. "Oh, so you can bite me?"

Tala blushed. "With your consent."

"Oh, look at you, comfortable all of a sudden. Is this why you've been so nervous around me?"

"Partly, but I'm also just a mess. That's me." Tala shrugged.

Citlali kissed the top of her head. "I like you. I want you to be able to relax around me and be yourself. You're not a mess." She twirled the end of a braid. "Are there other werewolves or supernatural creatures?" It seemed like there were at least other werewolves. Tala was born this way, so she probably had werewolf parents. And there was Kyra, who was panicked about Tala revealing herself.

"Plenty of werewolves, but no on the supernatural creatures. We're not really supernatural. Just a different type of sapien."

"Okay." That was interesting, but now her mind shifted. Kyra was so upset, so panicked. Something serious was on the way. "Why was Kyra so upset?"

"It's nothing."

"It didn't sound like nothing." She could understand Tala not wanting to tell her. She'd have to work to earn Tala's trust again.

"It's nothing to me. I did the right thing."

"You're in trouble for saving me." Those other werewolves probably wouldn't be happy with Tala letting people see that werewolves exist.

Tala shrugged. "Not really."

"What's going to happen?" *What did my stubbornness cost Tala?*

Tala shook her head. "We have family and pack. Pack is like our nation or whatever. There are rules to being in it. I broke the rules regarding revealing my wolf form to the outside world."

Citlali doubted it was nearly as calm as Tala was making it seem. After all, Kyra was bawling. "Well, what could happen?"

"They could kick me out."

Citlali's mouth dropped open. "Kick you out of your nation?" *How would werewolves deport another werewolf?* "Or would it be more like an excommunication?"

Tala scoffed. "Something like that. It's not a big deal. I hate them. They hate me."

"They hate you?" She would see people getting frustrated with Tala, but how could anyone actually hate Tala?

Tala sighed. "It's just...I'm weird, okay? You know that. Kinda...broken, I guess. You know how people are social creatures? Or how wolves are social creatures? Werewolves are like quadruple that, but...not me."

Citlali tilted her head. *Does Tala think she's broken because she likes to stay inside?* "Being introverted isn't abnormal."

"It isn't normal for a werewolf. Werewolves are all about being together and enjoying company and touching and blah." Tala shuddered. "My pack never let me forget how weird I am, ever since we were little. We have these big gatherings once a month, and we get to just be who we are out in the woods or in the mountains. Sometimes even houses, if they're big enough. The kids would change and run around, tackle each other, wrestle, tumble, and stuff. I didn't. I found a corner or a cave or a tree, did my models, read, whatever. That made me happy, but someone always came to pounce on me, to get me to play. And I'd play, but..."

"But?"

Tala swallowed. "I pinned them easy and then they didn't want to play. I was always stronger. They started excluding me and I didn't care. I'd go back to my models or books. My books didn't make fun of Kyra or my dad. My books didn't whisper about my mom."

"Kyra, your dad, and your mom?" There was so much she didn't know.

Tala blew out a breath. "Werewolf social norms. Like wolves, werewolves mate for life, but my dad...he's a rogue wolf. Doesn't have a pack. Just sort of wanders. Wandered into my mother's path and she fell in love with the big idiot. As a rogue wolf, it's not very likely for him to settle down to be a proper mate for her, but she gave him a chance. They had me. He wandered away for a couple of years. Even though he came back, the pack never let her forget it, never lets her forget that he's not her mate, that she bonded with someone who can't form that bond in return. My existence never lets her forget it. My weirdness." Tala sniffled.

Citlali scratched Tala's scalp. "Your mother loves you. I can hear it in the way you talk about her. You're down on yourself because you're looking at yourself through their eyes. You're a wonderful person who saved me. You care about your friend. You love your mom. And apparently you were enough for your rogue wolf dad to come back for."

Tala's brow wrinkled. "He didn't come back for me."

"Then, why did he come back?"

Tala opened her mouth, but didn't say anything for a few seconds. "I dunno."

"Have you ever asked?"

"Well, no."

"You should ask. And you should believe in yourself. You're amazing." Citlali kissed the top of Tala's head. Tala cuddled into her. Citlali smiled into her hair. She wanted to protect this brave, kind soul from the world. *Time to step up.*

Chapter Thirteen

TALA WOULD'VE STAYED CURLED on the couch forever if she could, wrapped in Citlali's warmth and comforted by the hint of jasmine buried underneath Tala's stingy soap. It was skin on skin contact as neither of them bothered to put on pants.

But her phone went off.

Tala leaned forward to grab her phone from the coffee table, and Citlali went for her phone at the same time, probably to check her messages. Surely she got a bunch considering what happened last night. Tala glanced at her screen. Her mother texted her. **Your father and I can't stop talking. We want to meet the woman who's captured your heart.** She smiled. Her parents would love Citlali, even though they'd embarrass the hell out of Tala.

"You look happy," Citlali said, caressing Tala's side with her free hand.

Tala felt that was right...for the first time in a long time. "My mom wants to meet you. Well, both my parents want to meet you." She wasn't sure if her parents knew about what happened, but she wasn't about to ask right now. She had enough things to handle as it was.

Citlali nodded. "I'd be happy to, but before that, we need to talk to a detective. I called him when you went to the bathroom and made an appointment." She gazed deeply into Tala's eyes. "You're going to come, right?"

If you stare at me like that while holding me, I'll probably do anything you ask. "Of course." The police could probably use more witnesses. "Besides, it'll be good to find out what they believe about the monster the goons said attacked them."

Plus, there might be video. She needed to find out if they had solid evidence.

"I need to go home and get new clothes." Citlali sighed. "And my car is still at The New Moon."

Tala snorted. "Rideshare it is. My bike's still there, too. I vaguely remember running us here."

Running was her method of movement as a wolf; she moved too fast in her wolf form to be more than a blur. *At least I got lucky in genetics*. It would still be a miracle if no one snapped a picture of her.

With a chuckle, Citlali rubbed her forehead. "Of course you did. Well, I told the detective I didn't want it to seem like I was dodging him."

"Considering you were the target, I think you're owed some time to get your head together."

Citlali nodded. "He seemed pretty insistent on my coming down as soon as I could. Maybe he's in a hurry to build a case."

"Maybe, but it sounds like he needs to work on his people skills. Who rushes a person who just went through a traumatic experience?" The idea left a bad taste in her mouth and gave her even more of a reason to go with Citlali.

"I don't know. I've dealt with the police on a limited basis."

Tala gaped at Citlali. "You've dealt with the police?"

"More often than we like, The New Moon gets accused of having prostitution or illegal drug use on the premises. And just so you know, we don't."

"I honestly don't care. I'm just not buying it."

Citlali laughed and kissed her cheek. "I love how open minded you are, but it's funny how you don't want to do any of these things you have no problem with."

"I live my entire life just wanting to be left alone. If it's not bothering someone, I don't mind."

"Ah, so your whole philosophy in life is leave people alone?"

When Tala nodded, Citlali leaned in and kissed her. Kissing Citlali was something Tala would never tire of, she was sure of that. It sent a gentle shock through her. The soft feel of Citlali's lips, moving against her own, made her head swim. She liked it.

"We should get going," Citlali said, pulling away.

Tala ordered them a ride while also trying to find pants Citlali might be able to fit in. *Why are her beautiful legs so long?*

"Are you going stare at my legs all day?" Citlali asked, tilting her head.

Tala blinked and yelped. "Sorry!" She ducked into her closet.

Citlali's laughter echoed through the room. "Don't be. You can stare all you want later. Right now, we need to go. You don't have any yoga pants?"

Tala frowned. "The waist will be too big."

"It's fine. I just need to make it down to the car and up to my apartment."

True. Tala grabbed a pair of grey joggers. They ended up as capris on Citlali, who didn't seem to mind. They fit with the t-shirt she had on anyway. Then they were off, making their way back to Citlali's apartment. *Oh, I still haven't told her.*

"Citlali," Tala said as she waited in Citlali's living room as Citlali changed outfits.

"Yes?" Citlali's voice came from her bedroom.

"I wasn't sure if I should tell you, but the reason I was up at the club last night was because Ruby confronted me that morning," Tala said.

Citlali rushed out of her bedroom, fixing a bracelet on her wrist. Tala's eyes widened. Her sky blue pants hugged her forever legs and the white heels hit just right. *Would she keep the shoes on if I put her legs on my shoulders?* She shook the thought away. She wasn't even sure Citlali would want that now that she knew what Tala was. Kissing was much tamer than sex.

"Where did you see Ruby yesterday morning?" Citlali asked, pressing her hands together and putting them in her mouth.

"She was outside here." Tala pointed her thumb behind her.

Citlali's eyes went wide, panic clear in them, and she went over to the glass door that opened to her balcony. "Outside my apartment?" She looked over the railing as if trying to spot Ruby.

"Yeah." Tala stepped over to the balcony door and looked out. It was a neat little area with a cushioned chair, small table, and a couple of potted plants. "I was coming to tell you because I thought you'd want to know in case you didn't tell her where you live."

Citlali's chest heaved. She pushed by Tala back into the apartment. "Of course I didn't tell her where I live! She's a customer."

Tala scratched the side of her head, braids uncurled thanks to her transformation. "You showed me where you live."

"You're my girlfriend." Citlali motioned to her with both hands.

Tala fought to keep from puffing up at that. "I started as a customer."

Citlali shook her head. "You're so different I can't even begin to explain it. How did she get my address? Oh my god, what has she been planning?" All of the color drained from Citlali.

Tala embraced her, wanting to remind Citlali how powerful she was. "She's not going to hurt you. Not while I'm here."

Sniffing, Citlali looked into her eyes. "But how did she find out where I live?"

"Um...if it makes you feel better, you can stay with me. Until you feel comfortable." *Wow, we are bold today, aren't we? She'll probably agree, but only because she knows you'll literally rip someone apart for her.*

Citlali searched her eyes for a long moment. "Are you sure?"

Not at all. In fact, her stomach dropped into her feet and she was a little lightheaded, but in for a penny, in for a pound. "Yeah. Pack a bag."

Citlali nodded and went to go do just that. Tala paced the living room to keep her brain from going to all sorts of horrible places. She named off video games to try to occupy her thoughts. She and Citlali hadn't spent more than a couple of hours together at once in one central location, and worries crept inside of her. Tala liked doing...inside things. Quiet things. Would Citlali like the same? *There's no way this will work. You'll never make it without her learning just how truly dull you are.*

Citlali rolled a luggage bag by her side. That seemed like a lot of clothes, but Tala didn't address it. When Citlali grabbed her hand and pulled her close, her sweet scent invaded Tala with every breath. Thanks to that, all thoughts flew from her head.

They were off again, using a rideshare to head to the police station first. Tala followed Citlali's lead, having never been in a police station and really wishing she could have kept things that way. She looked around while Citlali talked to someone about meeting the detective. *It's kinda weird how much this looks like stations on TV.* Before she could think more, Citlali took her by the hand.

"They told me we could wait over here." Citlali led her to a row of chairs by the wall.

It was almost ten minutes before a dark-haired man in a tan suit—Detective Letran—found his way to them. Ten minutes! *What the hell is that about?* Tala already wasn't impressed with him from glancing over Citlali's trauma, but now he was acting like they didn't matter. Rude.

"You the ones from the club last night?" he asked in a short tone, scratching the stubble on his pale chin.

Tala leaned back a little. His sour aftershave stung her nose.

"We are." Citlali climbed to her feet, bringing Tala up with her.

He looked them up and down, face tense and eyes hard. Tala could feel the judgment radiating off of him, just as powerful as his aftershave. Citlali squeezed her hand, as if to keep Tala from barking on the guy. *How did she know?*

"Follow me to my desk, please." He turned before they could answer. They glanced at each other and then followed him. The desk was obsessively neat. There were people milling about them, living their lives, not judging, and therefore doing better than the detective.

"So, I was told you need to speak with me about what happened at The New Moon last night," Citlali said.

Detective Letran pulled a notepad and opened a folder in front of him. "You're Sit—" he didn't get to finish.

"It's pronounced Seet-la-lee. Last name is Zhen, but I'm sure you'd have gotten that one." Citlali smiled. She probably had to correct people on her name all the time.

Tala was somewhat familiar with that pain, not just for herself, but also for Kyra's sake.

He nodded. "And you're a manager at The New Moon?"

"I am."

He glanced at Tala. "And you are?"

"She's my girlfriend. Here for support," Citlali replied.

"And I was there last night when the shooting happened," Tala said.

His dark eyebrow ticked up. "And your name?"

"Tala Grayson."

Citlali glanced at her, shock clear on her face. Tala assumed it was because her voice didn't shake. One-on-one, she could handle, even with someone so official as a detective. Plus, even though this was annoying, it was important, and once it was over, it was over. She had to support Citlali.

He jotted that down. "So, tell me what happened."

Citlali recounted the event, ending with Ruby leaning into her and how she thought the woman would rape her.

The detective scribbled it all down. "And what made you think she was going to rape you?"

"She had a bag of sex toys with her. She licked my face. I doubt she wanted a private room with her armed friends just to chat."

He nodded. "And why did the shooting start?"

Tala raised her hand. "That would be me. I was up there to talk to Citlali and I noticed them in the parking lot. I thought I saw a gun and panicked when I went inside."

"Where were you when the shooting started?"

"The hall where the shooting started," Tala replied. "I wanted to save Citlali."

"So, you saw the monster?" he asked with a straight face.

Tala blinked. "Saw the what?" *Does he believe that?*

"Monster." He rubbed his eyes with his thumb and forefinger. "Miss Quills and her friends claim they were attacked by a giant beast. A monster dog or werewolf. Did you see that?"

She snorted. "Of course not. I guess that's a better story than saying they got beat up by two women, one who's barely five feet in boots."

"They had strange cut marks on them."

Tala shook her head. "I didn't cut anybody."

As the words left her mouth, she could almost feel their blood on her fingertips. *How dare those bastards try to hurt Citlali.* The nerve of those men to kidnap someone just because their boss told them to. Paid them to. Disgusting.

The corner of his upper lip ticked up as he stared at her. "Do you have a weapon?"

Tala pulled out her knife. She carried it just in case she used her claws and then needed to lie about having a weapon. She put it down on the desk. "It's clean. Maybe the guys injured themselves and came up with that ridiculous story after they realized they had just been involved in an assault." She motioned to Citlali's injured face. "And unlawful imprisonment since they were holding her against her will. Hell, it might even be a kidnapping, right?"

"Let me work out the charges."

"It doesn't sound like you have any, and I'm feeling a little blamed over here," Tala said.

Detective Letran grunted and directed his attention to Citlali. "Miss Quills said you are her girlfriend, and you were planning for a romantic encounter when a monster interrupted."

Citlali rolled her eyes. "I'm sure you've spoken with enough club personnel to know that's not true. You can talk to anyone and you'll find I hadn't interacted with Miss Quills outside of the club."

"I imagine you know how to hide relationships," he said.

"So, we're going with the idea that a monster attacked and that's why those men opened fire rather than that they threatened me and were surprised when Tala showed up? The monster story is more believable?" Citlali arched an eyebrow, daring him to confirm that.

"I'm open to ideas considering you two want me to believe she beat someone up." He motioned to Tala.

Tala growled. "You don't know a thing about me. What if I'm a martial artist? What if I've just taken classes in self-defense? What if my dad happened to train me to fend people off?" *Does this guy know about werewolves? Is that why he's making this so hard?* "But rather than asking irrelevant questions, let's ask some relevant ones. Are the men who pulled guns in a crowded building and opened fire in jail?"

"They had licenses for those weapons, and they claimed self-defense," he replied. "We're investigating."

Citlali's mouth dropped open. "So they're just out walking the streets?"

"This investigation has only just begun. They were booked, but they made bail. We're trying to figure out what exactly happened."

Tala couldn't believe what she was hearing. "Well, can Citlali press charges?"

"We need to investigate," he replied.

Citlali's face was so tense, her teeth might shatter under the pressure of her jaw. "Are we done here?"

***

After spending more time than she liked with Detective Douchebag, Citlali was more than certain she would have to move. She couldn't chance Ruby knowing where she lived when it sounded like pressing charges would be a waste of time. Ruby wasn't even in jail! The detective seemed to think it was a weird sex thing that got out of hand because it happened at The New Moon. Never mind the gunshots.

"That guy sucked," Tala said as they made their way to The New Moon. It was only a few blocks away, so they walked. Citlali felt a little odd dragging her suitcase behind her, but it was necessary. She didn't stand out too much. With all of the casinos, boardwalk things, and the beach, this was a touristy area.

"He did. Just because sexual things take place at the club, it doesn't mean the place is sketchy or everything that happens there is sexual," Citlali replied.

Tala frowned. "He shouldn't be able to dismiss a victim like that."

Citlali didn't argue with that. "Well, as he said it's a matter of 'she said/she said', and he seemed hung up on the fact that Ruby claimed she's my girlfriend. I'm going to meet with Raul, The New Moon's owner, and see what he wants to do."

Tala's face scrunched up. "What do you mean?"

"I'm sure he'll ban her. A shoot out could mean metal detectors or searches, though, and our clients might not be into that. We'll discuss the security options."

Tala gave her a sidelong look. "Should I come?"

"You don't have to. I'm safe with him, and Daphne will be there with the other managers."

"Good."

"Text me your address, though." She wasn't observant on the run there last night.

Tala did. They walked into the parking lot of The New Moon. The building was taped off, but thankfully, their vehicles were not part of the investigation. Then, they drove off in separate directions.

Citlali tried to focus on driving, but all she could think about was that Ruby knew where she lived. Ruby had almost violated her last night. *But Tala saved me.* Citlali's heart practically floated out of her chest. *How did I get so lucky?* She would make sure she cherished Tala properly now.

The meeting was at a small pizza parlor Raul also owned. He had a knack for hiring people who were technically beneath the business' targeted audience, this pizza place included. The pizza was like ambrosia there, and was worth the insane price for a slice. *I should get some for Tala on my way out.*

"Oh, no! Look at your face!" Raul was on her as soon as she was in the restaurant. He loomed over her, standing six inches taller than she was. He cupped her face with both large, soft hands.

"I'm fine." *A pharmaceutical student patched me up.*

"You're not." He stepped back from her. "Did she hurt you in any other way?"

Citlali shook her head. "No." *Not physically, anyway.*

He clicked his tongue. "What a little monster. Come sit." He waved her to the table. "And please know you can take as much time as you want to bounce back from this."

Daphne patted the chair next to her and Citlali wasted no time sitting. Daphne put her arm around Citlali and kissed her healthy cheek. The other managers gave her encouraging pats and then got down to business. It felt good, normal. Her input was appreciated. She was still Citlali. She wasn't broken.

When the meeting was over, Citlali and Daphne went off for a walk, just the two of them. "Are you really all right?" Daphne asked.

"Shaken, but fine."

"How did you even get out of that mess? When I heard the gunshots, I thought for sure I lost you." Daphne put arm around her shoulders, pulling her close.

Citlali grinned. "You won't get rid of me that easy. Tala saved me." *Don't ask me how.* Usually, she told Daphne everything, but this wasn't her secret to tell. Beyond that, she didn't want Daphne to think she was insane.

Daphne leaned into her. "Remind me to buy Tala dinner for saving your ass."

Citlali laughed. "You'd go bankrupt, but I'll pass the sentiment along. Would you like to formally meet her?" Tala talked about Citlali meeting her parents, so Citlali should introduce Tala to the important people in her life, too. She wanted Tala to know she was in this for the long haul.

Daphne nodded. "Soon. You two need some time to yourselves."

"I almost blew it with her, blew it over something she was totally right about."

Daphne patted Citlali on the shoulder. "Well, you made a mistake, you recognize the mistake, and now you know not to make that mistake again."

Citlali looked to the cloudless blue sky. "Maybe. And yet you told me how to handle things and I just doubled down on my stupidity."

"Don't sell yourself short, especially if Tala is still willing to try with you. Respect her decision."

Respect her decision. Respect her opinion. Listen to her. Things Tala needed and deserved as much as the next person. She wanted to give Tala everything.

"She put so much on the line for me," Citlali said. She didn't mean to voice that.

Daphne gave her shoulder a squeeze. "You're not used to someone sacrificing for you, but you're worth it."

Citlali opened her mouth, curious if Daphne noticed any behavior to make it seem like she didn't know her worth, but decided against asking. Daphne would probably tell her something she didn't need to hear.

"Have you spoken to your parents?" Daphne asked.

"I talked to my father this morning, just assuring him I'm all right. I'll talk to him more later. I told him I had a lot to do today. My mother's out of the country, so she might not know. I'll call her later, just in case."

"Good."

Citlali opened mouth, ready to tell Daphne that Ruby knew where she lived, but she hesitated. Daphne would offer her a place to stay. She had the place she wanted right now. Besides, she didn't want to worry Daphne any more than she already had.

"So, when do you think you'll be back at work?" Daphne asked.

"I'm not sure." She had a lot to work through, like the fact that Ruby was possibly escaping punishment. The idea made her tremble, but if she was with Tala, she knew she'd be safe.

"Take as much time as you need."

Citlali nodded. The club was closed for the week, anyway. For now, she and Daphne shared a hug and went their separate ways.

Citlali went shopping at a nearby grocery store, secured the bags in the back seat since her luggage was in the trunk. She purchased a meat lover's pizza pie for Tala. Then she set off for Tala's apartment. Home...for now.

***

Tala tried to play a game to take her mind off of Citlali, but to no avail. One of the in-game NPCs looked too much like her. She also tried re-braiding her hair to keep herself busy, but all she managed were three chunky cornrows. She'd need Kyra to redo her beloved mohawk.

What if something happened to her? Her stomach butterflies were practically crashing into each other at the idea that Citlali might not actually come to her house. Citlali might have been all right with the werewolf thing this morning, but by now things might have sunken in. Maybe she didn't want to be with a monster. *Yeah, you were stupid to think she'd actually come back to a loser like you.*

A text message distracted her. Citlali. **Hey, I have groceries and pizza. I don't have enough hands for all of them. Little help?**

Tala's heart jumped. **Hell yeah!** She rushed out to go lend a hand.

Chapter Fourteen

TALA SIGHED, PATTING HER stomach. The meat-heavy pizza Citlali brought over had to have been made by angels, and possibly of angels, which held her over until dinner. Citlali cooked stuffed shells dripping with mozzarella and marinara, and smiled as Tala ate five out of the six she made. They soon shifted to the couch to make-out, then cuddled and watched a movie.

A text from Tala's mother brought it all crashing down. **Calling.** The clipped message wasn't a good sign.

"Bad news?" Citlali asked, twirling the end of one of Tala's braids. She paused the movie.

"My mom. She's about to call me." The call rang, and Tala forced a smile. "Hi, Ma."

"Are you crazy?" Her mother's scream hurt her ears.

She ducked her head to escape the sound, which, of course, didn't work. "Ma, let me explain."

The snarl made her nerves jump. "You have two minutes!"

Tala went through the whole story as fast as she could, doing her best not to stammer. Her breath caught in her throat a couple of times. She wasn't sure how this would play out, but her stomach twisted so many times it might not exist anymore. Would her mother be angry?

"My goodness, is your mate all right?" her mother asked.

Tala was pretty sure her entire body blushed. "Ma! She's fine." She whispered the next part. "And she's not my mate."

It was a rare day when a human mated with a werewolf, and it didn't usually work out. Kyra was a shining example. Her parents broke up early on, and her werewolf mother ended up hunted and dead based on lies from her father. Her father wanted nothing to do with Kyra.

Her mother snickered. "Sweetheart, she definitely is. You, the ultimate cool, calm, and collected wolf, lost your shit over her. You've got it bad."

"Ma!" Tala buried her face in her hand. She hoped Citlali couldn't hear the other side of this conversation.

"Remember that your father and I want to meet her."

Tala's face scrunched. She hadn't been looking forward to that in general, but now that her mother was talking about mating, she would rather space debris fell from the sky and kill her. Beyond that, she needed to know if her mother was angry or her stomach might never unravel. "You're not upset with me at what's probably going to happen?"

The exile. The shame that would hang over her family.

Her mother blew a raspberry. "I'm not upset with you. I'm upset with them if they go through with that piece of stupidity."

"Ma..." Tala wasn't sure what to say beyond what they knew to be true. "They hate me."

"Emotions shouldn't overrule law. You're allowed to protect your mate. If they kick you out of the pack for saving your mate, then none of us deserve to be in the pack. Every single wolf has done something stupid for their mate. That's just growing up."

"Ma, you know they don't care about that."

"But they should be fair with you." She said the words with the conviction of a person who knew they wouldn't be fair.

"I'm sorry."

"No." Her mother's voice snapped enough to make her sit up straight. "You never apologize for doing the right thing, especially to me." She took a breath. "Now, what time would be good to meet?"

Tala turned to Citlali. "Parents are eager to meet you. When would be good?"

Citlali tilted her head. "In a few days? I'd like to relax for a little while. Catch my breath."

Tala nodded. She'd do her best to make it happen. "Got it." Her attention went back to the phone. "Ma, I'll have to get back to you on meeting. Citlali wants some time to breathe."

"That's fair. Good job, hero. Take care of your mate."

"Ma!" She groaned. *Could the sofa just swallow me already?*

Her mother snickered and hung up.

Tala sighed, feeling both light and heavy at the same time. Her parents weren't upset, but they thought Citlali was her mate. Tala wasn't even sure she could form that sort of bond, and she just wanted to enjoy the little moment of heaven in her apartment. She tossed the phone on the couch.

Tala curled against Citlali and inhaled her scent. It filled her lungs, and her chest wasn't so tight anymore. She relaxed. *That doesn't mean anything. You like her scent. So what? She's not your mate.*

"You okay?" Citlali asked.

"Yeah. My parents are going to fucking love you." But that would just add pressure to not mess this whole thing up. *You're so going to blow this whole thing.*

"Does that bother you?"

"Nope."

Citlali regarded her with a tilt of her head. "Then what's bothering you?"

Tala blinked in disbelief that Citlali could tell something troubled her. She took a breath, but an answer didn't come out.

"I know I have to work on building your trust again, but I'm here for you, Tala. I want to hold your burdens with you. So, what's bothering you?" Citlali asked, her voice gentle and sincere.

Tala scratched the end of her nose. "Holding onto you. I didn't think you'd come back, and when you did, I was happy, and then my stomach dropped and the darkness came back. I thought you're being nice to me because I'm a monster, but then you handed me pizza and made dinner and I was happy again and..."

Citlali jumped right in and filled the silence. "Your stomach dropped and the darkness came. A cycle."

Tala nodded. "Then you kissed me."

"And you were happy again. I'm noticing the pattern. Have you ever spoken to anyone about your anxiety?"

"Not really." It was something she just lived with. She didn't have much choice.

Citlali's forehead wrinkled. "Why not?"

Tala shrugged. "Whoever I saw probably would've been in the pack. We try to stay within our community as best we can to avoid getting discovered. I couldn't tell a human therapist that people draining my energy is like a mental illness in my community. I'd have sounded crazy. And maybe I am. I dunno." She didn't feel mentally ill, but did people with mental illness feel like they were sick? She doubted it.

Citlali pursed her lips. "You try to stay in the werewolf community?"

"Yeah. It's a win-win situation. We help the community stay afloat and take care of each other. So like, there's a pediatrician in our pack because who do you take your werewolf baby to if they accidentally go into wolf form while they're sick? My mother's one of the pack's general practitioners, occasional surgeon, and the way the pack talks about my mother for chasing a rogue wolf, even though they need her, lets me know my problems would go through the whole pack less than an hour after my first visit."

Citlali pulled her a little closer. "Shit, that's horrible. Wait, is that why you wanted to be a pharmacist? To help your pack?"

Tala nodded. "Sometimes, certain drugs don't work for us and I get to learn to create the right mixes to help us and other people."

Citlali's face dropped, and for a long moment she didn't make eye contact. "And helping me could cost you your dream?"

Tala scoffed and waved that off. "I'm going to be a compound pharmacist. That's happening. I even have an internship lined up for next month thanks to my college advisor. I may or may not help my pack. Hell, I may not have a pack soon. My dad has survived his entire life without a pack. It's not impossible, so I'm not going to lament losing people who tormented me my whole life and make me feel broken for being a lone wolf." Tala locked eyes with Citlali. "They can't make me regret or feel bad for doing the right thing."

Citlali kissed her again. It was hot, heavy, but also…freeing, like she had been unleashed. There wasn't her anxiety or her secret between them. It was just her and Citlali's amazing mouth and tongue caressing her own. Citlali's hand warmed Tala's bare abdomen.

"Is that okay?" Citlali asked.

Tala grinned. "I'm happy."

Citlali caressed Tala's cheek. "Well, let's work on keeping you that way. No stomach drops or dark clouds. Just feeling good for as long as you can." She went in for a fresh kiss, which Tala accepted.

Citlali's lips, tongue, and hands were all nothing short of perfection to Tala. Every caress was perfect. Every inhale was filled with the aroma of jasmine. Tala's mind swam with pleasure. Her ears picked up every little noise Citlali made—a moan here, a groan there. A gentle sigh. She couldn't think of anything beyond how good Citlali made her feel, and that was beyond physical. Her instincts howled. *Shit, what if she is my mate?*

She pulled away, wanting to look in Citlali's eyes. Try to figure things out.

"Still happy?" Citlali asked with a grin.

"Yeah." Tala sighed, a pleased noise for once. She felt soft and comfortable. *I'm connected to her in a way I've never felt before. I want her around.*

Citlali's face was so bright. It touched Tala in a way she didn't know was possible. This whole thing seemed impossible, well out of the realm of Tala's imagination, yet here it was, happening.

"You make me so happy," Tala said.

"That makes me happy."

The kissing continued.

Tala wasn't sure when it happened, but she ended up on her back. Citlali's weight on her was nothing short of amazing. She clutched Citlali's back and Citlali didn't flinch, didn't seem to think about her claws. That relaxed her even more. After a while, Citlali pulled back and Tala's heart sank.

Citlali smirked. "Could I convince you to move this to your bed?"

Tala blinked. "You still want to sleep with me, even though I hid such a big secret from you?" *Even though you know what I'm capable of?*

The smirk morphed into a grin and her honey eyes grew molten. "Hell yeah. You are so sexy and, believe it or not, knowing you're a big, strong werewolf only makes it hotter."

It felt like a bomb went off inside her, sending jolts of energy through her muscles, her bones, her very core. She had never felt anything like it. *Ma said she's your mate. Maybe she's right.* This matter deserved a discussion. Citlali should know before they did anything more.

"I should tell you something," Tala said.

Citlali's brow wrinkled. "There's more?"

Tala scratched her head, sagging as the energy left her, and anxiety buried the good feeling. "I don't want to scare you off."

Citlali arched an eyebrow. "Babe, I watched you turn into a giant wolf. What more could there be?"

Tala blew out a breath, puffing out her cheeks. *So much.* "Werewolves aren't like humans when it comes to relationships."

"What do you mean?"

"We're…intense. For humans, anyway. It makes sense to us."

"Again, what do you mean? Take your time. I'm not going anywhere." Citlali searched her gaze, as if needing her to see that was the truth.

Tala rubbed her hands together and held them up to her mouth for a second. *Just go for it. Tell her in a more organized manner than when you showed her what you are.* "So, like regular wolves, werewolves are monogamous. A bond forms between mates and it lasts for the rest of their lives."

Citlali nodded. "Okay."

Tala waved her hands, defensive for no reason beyond her own nervousness. "I'm not telling you this to freak you out or anything. It doesn't have to mean anything on your end. The bond might not have even formed for me, but it might. I've done some pretty crazy things for you. But, my dad can't form that bond, and my mother bonded to him. He still lives his life."

Citlali held up her hand. "Wait, slow down. What do you mean by a bond?"

"Just if I form that bond with you, or for you, it doesn't have to affect you in any way. I just...I thought you should know."

Citlali caressed Tala's hands with her thumbs. Tight circle motions that made Tala's body calm. "So, what you're saying is, there's a chance you could fall in love with me like there's a chance I could fall in love with you?"

Tala scrunched her mouth up. Bonding was more than falling in love, but that was fine. The bond would be her burden and she could control herself. She wouldn't need to be around Citlali all the time or want to do stuff with her or need to fall asleep next to her unless it was something Citlali wanted. She wouldn't make a nuisance of herself. She ran her hand through Citlali's hair, enjoying the way it trickled through her fingers like onyx water.

"Do you think you could fall in love with me?" Tala asked, her voice quiet.

Citlali kissed her. "Definitely."

Hope fluttered inside her chest. *I'm so gone on her already.* Weird what a little attention could do for her. *It has to be the person. I hate attention from others.* Still, that only proved her point more. And Tala's stomach butterflies didn't freak out. That was something.

***

Citlali listened to Tala's relaxed breathing as they spooned in bed. Tala was the little spoon and it seemed like a trusting position, like she trusted Citlali to keep her warm and safe. They hadn't done anything beyond making out on the couch, and Citlali was fine with that. The idea of bonding, falling in love, seemed to trouble Tala, at odds with her antisocial personality. If Tala needed time to piece it together, Citlali would give her all of that and more.

"You deserve the world." Citlali kissed Tala's bare shoulder. Tala made a cute noise in her sleep.

Citlali felt like something was slowly blooming inside of her. She wasn't sure what it was, but it was warm and sweet. She was at peace here, like anything that went wrong or could go wrong couldn't touch her here. It was like nothing she ever felt before. *Maybe it's because I know Tala would move heaven and Earth to keep me safe.*

She kissed Tala's shoulder and Tala made the noise again. *My hero.* She gave Tala a little squeeze and fell into a peaceful sleep.

In the morning, Citlali woke before Tala. She showered, dressed in a t-shirt and leggings, made coffee, and then started on breakfast. Cooking in a new kitchen was challenging at first, but fun, too. Tala staggered out, yawning with her mouth wide open. *Is that the wolf part of her?* It was intriguing. Citlali didn't want to pick Tala apart like that, though, because if Tala noticed her doing it, Tala's anxiety would go through the roof.

"Morning," Tala grumbled. Not a morning person then. Her hair was twisted and tangled, braids going in several directions.

Citlali took a chance, embracing Tala in a warm hug. Tala gasped and froze for a moment, but then accepted the contact. They exchanged a soft, sweet kiss.

"You making breakfast?" Tala asked.

"Chilaquiles."

"Never heard of it."

A giddiness bubbled up in Citlali. She liked introducing Tala to new things. "You're in for a treat, then. It's my favorite breakfast."

Tala grinned and sat at the counter that divided the kitchen from the living room. She stayed out of Citlali's way as she cooked. Kyra had trained her well. Citlali served Tala, who shoved a tortilla into her mouth. She moaned after eating the first one and then quickly ate more.

Citlali sat down, watching Tala eat, scrambled egg and a dot of salsa on the corner of her mouth. The color bursts in Tala's light blue eyes were like fireworks. Pride straightened Citlali's spine. It might not seem like much to make something Tala would enjoy, but she was also used to having a great chef in Kyra to make meals for her. Yet Tala's face flushed with happiness as she devoured Citlali's cooking.

"So, what do you do with your time?" Citlali asked, digging the corn tortilla into the thick green salsa and putting a hunk of spiced chicken on top. She didn't want to invade Tala's space any more than she had.

Tala shrugged. "My internship doesn't start until next month, so I'll probably play games, read..." She dipped her head then looked up through long lashes. "Go out on dates with my girlfriend."

"I very much like that last one."

"Okay." Tala laughed. "I don't have any good ideas right now."

"Take your time. I have a few ideas, if it helps."

Tala nodded like a bobblehead. "Yeah. I wanna take you places you wanna go."

Citlali leaned over to kiss Tala's cheek, brushing away crumbs. "My ideas are for places you'd like." Tala blushed and Citlali felt a flutter of joy. "Think about when you'd like to go out. I'm going to go sit with Daphne and apartment hunt."

Tala's brow furrowed. "You can stay here."

"Thanks, babe, but I don't think we're the U-Haul type couple."

"Maybe." She looked around, as if assessing her space. "You're welcome to stay here for as long as you need to."

"Thanks, especially since I'll have to talk to my landlord about my lease. Ruby knowing my address is possibly the worst thing I can think of." It didn't help that Ruby wasn't in jail. The woman might be stalking around her apartment right now, waiting for Citlali, planning to snatch her out of her bed or in the hallway or the moment she stepped out of the building.

"I could go outside with you."

Citlali hummed, thinking. "The buddy system might be best. At least if I go to my apartment or job."

"If you need anything else, let me know."

Citlali nodded, even though she had no intention of bothering Tala with her moving nonsense. Instead, they could go to the carnival on the boardwalk, go to an arcade, and maybe even see a concert once she learned what sort of music Tala liked. *So that's what the feeling was, opening up to the possibility of adventure. I'm ready for this.*

They enjoyed breakfast and Tala took over doing the dishes. Citlali left Tala with a kiss and went to Daphne's apartment. She took her shoes off at the door while Daphne popped out of her bedroom, dressed in sweatpants and a loose tank that showed off her entire purple lace bra.

"Well, my, my, my, if it isn't my little lesbian cliché," Daphne said with a chuckle, her accent thick now that they were alone.

Citlali sighed and motioned to herself with both hands. "Come on, get it all out of your system."

Daphne hit her with every lesbian joke she could think of as Citlali set up her laptop and sank into the couch. Daphne sat next to her. Citlali went to a real estate website and started going through apartments.

"What about this one?" She turned the computer so Daphne could see the high windows, quaint kitchenette, and open floor plan.

Daphne shook her head, all jokes vanishing under her frown. "This is too close to your old apartment."

"Damn." She liked her neighborhood and wanted to stay close to it. "Do you think it's safe to stay in the area?"

Folding her arms, Daphne stared at the computer. "I dunno. It might not even matter. If Ruby found you once, maybe she can do it again." She scowled.

So I might not be safe anywhere. Citlali pinched the bridge of her nose, trying to keep the fear coiling in her chest away. "How do you think she knew my address?"

"She's got money. Probably a private eye, or she paid off people near you. Who knows? Her age blinded us."

It didn't help that Ruby had an air of innocence about her. Her obsession with Citlali always felt more "school girl crush" than anything else. Eventually, she'd meet someone real outside of the club and understand her feelings toward Citlali weren't anything more than a flight of fancy. "And she was recommended by a well-respected client. We obviously need more vetting."

Daphne looped an arm across her shoulders and hugged her. "I'm so glad you're all right."

"That makes two of us."

"I don't know what I'd do without you." Daphne's shoulders dropped.

This moment was too heavy, so Citlali brightened. "Never get another job again, I tell you that." They both chuckled, and though it was forced, it helped release some of the tension. *I could've been killed. But I wasn't.*

"Let's keep looking." Daphne turned her attention back to the laptop. "So, what's it like staying with Tala?"

"It's nice. I don't want to do it for too long. She values her space and I like mine, too."

Tala needed a sanctuary. Some place to recoup and quiet the demons of her anxiety. Citlali wouldn't dare encroach on that territory more than necessary.

"You're welcome here."

"I'll probably take you up on that."

Citlali needed space to recharge after spending her time doting on people. Some place where she just had to worry about herself. Yes, she would love to take care of Tala, but she needed to take care of herself as well. They had to learn to coexist, but not all at once.

"We should put your things in storage as soon as possible. Did they arrest Ruby?" Daphne asked.

"No. The detective seemed to think the club was hiding something shady, and Ruby told him I was her girlfriend." *And maybe he believes in werewolves.*

Daphne frowned. "Well, if he bothers to do his job he'll find out that isn't true, and you're in serious danger. Can you speak with another detective?"

"I didn't ask. I was so drained at the time. Do you think you could find out if they arrested Ruby? I'm sure the club would be all aflutter about it, and I'm not ready to deal with the club gossip."

"You know I got your back."

Citlali smiled. "Her parents want to meet me."

"That's good. Are you nervous?" Daphne winked.

"No. Tala has anxiety and she's nervous about everything, but she's sure her parents will love me. If she's not worried about it, then I'm not going to."

"And how are you feeling about Tala?"

"Fine. Better than I've ever felt about another girl." Citlali tried to fight it, but couldn't keep the giggle from escaping her. "Oh, she's got me feeling giddy now."

"So the hero thing does it for you?" Daphne knocked her with her shoulder.

She tittered. "I guess so."

Daphne patted her forearm. "I think she set you free."

Is that why I like Tala so much? Citlali had never been welcomed like Tala did when she shared her plans for life. *I can be me around her?* She could be herself, but also Tala appreciated it. That was new.

With girlfriends, she found herself acting like her club persona. It was exhausting to be on twenty-four hours a day, and they rarely noticed that it wasn't the real her. She didn't have to put on an act for Tala.

"We have to find a place as cute as your current apartment," Daphne said, breaking her from her thoughts.

They found several apartments to follow up on. Daphne acted as backup as she called her landlord to get out of her lease. At first the landlord resisted, but Citlali mentioned being attacked a few more times and he didn't stand a chance. After that, they found a storage space and arranged for Citlali's things to be picked up. It was a good day's work. She and Daphne parted with a hug.

Citlali returned to Tala's house to find her girlfriend still in her pajamas. Tala slouched on her beanbag, playing a video game, and eating chips. She kissed Tala's cheek as a greeting and glanced at the television to see what type of game it was. There was a knight on screen and a dialogue box below. Maybe an RPG. She made dinner.

"Can I help with anything?" Tala asked.

"Nope, you enjoy your game," Citlali replied.

She didn't need to tell Tala twice. She finished up dinner and brought the plates to the coffee table. Tala turned off the game without a word.

"You didn't have to stop," Citlali said.

Tala rolled her eyes. "Can't eat and play the game at the same time. Besides, I wanna spend time with you."

Citlali's heart thumped as Tala moved to sit in front of her plate, made obvious by twice the serving size of the other plate. Citlali needed a moment to gather herself, feeling Tala in a new way since her talk with Daphne, and used getting them something to drink as an excuse to go back to the kitchen. She poured them some wine, lingering for a moment to catch her breath. She felt giddy just being in Tala's kitchen.

"This looks good," Tala said.

"I hope it tastes good. It's been a while since I've made dumplings," Citlali replied, returning to the couch. It was her father's recipe, one close to her heart.

"It's tasty," Tala said around a mouthful of dumplings and vegetable fried rice.

Citlali chuckled and started on her own food. They ate while watching a movie. Once the food was gone, they cuddled, then made out a little. At some point, Tala put the empty dishes in the sink and returned with a blanket. They snuggled under the blanket, even though it was a hot summer night. Tala rested her head on Citlali's shoulder and Citlali put her arm around Tala's waist.

"By any chance, do you braid hair?" Tala asked. Her hair was free of the cornrows she had them in, crimped and curled around her head like a dark brown halo with streaks of white in it.

"No, but I could learn."

"You don't have to."

"I already like playing in your hair, though." Her hand got lost in soft curls. Tala seemed to have a thing for having her hair done in designed, tight cornrow braids to gather her hair to the center of her head and leave the rest as a fluffy mohawk. She would definitely take time to learn to braid.

Tala smiled. "You'd really do it, wouldn't you?"

"My day tomorrow will be nothing but hair braiding tutorials." She winked, even though she was completely serious.

"You can practice on me, but we'll have to start the day after tomorrow."

"Why the day after?"

Tala's grin widened. "Because tomorrow I'm taking you on a date."

That simple phrase filled Citlali with so much joy. Despite the terror Ruby caused her, she managed to shift Citlali's mindset concerning Tala. She saw what she had in front of her and appreciated the sight, awkward as Tala was. This whole Ruby incident just might change Citlali's life for the better.

Chapter Fifteen

THE DAYS WENT BY. Citlali tried to press charges against Ruby, but the district attorney wouldn't go for it. The fact that it happened in a sex club didn't do Citlali any favors. Citlali hated that the location meant anything, but she was sure Ruby's name had something to do with it, too.

The Quills family was well-heeled and had their fingers in a lot of pies around the city. Citlali could possibly impose on her relationship with other big shots in the city who frequented The New Moon, but that seemed like a good way to burn some bridges. She wasn't ready to do that, yet.

Beyond that, she managed to find a good apartment, and she enjoyed her time living with Tala, making meals and deep conversations mixed with intense make out sessions, but by the end of the week, she moved in with Daphne. Their relationship needed space to go at the right pace. And apparently the pace called for meeting Tala's parents, who insisted.

"What do you think of this outfit?" Citlali asked Daphne as she stepped out of the bathroom. She had on one of her yellow work suits. A favorite. It'd give her confidence as she sat down with werewolf parents this afternoon. She could only imagine how protective they were of Tala.

Daphne arched an eyebrow from her space on the couch. She was still in her pajamas—shorts and a black camisole. "You're colorful."

"I like flare," Citlali replied. She learned this from Daphne. Yellow was her favorite color. It was empowering.

"You don't want to wear the blue one?"

Citlali shrugged. "Maybe the orange one?" It was the same design as the blue one, but again, she loved the flare.

Daphne grimaced and waved both hands to get Citlali to stop talking. "No. Just no. You always wear a halter top with that. You don't want to meet the parents in that."

"And Tala said they wouldn't mind how I look."

As she was coming to understand "werewolf culture," there were some things that she might not get used to. Tala told her they wouldn't care how she looked, but requested she come "smelling like you always do." Citlali made sure to shower with her usual jasmine body wash.

Daphne sighed, rubbing her forehead. "Fine, but put on a different shirt. And by that I mean put on an actual shirt."

Citlali glanced down at herself. She had on a sheath. "That's fair."

"Is she going to meet you there?"

"Near there. She wants to take me somewhere first, like a mini-date." They had managed one date while Citlali lived with Tala, dinner at a restaurant and a movie in a theater. She delighted in watching Tala be bashful in public.

Daphne burst out laughing. "Oh, god, she's too cute! How have your dates been?"

"Good. She's out and about with me, which is huge." Tala confessed to spending all of her free time indoors, away from people, but she liked outside and air. They had taken lots of long walks. She wasn't sure if they counted as dates, but she enjoyed them all the same. Beyond that, they spent a lot of time on Tala's couch, talking, watching movies, and just enjoying each other.

Daphne smiled. "Guess I'll make sure to keep her name on our partner list when you come back to work."

"I love that you think she wants to come in. Although, she loves the food."

"I'll make sure she can get into the restaurant part then. She deserves at least that for saving you. How did her little ass save you?"

Citlali shrugged. "She's just feisty."

Daphne laughed, but didn't ask any more questions, probably tired of the way Citlali deflected whenever the topic came up now. Apparently, it was impossible to believe Tala could fight.

Citlali finished putting together her outfit, dabbed on some light makeup, and went to meet Tala and her parents. They met in Wells Park, a huge park in the heart of the city. Finding parking was a hassle, but at least Tala met her nearby, so she didn't have to hike all over the park. Meeting her parents clearly wasn't a formal event, as Tala was in a basketball jersey and shorts. Her casual attire was a little reassuring.

They kissed and automatically held hands. Tala seemed more confident, standing tall and holding firm on Citlali's hand without it seeming possessive.

"So, where are we headed?" Citlali asked as they started walking.

"There's a go-cart course in the park. Have you ever been?" Tala's eyes sparkled.

"Can't say that I have." No one would think to take her to a go-cart track, but she was happy to be asked.

"I used to do it a lot with my dad. It was always a lot of fun."

"He sounds like a good guy."

Tala pursed her lips and tilted her head, thinking about it. "He is. He's a good dad, too. How you said he came back for me, I'm not sure if I believe that, but I always judged my dad in the light my pack sees him. My mom accepts him like she accepts me, and he's always there for me and supports me, and he never makes me feel weird. He's a good person."

Citlali smiled. "I'm glad I could help."

Tala grinned. When they got to the go-cart track, Citlali worried for her hair. She had taken her time to do it to perfection, blow-dried and combed straight down her back, shining like polished onyx in the sun, and didn't want her work to be in vain. And, even if Tala's parents wouldn't care about how she looked, she didn't think hurricane hair would leave a good impression.

"Can we do this some other time?" Citlali asked.

Tala's expression twisted. "You okay?"

Citlali squeezed Tala's hand. "I just don't want to meet your parents with wind swept hair."

Tala patted her hand. "They're not going to care, but I know your appearance matters to you, so I won't press."

"Confidence looks good on you."

"I'm only confident in you and my parents' reaction. I know they'll be happy for me because you make me happy."

Citlali held her chin up. She wasn't a source of anxiety for Tala anymore. *That's huge.* She wrapped her arm around Tala's shoulders and flicked her hair.

Tala laughed. "You're trying to mess up my hair because you can't make a mohawk like this?"

"Hey, it was my first try!" Citlali gave her a light hit to her shoulder. She had practiced braiding Tala's hair several times, but she wasn't advanced enough to do the different mohawk designs Tala sported. Tala went to a professional for some of them, and others Kyra did.

"Are you okay to walk around? Those shoes don't look like they're made for strolling," Tala glanced down at Citlali's footwear. Practical heels, not high but not flat either.

"Maybe we can sit and talk? Where are we meeting your parents?" Citlali asked.

"At Dila's Lunch. Have you been there?"

"No. I've heard it's a nice little cafe."

Tala nodded. "The scenery helps. It has a good view of the park. My parents love the place."

"Is it a werewolf-owned place?"

"I actually don't know. I just know we can get all the food we want and it's not weird." Tala grinned.

Citlali laughed as they found a bench to sit down. A few people walked by and looked at them holding hands. They were probably quite the mismatched sight, Tala in her sports apparel and Citlali in a suit. She was so much taller than Tala. Her dolled up face while Tala's face was natural beyond lip balm. Citlali's hair bowed to gravity while Tala's defied. Yes, they were quite a sight, but Citlali had never felt better paired with a girlfriend than she did now.

"How did your parents take your coming out?" Citlali asked.

Tala's brow wrinkled. "I didn't really have to come out. My parents just sort of accept things about me. When I was little, I'd comment about how I was going to marry celebrity crushes. They all happened to be women. No one batted an eye."

Lucky. Citlali nodded. "And the other werewolves?"

Tala shook her head. "Homosexuality is accepted in werewolf society. You bond with who you bond with. As long as you're social, it's fine. You actually find a lot of werewolves who are bisexual or pansexual. I am not one of them."

"Completely homosexual, huh?"

"Yup." Tala wiggled her eyebrows. "Girls just look nice and smell the best. What about you?"

Citlali took a breath and looked away for a moment. "It was a struggle for my parents in a way I didn't expect. They were with me through so much, always standing by me, but I told them I wanted to get a girlfriend and you'd have thought I told them I wanted to poison some wells."

"That's my pack whenever I tell someone to leave me the hell alone."

Citlali stroked Tala's hand with her thumb. "I'm sorry you know how it feels like. My dad came around first, but I think it's because he blamed himself."

Tala squinted as she tried to follow along. "He thought he made you gay?"

"It's weird. My father's a horrible flirt. In fact, most of my personality is just him. He flirts with almost every woman he encounters, and I've been flirting with people since I was five. Men and women alike."

Tala's face didn't clear up. "So, you're attracted to women because he's attracted to women?"

"According to him, yes, I like women because he likes women. I can see why he thinks that, though, as much of my behavior is modeled after him. He's my hero."

Tala nodded. "And what about your mom?"

"She was easier, even though it took her longer to accept, because my abuela didn't care. If she dared to say anything, my abuela would get on her case. 'You leave that child alone. She likes girls because boys are trouble.'" Citlali laughed, thinking of all the times her grandmother tried to justify why she liked girls.

"Your grandmother accepted it?"

"Yeah. I was hardly her first gay grandchild. My cousin, Freddie, went through hell when he came out, and my grandmother didn't want to see it ever again."

"Good woman."

"I think it bothered my mom for longer than she let on, but she's all right with it now. I do find it amusing that she took to me working in The New Moon better than she took to me being a lesbian."

"I can't imagine."

"I'm glad."

Tala smiled, tightening her hold on Citlali's hands. "Any other questions?"

Citlali hummed, thinking. "I'm wondering if there's something I should do when I meet your parents."

"Nope, just be your wonderful self."

"Hey, hey, hey. I'm the sweet talker between the two of us."

Tala laughed and leaned into her. "Lemme have it just this once."

She kissed the top of Tala's forehead. "You can have it whenever you want it, babe."

They sat for a little while longer before getting up to go to the cafe. Perhaps her low heels weren't the best option. She winced with each step, her feet throbbing.

"Should I carry you?" Tala asked.

Citlali chuckled. "You're sweet for offering, but I'll manage. I think you carrying me would raise a lot of eyebrows."

Tala nodded. "Probably."

"But I really appreciate the offer."

"Come to my place after and I'll massage your feet."

Citlali could feel herself light up. "Well, who could turn that down?"

The cafe was larger than Citlali expected. A dozen outside tables with a breathtaking view of the park, especially a grand fountain not too far away, where water shows took place at night.

"Tala!" A tall man grinned and climbed to his feet from a table. He was built like a football player with familiar, warm gray eyes with similar color bursts in them. His goatee was neatly trimmed with a spot of white in it, and his striking black suit had Citlali preening that she chose hers. His hair was short with waves. His smooth skin glowed with a lovely red undertone to the chestnut brown. Tala's skin would probably glow like his if she went outside more.

"Thank you, Dad. I really need the world to know my name," Tala said as a woman popped up by his side, like magic. She was a tiny thing, just like Tala, and had to be Tala's mother. The woman elbowed him in the side.

"Ow!" He rubbed his rib.

"I've told you about doing that to her," the woman said, and then turned her attention to Tala. Tala was the spitting image of her except the eyes. She even had the white streaks in her hair, which zigzagged through her braids that formed a bun at the back of her head.

"Let's sit down and order," the dad said.

The mom glared at him. "And get to know Tala's girlfriend."

"Right! Right!" He clapped his hands and grinned, showing off perfect teeth.

They all sat down. Tala did the introductions. "So, that's my dad, Amarok. Everyone calls him Rocky, even though he's a forty-five year old man."

"Who still looks good." He posed, finger under his chin and a half smirk.

Tala rolled her eyes but smiled. "He acts like that's his only redeeming quality, but there has to be some substance there because my mother keeps him around." She motioned to her mother. "My mother, Doctor Rashida Grayson."

"It's a pleasure to finally meet you, Citlali." Doctor Grayson leaned over to shake Citlali's hand. Her amber eyes were as warm as her smile. "Please, feel free to call me Rashida."

"I'm not sure—" Citlali didn't get a chance to finish that objection.

"I insist," Doctor Grayson said.

"Rashida it is then." Citlali smiled.

"We've been so excited about this! I always knew this kid would charm a beautiful woman eventually. She is my kid." Rocky tilted his chin in the air.

"Dad!" Tala blushed.

"She's a good person." He stared Citlali down with hard eyes, reminding her of how Tala looked in her wolf form. "Treat her with care."

Citlali wasn't intimidated. "I will. She's very special."

Tala scrunched up in her chair, like she wanted to disappear. "Citlali."

"It's true. I had to realize I was an ass to understand how special, but you're amazing," Citlali said.

Rocky nodded. "I know the feeling. At least it didn't take you a year. I had to come back with my tail between my legs, literally and figuratively."

Tala scoffed. "You're not even with Mom."

Rashida laughed. "He means you, Tala."

Tala blinked and looked between her parents. "Me?"

"Yes, you." Rocky's forehead furrowed. "Me and your mom are great friends, always have been, but it was pictures of you that eventually bought me back. I didn't think I was ready to be anyone's father, but you weren't just anyone. You were my freaking pup and I couldn't stay away. Still can't, even though you're too cool for me now." He winked at Tala.

"I'm not cool. You're annoying," Tala grumbled, slapping a hand over her face.

Rocky's personality did seem a little full on for Tala, and he didn't seem to know how to turn it down, but he never stopped smiling at Tala. It was cute, and Citlali couldn't believe that Tala didn't think he loved her. Her anxiety got the better of her for sure.

"Honestly, she's been too cool for me. When she was six, Rashida bought us matching leather jackets and I took her out on my bike. We went to the park and she picked up all the girls," Rocky said.

"Is that the day my mom called me and said Tala was getting free ice cream at the park when she brought Kyra to spend time with you two?" Rashida asked.

"Yes! Kyra coming along made it even worse. All the women were just cooing over Tala hugging Kyra and making sure she was safe on all the stuff." He laughed.

Citlali watched Rashida as Rocky monopolized the conversation, but Rashida leaned into the conversation, eyes only for her ex. Tala blushed, grumbled, and managed to ignore him until a waiter came over to take their order. Once the waiter stepped away, this allowed them to redirect.

"Rocky, you do realize we're supposed to be learning about Citlali rather than embarrassing Tala?" Rashida said.

"Thank you!" Tala had her knees pulled tight to her chest and her chin on her knees.

Rashida smiled as she focused on Citlali. "Tala said you work at the same restaurant Kyra does. You're the manager."

Citlali nodded. "One of the managers, yes. Looking to get some experience before I start my own club."

"Will your club have the sex shows?" Rocky asked, as if it was normal conversation. It was a breath of fresh air.

"I'd like to have sex shows. I want to help people get comfortable with sex, with kinks they might have, and things like that. Maybe give couples some ideas on how to spice up things in their bedroom, reconnect, or just start a conversation between them about things they might like," she replied.

Rashida tilted her head. "Sounds more like sex therapy rather than sex entertainment."

"I think I want something in between. I'm not completely sure, yet. I just want people to be comfortable," she replied. It was refreshing to have someone to discuss her ideas with beyond her own parents and Daphne. And Rocky and Rashida hung on her every word.

Tala sat back, ate when the food showed up, and grinned the whole time. She never said a word and no one pressured her to do so.

The meeting went well enough for Citlali to feel confident that the Grayson's didn't have to worry about their daughter with her.

"Oh, we have to meet with the pack elders tomorrow," Rashida mentioned, right before they parted ways.

"I wasn't invited, but I'm going to come anyway," Rocky said.

"They're just going to push you out," Tala replied.

"Let 'em try." He grinned.

Tala didn't put up an argument, taking Citlali's hand. Tala didn't seem moved, but a nugget of worry sank into Citlali's stomach. Was this meeting about seeing if Tala was to be excommunicated? To find out if Citlali was worth Tala's reveal? The family didn't seem bothered, like they knew the outcome already, but Citlali couldn't help but be nervous for her girlfriend.

***

"You don't have to wait around for me," Tala said to Citlali, who was curled up on her sofa. Tala was about to leave to meet with the pack elders. She straightened her dark grey capris sweatpants and t-shirt with a demon fox.

Citlali tucked her feet underneath her. "I want to be here for you when you come back."

Tala shrugged. They exchanged a kiss, then Tala left her apartment. It was disappointing to leave Citlali behind, but pack business was only for the pack, which was how they'd try to keep her father out. He might be irksome enough to get in, but Citlali was neither annoying nor a werewolf. She wouldn't make it through the door, even with all her charm.

The meeting happened in an elder's house tucked into a posh neighborhood, surrounded by old Victorian homes. Most of their neighbors were also werewolf elders. It was safer to live together. Youngsters were encouraged to stay home until they saved enough money for their own homes. No one was ever forced out of their houses, unless they broke a big rule. Tala was out on her own just for the quiet, really.

Her parents stood on the porch of the house, waiting. They stepped inside together, greeted by the scent of sage and vanilla. With barely a foot in the door, a hand pressed to her father's chest. He grinned at Dante, one of the pack's larger members.

"This is pack business," Dante said.

"This is my daughter," her father replied.

"Dante, it doesn't matter," a voice called.

Dante growled, but let them by. They stepped into the living room to find six elders playing cards around a squat wooden table. Tala would bet money on her father flipping the table on their way out.

"We'll make this fast. We've decided to banish you, Tala," Elder Bryer said without looking up from his cards.

"You didn't even hear her side!" Her mother stepped forward as if she wanted to slap the cards away, eyes flashing.

"She's endangered us all by revealing herself to humans. Now, we have to watch for Hunters."

Tala held in a wince, refusing to show weakness. Hunters were definitely bad news. They had the means to kill a werewolf and would do so to protect human society.

"The reason why doesn't matter?" her mother asked.

"Ma," Tala said. It wasn't right to talk back to the elders. She may be banished, but her mother didn't have to be.

"No! She's not the first one to reveal herself, and she won't be the last. She did it to protect her mate, which is perfectly legal, so there won't be any damn Hunters," her mother said.

"Only if her mate's a fellow wolf, and we know that's not the case with Tala. It would be too normal for her to settle down with a wolf," Elder Bryer replied.

"Tala is perfectly normal," her father snarled. The noise didn't even register a twitch from any of the elders, who kept playing cards. Poker, if the chips were any indication.

The elder sniffed. "We never really expected much from her considering her packless rogue father. Mental illness is hereditary."

That struck a chord in Tala. "Leave my dad out of this. You've spent my entire life shaming me for being his daughter, and it worked for so long that I've looked down on my own damn dad, but he's a damn good dad. He's never made me feel bad or wrong for being me, which is more than the pack ever did. Screw you guys for trying to act like there's something wrong with him, me, or my mom for loving him. There's nothing wrong with any of us."

Elder Felan sighed and looked up from his hand. "Says the lone wolf. There's obviously something wrong with you. You're broken."

"Bastard!" her mother said, stepping closer to them.

"Ma, I got this." Tala stared down the table. "I know how you feel about me. You think I'm mentally ill because I don't want to be around a mob. No one ever bothered to ask why. Crowds of people drain me and there's nothing wrong with that. I'm just an introvert. We exist. You're the assholes. Don't even get me started on how you abandoned Kyra when her mother died. You can't have the moral high ground when the whole support system abandoned a six-year-old because she's half human. So, fuck you guys."

Her father applauded. "Well said."

All of the elders leaned away. Elder Bryer gasped. "Now, see here!"

"I don't have to. Since you banished me, we don't have to worry about each other anymore," Tala replied.

Tala turned to leave, but her mother grabbed her hand. She gave the pack elders a withering gaze. "Be aware that when we leave, the pack has banished the entire Grayson family. You've lost access to all of us, including my mother and Kyra."

"Ma," Tala's energy flagged. That was too much. She could stand losing the pack, but her family didn't have to.

"Our family will support Tala and her mate in ways this pack obviously never would. From this moment forward, the pack loses this family." None of the elders objected, and the Grayson family walked out with their heads held high, which made more of a statement than flipping a table could.

With them went a doctor, a mechanic, an up-and-coming pharmacist, a budding master chef, and a retired nurse. It might not seem like much, but they were good people. The pack didn't have many of those.

As the door closed behind them, she grabbed her mother and father into a hug. A rare gesture for her, but a necessary one. Worry came back as she let go. *Hunters.*

If Hunters came, Tala was on her own. Her small family wouldn't be enough to fight off Hunters, and she would never put her family in a position where they'd have to physically defend her. *But Ma seems confident there won't be Hunters.*

"Look, I'm living proof you don't need a pack to survive," her father said gently.

"Which is why I'm not worried about that," Tala replied. "But do you really think Hunters would come after me? I was defending a human." Yes, she hurt humans, but to protect a human. That counted for something, right?

"Hunters aren't supposed to operate without a legitimate reason. You saved someone. Everything you did was perfectly legal, even shifting. The pack elders just used that as an excuse for their behavior. We'll be fine," her mother said.

Tala wanted to believe that, but her luck had never been *that* good.

Chapter Sixteen

PUTTING THE GROCERIES ON the counter, Citlali grabbed a pot from Tala's kitchen cabinet, wanting to prepare a big meal for Tala when she returned from meeting with her pack elders. The door opened and closed. She stepped out of the kitchen.

"That was fast," Citlali said before realizing it was actually Kyra, not Tala. Kyra had her hands full of grocery bags. Behind her, there was an older woman and younger woman with even more bags.

Kyra smiled. "You're waiting for her."

Citlali grinned. "You're about to make food, aren't you?" She should've known she wouldn't be the only one with this idea.

Kyra shrugged. "It's one of the best ways to comfort Tala."

"Well, it's basically your kitchen. Mind if I join you?"

"The more the merrier." Kyra turned around. "That's my guardian and Tala's grandmother, Sofi." The elderly woman was just as small as Tala. "And that handsome thing behind her is my girlfriend, Raina."

Citlali eyed Raina. Handsome was the best way to describe her.

"I'm Citlali." She waved at them.

"Pleased to meet you. I've heard tons about you, but none of them included cooking. Good to know someone will feed Tala when Kyra's career takes off. Can't see her cooking for that girl too much longer." Sofi shook her head as she put her bags down.

Kyra snickered. "I'd feed Tala until we're both dead, but I'll leave the job to you whenever you want it."

Citlali laughed. "Thank you."

They began cooking through several different meals. Citlali watched Kyra and Sofi interact and listened to their conversation, earning even more understanding about Kyra's relationship with Tala. Kyra was basically her little sister.

When all the meals were cooking merrily on the stovetop, Kyra stepped out of the kitchen, yanking Raina with her. As soon as she was gone, Sofi turned to Citlali with fire in her bright yellow eyes. The sun had nothing on this tiny woman.

"All right, I'm gonna make this fast between you and me," Sofi said. "Tala is special, and people who don't get that have made her feel bad about her entire life, and I'm not going to stand around and let someone else hurt her."

Citlali held up her hands. "I only want to be there for her, support her, and love her if she'll let me." *Love? That's fast, isn't it?* It should've bothered her, but she really wanted to love Tala.

Sofi looked her up and down with a sour expression. "We'll see. Be aware, a sixty-year-old werewolf is still a werewolf."

Citlali nodded as Kyra popped back in and they all went back to work. If Kyra heard the conversation—and it was almost certainly a guarantee she did—she didn't mention it.

Raina stayed out of the kitchen on Kyra's orders. Apparently, she once set their toaster on fire and was banned from using kitchen appliances. The three of them were able to navigate around each other. At one point, Kyra was practically on her back, leaning over her while she simmered the milanesa.

"Yes?" Citlali arched an eyebrow.

"You're making milanesa?"

"I am."

"It smells good."

"You want the recipe?"

Hearts practically appeared in her eyes. "Would you?"

"My abuela would want people to enjoy her recipe." It was one of the reasons she was making it now. Her grandmother made it for family gatherings.

Kyra gasped. "Thank you!"

Citlali chuckled as Kyra practically floated back to her jambalaya. When things were all done, Citlali stared at Tala's poor excuse for a table. There was no way all of the food would fit.

Sofi patted her arm. "Don't worry. It's all staying in the kitchen, right here on the counters."

Citlali pursed her lips. "Really? My family would sit at the table."

"We make our plates from the dishes in the kitchen then sit down together. Although, I don't see how we'll fit there." Sofi looked at the table and then turned her attention to the living room. "You youngsters might have to eat on the sofa."

Kyra laughed. "You know she purposely chose an apartment this tiny so we'd never host anything here."

Sofi smiled. "That poor girl. We're never going to leave her alone."

"I don't think she would want you to leave her alone. She just needs space to recharge," Citlali said.

Tala was always happy to see Kyra and she enjoyed her parents, especially when they didn't try to pull her into the conversation.

Sofi shook her head. "One of the many reasons I took Kyra in was to have some noise in my house while my crazy daughter tried to live with her crazy daddy baby."

"They don't live together now?" Citlali asked.

"No, she's thankfully back where she belongs, in my house. I was glad when she moved back in and Kyra got to be around Tala more. Had all my babies at home where they belonged," Sofi said with a smile.

Citlali had to ask. "A doctor living at home?"

"I'm a retired werewolf. I need someone around all the time. She needs the company when Rocky's busy, like when something shiny catches his attention." She grunted when Kyra gave her a reproaching look. "Anyway, that's how we are. You all live together, be together, until you run out of space. Technically, Tala should still be at the house, too."

"So, what do you do for privacy?" Citlali couldn't imagine still living at home as an adult, and her parents weren't even together.

"I know when to stay out of Rashida's way. If Kyra and Tala decide to come back home, we'll look into a bigger house," Sofi replied.

"It's not weird for us to have several generations living under one roof," Kyra said.

That made sense, from what Citlali knew about werewolves. And Tala was the exact opposite. It had to be hard growing up wanting to be alone while it was expected to be social almost all of the time. Maybe that was why she didn't mind being thrown out of the pack.

"What will happen with you if Tala is kicked out of the pack?" Citlali asked.

"We're all leaving if they cut her off. They shouldn't punish her for protecting you," Sofi said.

"Yeah, that's just dumb," Kyra said.

"Not that our pack is known for making smart decisions. Look at what they did with you. It didn't even occur to those idiots that you had a wolf form. Had I listened to them, we'd have been discovered before you could walk. Every time you sneezed, your tail popped out." A soft smile settled on Sofi's face.

That sounded cute. "Can you join another pack?" Citlali asked.

"We'd have to move and find other werewolves. We can also just be our own pack. Small, but better than those idiots," Sofi answered.

Citlali nodded. She'd probably learn more about it as she spent time with Tala and her family. The door slammed again, and Tala entered with her parents, their expressions firm.

"We are now our own pack," Rashida said, throwing her hands up.

"Well, we'll be well fed." Sofi motioned to the kitchen. No other words were needed. Everyone just went to get food. So, this was where Tala got it.

Tala turned to her, a full plate of milanese with fries along with a bowl of Kyra's jambalaya with cornbread.

She tilted her head. "You're not eating?"

Citlali could hardly imagine going into the cramped kitchen. "When you guys are done, I'll get something. Your kitchen is tiny."

Tala put her food down and ventured back into the kitchen. When she emerged again, she had two plates. One had a little of everything and the other had lamb chops, rice, mashed potatoes, and greens.

"Here you go." Tala handed the plate with everything to Citlali.

Citlali smiled. "Thank you."

Tala went to sit on the couch, and Citlali followed. Chatter continued as Rocky handed out beer bottles. They ate, drank, and conversed, like a regular happy family. Tala smiled the whole time.

"Should you be worried about Hunters, though?" Raina asked. She was on the floor with Kyra close to her. Raina nursed her second beer while Kyra had thirds...or maybe fourths.

Sofi waved that concern away. "Hunters need permission to come after us, and if anyone looks at the facts of this, they'll know Tala did the right thing."

Citlali twisted her mouth up. "Hunters?"

"People who hunt and kill werewolves," Tala replied.

"People are out to kill you?" Her memory flashed to guns firing, the shock of pain as her head hit the wall. Ruby's attack. Her breath hitched.

"They won't. Hunters can't just operate willy-nilly," Rashida replied.

"They have rules. They also understand werewolves live in human society. Every now and then, things happen. It's not like we're out hunting humans for sport. We're all civilized now," Sofi said.

"Was that once a thing?" Citlali asked.

"Look at it this way: have there been werewolf serial killers? Yes. Have there been human serial killers? Yes. Every group has horrible people in it," Sofi replied.

Citlali nodded as that made sense. "So, everything should be all right?"

"Yeah. Tala has a right to protect her mate, but also, she saved a human life. If the Hunters punished people for saving human lives, they'd have to kill each other," Rashida said.

"Can we watch?" Rocky grinned.

Sofi groaned. "To think my daughter bonded to this." She shook her head.

"You love me, Sofi." He blew her a kiss.

The way Sofi only rolled her eyes gave truth to his claim. The rest of the night was just the family reminiscing. They seemed close. It reminded Citlali of her mother's family when her abuela was alive. There was a clean up, and then everyone was gone.

Tala collapsed in her bed. Citlali followed and wrapped herself around Tala.

"Is it all right for me to stay the night?" Citlali asked.

"I'd like that."

"Loan me some pajamas?"

Tala looked deep into her eyes. "Or not?"

"Are you sure?"

Tala's smile grew. "You might as well know all of my secrets, and I'd like to know some of yours."

Citlali chuckled. "I'd let you learn all my secrets."

Tala came in for a kiss, a sweet caress of Tala's lips. It was warm and safe, like a cocoon of silk. Citlali moaned. She wanted the entire experience, yearned for Tala to pour herself all over Citlali and never leave.

Citlali deepened the caress, passing her tongue over Tala's lips. Tala granted her permission, and she slid her tongue into Tala's mouth. She drew a cute whimper from Tala and craved that noise again. Reaching between them, she cupped Tala's breast. Tala arched into her hand, then pulled away, staring into her eyes.

"You're beautiful," Tala said.

From the way Tala was looking at her, Citlali believed it. "And you're amazing. I feel so lucky to know you." She meant that with all of her heart. "Thank you for not giving up on me."

Tala stroked her cheek. "Thank you for taking a chance on me."

"Best decision I ever made." Citlali had to kiss Tala again. She ached to touch, kiss, feel every inch of Tala.

Citlali's body buzzed with each move of Tala's lips. Settling and simmering, it was a long promise, a vow of sweet days and comfortable nights. She shifted her body and Tala gave way, lying on her back. Tala's hand went to Citlali's breast, causing delightful jolts through her body, and then she squeezed enough to draw a moan. It was her turn to pull away just enough to look into Tala's eyes.

"You're sure?"

Tala nodded. "I'm definitely sure. Nothing about you was ever holding me back. You're great and I looked forward to being with you, but I couldn't do this to you without you knowing what you got with me. I wanted you to know me before we went too far."

Citlali swallowed as emotion bubbled up from her chest to her throat. This was a special moment, an event in her life. She should savor it.

"You okay?" Tala asked, caressing Citlali's cheek down to her neck.

"I'm happy to be exactly where I am."

Tala nodded. "I'm happy you're here, too."

She took Citlali by the back of the head and sat up a bit to start a fresh kiss, hot, burning, and full of promise.

Citlali melted into Tala. Lips and tongues glided against each other while their hands caressed their breasts. At some point, Tala's other hand, the one on Citlali's back, made its way under Citlali's shirt. Flesh on flesh. Citlali purred from the simple contact. She pulled away from the haven of Tala's mouth, earning a disappointed whine from Tala.

"I need skin contact," Citlali said as she popped open the buttons on her shirt.

Tala's eyes went wide as she watched Citlali work. Citlali smirked, slowing her movements to let Tala enjoy the show. Tala's hands fell to Citlali's thighs, and Citlali sat up. When she made it to the last button, she shimmed her shoulders a little, so her shirt fell open and dropped off.

Tala's breath hitched. "You're gorgeous."

Citlali smiled. "This is just a sneak peek." *Good thing I put on a cute bra.* The low cut, hot pink lace had Tala's full attention.

Citlali took Tala's hands and eased them up to her abdomen. Tala's hands on her skin were paradise, and she bit her lip to keep from moaning. Tala hissed as she touched Citlali gently, like she feared Citlali might break. The care caused Citlali to shiver.

"Could you...?" Citlali wasn't sure exactly what she should say.

Tala added some pressure, but explored Citlali at her leisure. Palms wandered Citlali's torso and it set her body aflame. To further encourage her, Citlali let her shirt drop further, caught by her elbows. Tala's hands made their way to Citlali's bra and stroked her breasts through the lace.

"I've got to get all of this off." Citlali was desperate for contact, and she tried to almost tear out of her shirt.

"Yes," Tala whispered.

As Citlali got rid of her shirt and bra, Tala sat up to do the same. One by one, the clothing fell off of them until they were both nude.

"You are as cut as I imagined." Citlali traced Tala's abs with her index finger.

Tala shrugged. "Werewolf."

Citlali's face scrunched up. "So you all look like this?" She could believe it from the few she met, but that was a small sample.

"I guess. Since we both know I just sit on my ass all day, playing games and eating."

Citlali laughed and leaned down, laying claim to Tala's mouth. Tala pulled her down until she was lying on Tala. Tala's whole body was hot and solid. Perfect. The skin contact was electric, buzzing down every nerve, making them beg for more. Tala squeezed her ass. Citlali ground against Tala.

"Fuck," Citlali said, mouth barely a breath away from Tala's. "Touch me, baby, please."

Tala granted her wish, flipping them over. Before Citlali could marvel over her strength, Tala had her legs open and stroked her. She hissed as pleasure zipped through her. She moaned as Tala kissed her neck down to her chest. Tala wrapped her lips around Citlali's nipple while adding pressure to her clit. The pleasure came in waves, growing as Tala grazed her nipple with her teeth. Citlali bucked against Tala's hand.

"Babe, more," Citlali said, her voice a whine to her own ears. She dug her nails into Tala's shoulders.

Tala gave her nipple a light bite. "Is it okay if I go inside?"

Citlali nodded. "Do it."

Tala eased a finger into her and Citlali arched. Tala slid her tongue down Citlali's chest and belly, a unique warmth. Citlali squirmed, needing something to do, so she hooked her leg around Tala's hip, anchoring herself, and bucked against Tala's finger. Tala curled her finger in response.

Citlali moaned. "Yes!" Her hips pushed against Tala, trying to take more of her in, but Tala took her time only granting what she wanted to give. Citlali's body hummed as she lost her mind with desire.

Tala kissed right above her trimmed patch of hair before going lower. She slipped a second finger inside of Citlali as she wrapped her lips around Citlali's clit. Citlali cried out, body trembling. She dug in harder. Tala moved her fingers faster, twisting them as she pressed her tongue against Citlali's gem.

The waves of pleasure came faster and harder. The stretch around those talented fingers as they worked to perfection and the way her mouth adored Citlali, it was too much. Citlali didn't stand a chance. She climaxed, drowning under the massive waves of pure ecstasy. With a loud cry, Citlali collapsed against the pillow, panting as Tala continued to stroke her.

"Sweetheart," Citlali said, voice weak as tremors swept through her.

"Hmm?" Tala's tongue lapped at her clit.

Citlali shivered as a joyful chill ran up her spine. "I want to do you now." She wanted to spend the rest of the night worshipping Tala, letting her know how wonderful she was.

Tala looked at her. "Are you sure?"

"Yes. I want to worship you all night long." Citlali caressed Tala's cheek. "Babe, I need you to understand that I want all of you." Tala's face scrunched up and Citlali's heart broke a little. She would mend that and help Tala understand that she wasn't going anywhere.

***

Tala enjoyed lying between Citlali's legs, but her heart melted when Citlali wanted to return the favor. Tala had been led to believe that she was weird and unworthy of any attention outside of her family. For a long time, she didn't want attention outside of her family, but she wanted Citlali.

"I don't get why you want me. You could have anyone," Tala said.

Citlali sat up, thumb rubbing Tala's cheek. "You listen here, sweet girl. I want you. I've wanted you since the moment you walked through the door at The New Moon. I almost lost you due to stupid pride. Never again. So get on your back and let me love you."

Tala's brain sort of short-circuited at the word "love." Citlali didn't mean it like that, but Tala couldn't get that out of her mind. She was distracted enough for Citlali to use leverage and flip Tala onto her back. Citlali smiled. Her straight, black hair spilled over her shoulder like an onyx waterfall. Tala's heart filled and her stomach butterflies fluttered to life, but it wasn't like their usual chaotic flight pattern.

"What's going through your mind?" Citlali asked.

"I'm used to my chest being tight, but you make me feel it in a different way. A good way."

Citlali kissed her. Tala smiled against Citlali's mouth before their tongues met and caressed each other. Distracted by the brilliance of Citlali's tongue, Tala couldn't be sure when Citlali eased her thigh between Tala legs. Jolts of bliss rocketed through her body. She hissed and broke their kiss.

Citlali nipped Tala's bottom lip. "You like that?"

Tala sighed. "Uh-huh."

Citlali's hands settled on Tala's narrow hips and she lifted Tala, moving Tala against her thigh. Tala gasped. Just watching it made it a thousand times better, flooded her with pleasure.

"Tell me what you want, sweetheart," Citlali said.

"This is good," Tala replied. It was more than she could hope for.

"But not great." Citlali leaned down. Tala expected another kiss, but Citlali bit her collarbone. Tala moaned and squirmed. Citlali moved Tala's hips and dragged her teeth down Tala's chest. And then she grazed a nipple with her teeth. Those bolts of pleasure boomed through her like thunder. She moaned, louder than she had ever done. Her hips moved with Citlali's hands.

"You feel so good against me, babe. Nice and wet and perfect," Citlali whispered, and Tala could only whimper. "I want you to come all over me."

Tala moaned, the words sending lightning through her. No one had ever talked to her like that. Citlali slid a hand between Tala's legs, easing a finger inside of her. She sucked Tala's nipple into her mouth. Tala cried out and spread her legs wider, begging for more. Citlali obliged, palm pressed against Tala as one finger became two. She worked up a wonderful rhythm.

"Let me hear," Citlali said.

Tala whimpered. She didn't usually make much noise during sex, but now she found herself crying out. Citlali rewarded her with a swirl of her tongue around Tala's nipple as she made the same motion with her thumb against Tala's clit. It caused a storm of pleasure inside of her.

Tala arched. She panted, clawing at the bed. It was like she was about to come out of her skin. She got louder as Citlali curled her fingers and things went from blazing through her to exploding outside of her.

Tala wasn't sure when she dropped to the pillow, but by the time she realized it, Citlali was covering her shoulder in wet kisses. Citlali pressed against her, sharing body heat. If there ever was a perfect moment, it was now.

"You okay?" Citlali asked.

Tala reached for her. "Of course. You're amazing."

"So are you." Citlali curled around Tala, blanketing her in comfort.

Tala sighed. "This was worth the wait."

"Yes, it was. I'll be wanting more, and often."

Tala chuckled, but she felt so warm and like she was floating. She would go to sleep right now and possibly sleep through the night. "We can do this as much as you'd like."

"Promise?" It shouldn't be a question, but it was good Citlali asked. It made Tala feel desired, and her mind didn't jump right to thinking that this was somehow all a cruel joke. She trusted Citlali.

"I promise."

With a content sigh, Citlali snuggled closer. "Thank you for sharing so much of your life with me."

Tala wasn't sure what to say to that. Citlali was willing to put up with her anxiety, self-doubt, and being a werewolf. It was more than she ever expected.

"Hey, since I've met your whole family, would you like to meet my parents?" Citlali asked.

Tala gasped. *She wants me to meet her parents? She does want me.* She wasn't sure if she'd ever get used to it. *I wonder how long it'll take me to just believe in her without my stomach dropping.*

"Tala, sweetie, I'm sure your thoughts are vast, but I need an answer," Citlali said.

Tala yelped. "Sorry. You sure you want me to meet your parents?" All sorts of things could go wrong there. She'd never done that before.

"Look at me," Citlali said.

Tala didn't hesitate, and it was like Citlali was staring into her soul. Instead of making her uncomfortable, everything inside of Tala felt toasty. Light bloomed in her chest.

"I want you in my life, as a huge part of my life, as my partner if possible. I'll show it whenever I can and tell you as much as I can. I am here for you, completely." Citlali asked.

Tala's eyes stung. *You're wanted. You're wanted. You're wanted.* She was understood and accepted. Her voice caught in her throat, so she nodded.

Citlali smiled. "Now, do you want to meet my parents?"

Tala nodded again, heart touched by even more light. "Please."

Citlali kissed Tala. A soothing, soft, wonderful kiss.

Maybe Citlali will be all right with being my mate. The thought drifted through Tala and snagged. *We should talk about it.*

Chapter Seventeen

CITLALI DIDN'T WANT TO be nervous, as Tala would pick up on that and she might buckle under her anxiety. To be fair, she didn't know how her parents would react. So, she had the brilliant idea of introducing Tala to Daphne first. It would calm them both down.

They sat at a little cafe Daphne liked, waiting for her at a small table outside. Tala had already inhaled two giant apple turnovers and an iced coffee, and Citlali nibbled on a glazed donut.

With all of her focus on Tala, Citlali almost jumped out of her seat when Daphne sashayed over. "Citlali, you're practically glowing," Daphne said as she hugged Citlali.

"You have Tala to thank for that." Citlali laughed. She motioned to Tala. "Tala, this is my best friend Daphne. Daphne, my girlfriend Tala."

Tala began to climb to her feet, but Daphne stopped her. "Don't stand. It's a pleasure to meet you. Officially, I mean. We bumped into each other at The New Moon." Daphne shook Tala's hand before sitting down. Her eyes never left Tala. "First off, I want to thank you."

Tala's forehead wrinkled. "Thank me?"

"For taking care of Citlali. She's so good on her own, she forgets she needs others sometimes. You've been there for her."

"Well, she's been there for me through stuff, too," Tala said with a shrug.

Daphne smiled. "That's good. Citlali said you're going to be a pharmacist."

Tala nodded. "I've got an internship that'll start in a couple of weeks. I'm planning on getting a doctorate before I start working."

"You're really smart, huh?" Daphne asked.

Tala's mouth twisted up.

This was probably too many compliments too soon, and too much pressure to come across as "good enough." Daphne's opinion mattered. So, while she had no problem talking to the detective, Daphne posed the problem of being able to judge her and change her life. Of course, Daphne didn't have that power, and Tala needed to understand that.

Citlali patted her leg as silent encouragement. Tala glanced down at the hand and then at Citlali. Citlali nodded. Tala took a breath and then looked at Daphne again.

"School's easy." Tala nibbled the corner of her bottom lip. "What about you? You're going to run a club one day with Citlali?"

Daphne had mercy on Tala and monopolized the conversation from that point forward. That was good. Citlali's parents might do that, but they might also ask a bunch of questions and Tala would wither. *I hope that doesn't happen.*

"I'm going to get a smoothie. Do you guys want anything?" Daphne asked.

"Get two apple turnovers. I'll pay you back," Citlali answered. Tala earned it. She would've gotten Tala another iced coffee, too, but she probably didn't need any more caffeine. Daphne nodded and was off.

"You okay, babe?" Citlali asked, giving Tala's thigh a squeeze. Her leg trembled.

Tala nodded. "Fine. I'm just not used to direct conversation with someone I hardly know that I actually want to impress. She likes me, right?"

"Liked you from the moment she realized you were my type." Citlali kissed her cheek. "She's actually the one who pointed you out to me the first day."

Tala sighed. "I'm glad."

"She's not too much for you?" Citlali wasn't sure what she could do about that, except ask Daphne to tone it down. Daphne probably would.

"I think I can handle it. I'm just trying to coach myself on what to say and figure out where the conversation is going," Tala replied.

Citlali cooed. "You don't have to do that."

"If I don't, I'll say something I'll dwell on for weeks, months, possibly years."

Citlali patted Tala's knee. It would probably be better once she was more comfortable with Daphne. Daphne slid the pastries over to Tala.

"Thanks," Tala said, and Citlali was relieved when Tala didn't tense.

Daphne waved the matter off. "After what you did for my girl, I'd gladly buy you a lifetime supply of apple turnovers."

Tala blushed and stared down at the table. "Uh...thanks."

Daphne smiled at Tala and graciously turned her attention to Citlali. "So, when are you coming back? Raul is starting to grill me if I'm about to skip out, too."

"Wow. I love that he thinks we're ready to start our own place, but I've been in contact with him. I'm going to try for next week, granted it's safe. He tried to assure me it is, but I'll need to see it for myself."

Daphne sipped her smoothie and broke off some of a giant corn muffin she brought. "We have definitely ramped up security measures." She popped the piece of muffin into her mouth. "Ruby hasn't come around. We do think the police are sniffing around, wanting to catch our famous prostitute ring that surely you're a part of. They're annoying as hell."

Citlali groaned. She had gone from a survivor to confused girlfriend and now to a prostitute. They weren't investigating because she had been attacked; they didn't seem interested in that at all. *At least they're not looking for a werewolf.* Or so she hoped.

"You know they're trying to come in when we have people in there, too," Daphne said.

Citlali sucked her teeth. "They're just doing their greatest hits, aren't they? You keep telling them to buy a ticket?"

"I exaggerate my accent, too, so they don't know what the hell I'm saying. It's hilarious." Daphne snickered.

They spoke for a while about work. Tala was quiet, but content with her food, a soft smile on her face.

"You like the apple turnovers?" Daphne asked Tala out of the blue. Apparently, she needed to have some kind of conversation with Tala, even though Citlali told her how shy Tala was.

Tala nodded. "I gotta come back here."

"Yeah, they make good stuff. You like West Indian food?"

"Yup."

"I know a few places. I'll text them to Li, so she can treat you. For each of them, try everything. It's all delicious. You like black cake?" Daphne asked.

Tala grinned. Daphne was speaking her language. Now, Citlali sat back. Tala didn't talk much, just listened as Daphne waxed poetic about different restaurants and foods.

It was a good visit that ended with hugs. Tala looked like she might throw up, but she made it through. Daphne gave Citlali a one-armed hug, which she returned.

"That went well," Citlali said as she got into the driver's side of her car.

"It did." Tala sighed and leaned her head on the window. "She's cool."

"She likes you a lot. Meeting my parents will be similar." Citlali reached over and took Tala's hand. Tala covered Citlali's hand with both of hers.

"Are you going to go back to work?" Tala asked, fastening her seatbelt.

Citlali's stomach dropped, pulling away from the curb. "As soon as my nerves calm down. Right now, mentioning work makes me a little jumpy. I don't want to have Ruby pop up in the parking lot. I don't know how I'll react to that."

Tala's expression hardened. "I could meet you when you get off."

Citlali's heart thumped in a way she never felt before. She melted at the very idea of Tala doing something so selfless for her. "That's sweet, but you're going to start your internship soon. You need your rest and a regular schedule."

"I love that you think I have regular hours." Tala chuckled. "But I want you to be safe and secure."

"Let me think about it." She would feel better if Tala was waiting for her, but she couldn't take any more from Tala. After all, Tala probably wouldn't be able to come around every time Citlali got off work. She needed to know she could do it by herself, too.

***

Tala sweated through her second shirt. She didn't even need to look at her bedroom mirror. Citlali came up behind her, pulling her close. With a whine, Tala tried to pull away, but Citlali yanked her back.

"Wow, Tala, you're nervous. You don't have to be," Citlali said.

"I'm all sweaty. I don't want to mess your outfit up, too," Tala replied, trying to step away. If she was sweating this badly in an air-conditioned apartment, she didn't want to think about what would happen when she stepped into the summer air.

Citlali chuckled. "Don't be silly."

Tala shook her hands, trying to shake off the nerves. "I don't want them to think I'm weird."

Citlali laughed. "We're all weird. They're going to love you, though; I know that for a fact. You know how I know that?"

Tala shook her head, and it was like she shook her torso too because her damned stomach butterflies went crazy. "How do you know?"

Citlali locked eyes with her in the mirror. "Because I love you."

Tala gasped, certain her heart exploded in her chest. Butterflies expanded throughout her. *Citlali loves me?* The idea of someone outside of her family loving her was more than enough to short circuit her brain. She froze, like her entire body ceased to function. Citlali caressed her cheek.

"Tala, you have to at least breathe," Citlali said.

Tala couldn't remember how to breathe. What was breathing? What was anything?

Citlali rubbed the small of her back. "Are you okay?"

Tala's breath hitched. "You love me?"

Citlali smiled. "I do."

"How can you be sure?" She had already resigned herself to a fate similar to her mother's, to form a mating bond with someone who couldn't return it. Love wasn't a guarantee, but it was as close as a human could get and well beyond what Tala ever expected.

Citlali's brow wrinkled. "Sitting down with your family solidified it for me, but I could feel it down to my toes when you offered to wait for me at work. You're so genuine in your care for me and I want to give you the world."

"I don't want the world. I just want you."

"Well, you have me."

Tala settled. She took a breath, purposely inhaling Citlali's scent, and her sweet musk calmed Tala down. For once, it didn't feel like she was coming apart at the seams.

"Are you okay now?" Citlali asked. Tala nodded. "Then let's get you another shirt."

Citlali stepped away, going through Tala's closet. Tala was glad for the help. She didn't know what was appropriate for meeting parents.

"Oh, do you have a tie?" Citlali asked.

Tala scratched her head. "Yeah, plenty. They're pushed all the way to the right. Is this formal now?" She didn't need to sweat through a shirt and a suit jacket. *Damn werewolf genes.* It had to be the werewolf in her. No way a human could sweat so much.

"It's not. I just think you'll look cute with the tie."

Tala didn't argue, and soon Citlali emerged with a new shirt and tie. The dark maroon tie matched Tala's lipstick and contrasted with her pink shirt. She slipped it on, leaving the top button left open and the tie loose.

"I look all right?" Tala asked.

Citlali kissed her cheek. "You're beautiful, babe."

Tala smiled. "Thanks for doing my hair last night." Citlali had surprised her with learning how to cornrow so quickly, and she wove Tala's hair just the way she liked it.

"It was a labor of love." Citlali grinned. "And Daphne let me practice on her. Told you she liked you."

Tala knew that was supposed to make her feel better about meeting the parents. Daphne liked her enough to allow Citlali to play in her hair, but parents and best friends were two different creatures. She didn't even pay her own bills. Her parents took care of everything.

"Tala, you really need to relax. You'll be fine," Citlali said.

"Famous last words," Tala muttered.

They were off to meet Citlali's parents for lunch. It took a minute to click, but they sort of matched. Her pink shirt went with Citlali's pink suit, and Citlali had on a maroon halter-top, which matched Tala's tie. It helped. Like a united front.

Citlali drove to the restaurant. It was a little fancy, but Tala didn't have a chance to be nervous as Citlali took her hand. Citlali seemed familiar with the place, spotting her parents easily enough in a cushy corner booth, like they sat there all the time. And from the exchanged waves, maybe they did.

"My baby!" Citlali's mother jumped up.

She was short, but still taller than Tala. Business-like, in white pants and a navy sleeveless shirt with a white bolo tie. She was elegant with light makeup and perfect teeth. She smelled of shea butter and jasmine, like her daughter. She was Citlali, though four inches shorter and a darker complexion.

Citlali and her mother began speaking Spanish to each other. Tala didn't speak the language. The tall man behind Citlali's mother, probably her father, smiled, like he didn't speak Spanish either.

"Are you just going to pretend I don't exist?" Citlali's father asked, hand pressed to the center of his chest. Dressed dapperly in a short-sleeve, pink checkered shirt, he almost matched Citlali, too.

Citlali transitioned from excited Spanish to excited Cantonese as if it was the most natural thing ever. Tala blinked as they gestured to each other, surprised by how similar their mannerisms were already.

"Mami, Papa..." Citlali reached out for Tala. "This is Tala Grayson, my girlfriend. Tala, these are my parents, Albert Zhen and Laura Santiago Rodriguez."

"Nice to meet you," Tala said as she held out her hand to them.

Both of them shook her hand, but the disappointment was so intense, it could've choked Tala. Thick, heavy waves of disappointment, sharp like acid, flowed toward her. Though smiling, their posture got almost defensive. Her stomach dropped as they all sat down. *Citlali's just looking through rose-tinted glasses because she likes you.*

"Citlali's told us a lot about you," Mr. Zhen said.

Tala did her best to not squirm in her seat. "She has?" *That explains it.*

"A lot of it revolves around cooking meals for you," Ms. Rodriguez replied with a barely concealed sneer, the look of a mother who had high hopes for her daughter and wouldn't see them derailed by the likes of Tala.

"I like cooking for Tala," Citlali said.

"You haven't been to work in two weeks, and whenever you call either one of us, you talk about what you're doing for her," Mr. Zhen said.

Tala wanted to sink into the floor. Citlali's hand on her thigh didn't help. She tried to breathe in Citlali's scent, but the sharp anger rolling from her parents overwhelmed Citlali's quiet scent. *See, no one likes you*. The conversation paused when a waiter came over to take their drink orders. Tala couldn't even think of what she wanted and knee-jerk ordered iced coffee.

"Babe, maybe an ice tea," Citlali said.

That would definitely be better for her nerves, and Citlali ordered her some onion rings as well. She would've felt better if only the parents weren't glaring at her. *Is it bad for Citlali to order for me?* Maybe because it seemed like Citlali was doing everything, like a servant.

"Maybe you've decided on a different full time job." Ms. Rodriguez gave Tala a pointed glare.

Citlali frowned. "I haven't been back to work because I almost got shot, and the only reason I didn't is because of Tala. You know that."

Mr. Zhen shook his head. "Of course we're grateful for that, but you'd have gotten yourself out of that situation."

"You're resourceful," Ms. Rodriguez agreed.

Citlali's eyes widened and she rubbed her forehead. "Wow. I know I downplayed the situation, but not to the point you guys don't understand the actual danger I was in. I could've died if Tala wasn't there."

"What was she doing there, anyway? Your girlfriend shouldn't be allowed inside The New Moon," Mr. Zhen replied.

Tala couldn't stop from squirming now. That did look bad. She had been at Citlali's job when she shouldn't be. Broken the rules. Everything they had a problem with hit her hard. *Am I toxic?* Her chest hurt.

"She was there to warn me. She also went with me to talk with the police and held my hand as they basically accused me of being a liar and a whore. She's the main reason I haven't had a breakdown. I can't believe you're not thanking her," Citlali said.

"Cariña, we're happy you're all right, but this doesn't seem like a healthy relationship," Ms. Rodriguez said.

This conversation was so uncomfortable, Tala wanted to make a mad dash for the door, but she couldn't abandon Citlali. So she sat there, shame filling her so completely she couldn't think, couldn't breathe. Citlali's parents really seemed to hate her. Citlali's parents would eventually talk Citlali into leaving her. *Would they be wrong?* It certainly sounded like she was holding Citlali back. *You already knew that.*

Citlali pursed her lips. "I don't understand this."

"What's not to understand? In the time you've met her, you've turned into her housewife. You just ordered for her. She's barely said two words, but you pretty much hop when she snaps. That's not like you," her mother said.

A frown conquered Citlali's face. "Why, because I'm not like you? Because you couldn't stand being a wife and mother?"

The subtle scent of shock flashed from Mr. Zhen, quickly smothered by anger, and he pointed at her. "You are way out of line."

"No, you both are out of line." Citlali glared at her parents with a fire in her eyes. "Do you not understand how hard this was? You're treating Tala terribly right now. Was being there for me when I needed it wrong?"

Mr. Zhen's face twisted in the same way Citlali's did. "Of course not."

"That's what it sounds like." Citlali grabbed Tala's hand and put their joined hands on the table. "And I don't understand why."

"It just seems you've made drastic changes to your life since you met her," Mr. Zhen said in a forced, calm voice.

Citlali blinked, her lip trembling. Tala could see how much it hurt her, having her parents be like this. Citlali took a deep breath before she spoke. "I was living my life as always until a stalker almost shot me.

Would you have rather I'd gotten shot? I was in danger and Tala saved me, even though she didn't need to, even though I had just been awful to her, and even though she knew it'd cost her everything."

Tala sat up, like a switch was flipped in her head. She needed Citlali to understand it didn't cost her anything to do the right thing. "You are everything! If something happened to you, I wouldn't be able to live with myself." *What would it be like if Citlali got hurt?* She didn't want to think about it. "The people who are gone don't matter. I have you and my family. I can deal with whatever else."

Citlali smiled. "Thank you."

Tala's cheeks burned. Citlali kissed her cheek, which didn't help. Tala ducked her head again. Citlali's parents were quiet for a long moment. Tala stared hard at the wooden table, the lines in the wood, holding Citlali's hand tight. Their drinks finally made it to the table, but no one touched a thing, even though the onion rings smelled awesome.

"You folks ready to order?" the waiter asked.

Tala couldn't believe the dude didn't feel the tension, but he powered through all of their orders. Tala hadn't even thought to look at her menu. Citlali ordered for her—steak, roasted potatoes, and broccoli. It was probably delicious, but with the way things were going, it would be ashes in her mouth.

Citlali bumped her with her shoulder, and Tala wasn't sure how she didn't fall over. "I got shrimp you can try."

That should've made Tala feel better, but Citlali's parents kept eyeing her. Maybe she shouldn't eat. They'd definitely find a problem with how much food she usually consumed.

"What happened?" Mr. Zhen asked.

Ms. Rodriguez nodded. "What did she lose for you?"

Tala glared down at her lap and Citlali squeezed her hand. They stared at each other for a long moment. Tala shrugged. "You tell them. It's not really a big a deal."

Citlali sighed. "It is a big deal." She turned to her parents. "Tala was forced out of her community when they learned she was dating me. So, while you're accusing her of trying to control me, she actually gave up a huge chunk of her life for me. You guys just ripped her apart based on some idea of me being able to fight off armed men while I was locked in a room."

Ms. Rodriguez studied them for a moment. Silence somehow moderated the tension. "Maybe we should start over. Tala, tell us about yourself."

Tala squirmed. *What's there to say?* They didn't like her already. She didn't want to make it worse by saying the wrong thing. Her stomach crunched into a ball. *Am I sweating? Damn it, please don't sweat through everything.* Citlali ran a knuckle down her cheek.

Tala took a deep breath. "I'm…" She blew out the breath. "I'm not great with people, but your daughter makes me feel comfortable in my skin. I'm gonna do my best to honor her for that alone." She quivered, not sure what to say beyond that. *Do I have to keep talking?*

"It's okay, sweetheart." Citlali focused on her parents. "How about we have lunch and let Tala jump in when she's comfortable?" Her parents thought about it for a moment and then nodded.

As much as she tried to calm herself down, Tala just never felt comfortable enough to jump in on the conversation. She barely listened, but this was possibly the longest lunch of her life. She was so tense that she could barely get up when it was time to leave.

"It was a pleasure to meet you," Mr. Zhen said.

Tala shook both parents' hands, and then they were gone. Citlali led Tala outside. She gulped down the hot air, the salty air clinging to her clothes to mix with her sweat. Citlali rubbed her back.

"Sorry about that," Citlali said.

Tala wiped her forehead. "It's not your fault."

A moment of silence let her know Citlali thought she was to blame. "There's a park not too far from here. Want to go for a walk, or do you just want to go home?"

Tala wanted nothing more than to retreat to her apartment, curl up on the couch, and play video games until she forgot this whole thing happened, but she resisted. Walking with Citlali would help calm her down, and they hadn't been on a date for a while.

She managed a smile. "Let's take a walk. I want to admire you in the sun."

"Oh, listen to you being smooth!" Citlali kissed her cheek.

Tala tried to laugh, but she didn't have it in her just yet. Citlali kept her hand on Tala's back and led the way. The park was small, but green and filled with laughter. Kids on the playground, a pretzel cart, and fresh cut grass wrapped around her. The knot in her stomach eased. Citlali bought her a pretzel.

"Do you want mustard?" Citlali asked. Tala shook her head and Citlali handed her the hot pretzel.

The warm, salty bread smelled delicious, and Tala finally grinned. "I feel better already." It was the truth.

Citlali pulled her close. "I'm sorry they reacted that way. I really didn't consider the way they'd see it."

Tala shrugged and took a big bite of the pretzel. "They love you and have high hopes." She didn't mind that. She held up the pretzel for Citlali, in case she wanted some. Sharing food was a big thing with werewolf couples.

Citlali tore off a piece, popping it into her mouth. "They were fine with you in the end, but I know you checked out at that point."

Tala nodded. "I did."

"They shouldn't have done that to you, and they even admitted that during lunch. I think they'll like you more as they interact with you more."

Tala nodded, even though she doubted it. After her initial outburst, she couldn't even say three words to the pair. Not a great impression, but everything would be fine for her as long as she had Citlali.

The smell of silver mixed with gunpowder and the sickly sweet scent of wolfsbane caught her attention. *Hunters.* Her gut clenched. *What the hell?* She wrinkled her nose.

"Are you okay?" Citlali asked, giving her shoulders a squeeze.

Tala let out a breath, needing to calm down and clear her head. *My mind's playing a trick on me.* She looked around, but didn't see anyone suspicious. Kids, teens, parents. No Hunters. No other werewolves. *I can't be smelling wolfsbane.* She was just stressed after that lunch. Still, they should get out of here just in case. "Want to go on a real date?"

Citlali's smile was so bright it put the sun to shame. "Where do you have in mind?"

"I know a tea shop not too far from here. I bet you'll like a tasting."

"I've never done that. Let's go."

Tala led the way while trying to locate the source of the dangerous aroma. The scent faded once they were out of the park. Strange. *Probably just my imagination.*

Chapter Eighteen

CITLALI TOOK A BREATH as she stood before The New Moon. She purposely wore her yellow suit with black trim and a black sheath, feeling the most confident in this outfit. Tala held her hand, lending her strength. The building loomed, and Citlali's heart jumped to her throat.

Tala must have sensed her fear and embraced her. For someone so small, she felt massive against Citlali. "It'll be fine. We're strong, and I'm right here."

Citlali nodded. "Thank you."

"No place I'd rather be." She said it like it was the most natural thing in the world.

Citlali chuckled, taking a deep breath to steel her nerves. They walked into the lobby where people were milling about. Customers ate dinner in the restaurant. She glanced at Tala, checking to see if she wanted to sit down in the "innocent" portion of the business. Tala didn't even pause. They continued to the double doors of the main hall. Citlali froze. Her chest tightened, nerves humming through her body. *Do it.* She threw the doors open.

"Citlali!" A barrage of cheers hit Citlali, and party-poppers went off.

"We've been waiting for you!" Daphne grabbed Citlali in a hug. She then turned to Tala. "I suspected you'd be here. I asked the kitchen to make you something special."

"I'll sit out there." Tala pointed to the lobby. It probably had to do more with the rules rather than her discomfort. Tala kissed Citlali on the cheek. "This is your show."

Citlali snickered, not surprised by the decision, but as soon as Tala wasn't at her side anymore, Citlali's heart clenched. *Calm down, girl. Ruby isn't here.* She took a breath and slowly released it.

Daphne hooked her arm around Citlali's elbow. "We'll get you up to date on what you've missed."

Citlali nodded. "I read through the email with the new security protocols. No one minds coming through a metal detector?"

"Not yet. It probably has to do with the detector fitting the door so well you don't notice it. I mean, did you notice it when you walked in?" Daphne asked.

"I didn't." But she was more worried about keeping her wits about her as she stepped inside.

"Good. We've got people in the lobby who watch the sensors. People are also willing to do a bag scan. Everyone wants to feel safe."

I know the feeling. Unlike most people, she had a werewolf willing to defend her. "That's good news." It made sense that they'd want security while they tried to enjoy themselves. Hell, even amusement parks did bag scans.

"It'll be better. We also have metal detectors set up at the entrance of the private rooms, and three guards stationed in the hallway."

"Sounds good."

"Oh, but you should know that Marco resigned. People blamed him for bringing Ruby here."

Citlali pouted. "Oh, no. Marco was so fun."

"Yeah, but he vouched for a psycho, and no one, not patrons or staff, let him forget it. It sucks, but it helped start the healing process. You coming back is also part of that process. He's always welcome to come back, but now isn't the time."

Citlali definitely agreed with that. It was enough to kick Citlali into gear and start working. The job was easy, familiar, and with the lack of customers, she felt at ease. That would be the true test.

***

Tala sat down at a table in a corner in the dining section of The New Moon and swore she could smell silver and wolfsbane again, but it was faint. Maybe she was paranoid. There was no reason for Hunters to be there, to be after her. As her mother kept saying, she did the right thing. Before she could overthink the matter, Kyra delivered her meal. Kyra sat down with her, grinning.

"Have you by any chance smelled any wolfsbane around here?" Tala asked, even though she was sure she was just going crazy.

Kyra wrinkled her nose. "No, but then again, I'm in the kitchen most of the time and I smell a lot of things there. Sometimes, things mix together and fool my nose. You okay? Hunters show up?"

Tala shook her head. "No. I just keep thinking I smell it."

"You're probably just worrying yourself because of the stress. I know you say you don't care, but our pack was still our pack, even if they were assholes. It's okay to be a little upset."

That wasn't it at all, but Tala didn't have a better explanation right now. "You on break?"

"No. I'm able to visit with my friend, who also happens to be a hero around here," Kyra replied.

Tala dived into her food. A perfectly seasoned, massive steak with mushrooms along with mashed potatoes, string beans, and mac and cheese. Delicious.

"Hero?" she asked after swallowing several forkfuls.

Kyra rested her chin in her palm. "Yup. Everybody knows you saved her from a crazy person. They talk about how obsessed Ruby was with Citlali, more than Citlali ever knew."

Tala frowned. "Do they think she'll be back?" *Maybe I should hang around here, just in case.*

"That's the fear, but nobody's letting her stroll in through the front door."

"Are you sure?" Tala asked. Money went a long way, and from her understanding, Ruby had money. She employed four full-grown men who helped her kidnap a woman, after all.

"Pretty sure, but there's only so much they can do. Security's certainly better now, but they don't think they'll be able to completely stop her if she really wants to be a problem. I know you're going to worry no matter what, so you should know the situation."

Tala nodded as she made a point. Too bad Kyra couldn't keep an eye out for her. As long as Citlali stayed in the main hall, there would be eyes on her. Tala would come pick her up, showing up early to make sure things were all right. Citlali couldn't live in fear, especially after the way her parents reacted to her time off.

"So, how's your relationship going?" Kyra asked.

Tala ate some more as she considered how to respond. "Good. I met her parents last week." Hurt bloomed in her core, and she glanced down.

Kyra whimpered and grabbed Tala's hand. "Oh, no. They didn't like you?"

Tala's bottom lip trembled. "They think I'm controlling her. They told Citlali they changed their minds, but I didn't hear it."

Kyra scoffed. "It's like they didn't even try to get to know you. I'm sorry."

"It's okay. I didn't think they'd like me anyway."

Kyra scowled and sat back in her chair. "I wish you wouldn't say that like it's a forgone conclusion. You're such a good person."

This wasn't the first time Kyra made this speech. And truthfully, Tala knew not everyone she met hated her. It came from rumors pushed by their littermates. They went to school with pack members, who would tell the human children all sorts of terrible things about both of them. Eventually, it was too much of a bother to prove otherwise, but as an adult, it was hard to shake that feeling.

Tala smiled. "Thanks for saying so, and thanks for making my favorite."

Kyra chuckled. "I actually didn't make it. The head chef did. Like I said, you're a hero around here. So much so that I didn't even steal a piece like I did when we were little."

"Wow. Make sure to thank them. Guess Citlali is well loved around here." Worry trickled back into her mind, and she glanced around. "You sure you haven't smelled silver or wolfsbane?"

Kyra sucked her teeth. "Silver is all over this place. I'm lucky I'm only half or I'd choke to death. Wolfsbane, I've caught whiffs of it every now and then, before all this happened. So I figured it's actually all of the smells in here mixing. I mean, why the hell would wolfsbane be in here?"

Why indeed. "Be careful, okay?"

Kyra snorted, like she was being ridiculous. "The kitchen is hardly dangerous."

"Yeah, but Hunters would be looking for a wolf in The New Moon. You fit the build." If Hunters were on the prowl, they could mistake Kyra for her just because Kyra was another werewolf who happened to be in the right location.

"I'm careful, but it's like Auntie said, they don't have a reason to hunt you. You did the right thing."

"I know. Just, be on guard, okay?" She'd be ready for the worst rather than hoping for the best. For now, she enjoyed her meal. Kyra went back to work, so once she was done with her food, Tala went back home. She played video games and took a nap until she had to pick Citlali up again.

As Tala waited outside of The New Moon, she thought about her schedule. It could work. She got a full night's sleep during that nap, and her internship started at nine in the morning, so she could spend a couple of hours with Citlali before she had to be off. Life seemed to be good. Too good.

Silver, gunpowder, and wolfsbane distracted her again. Not good.

Citlali came out with Daphne and a few other New Moon employees. They were all laughing.

"You're going to follow her home?" Daphne asked Tala.

Tala shrugged. "If that's where she's going."

"You are so sweet." Daphne grinned at her before she turned to Citlali. "Li, you did good here. Hold onto her." Daphne slapped Citlali on the shoulder.

"I plan to." Citlali moved to Tala's side, grabbing Tala's hand. "Let's go home."

"Mine or yours?" They didn't spend much time at Citlali's new apartment.

"Mine. Let's get you comfortable with the space."

Tala could only nod. Sometimes, she was certain Citlali could read her mind. It was comforting, spreading warmth through her, and settling all those jittery bits about her.

***

Citlali flipped pancakes and scrambled eggs, making a big breakfast before Tala left for her internship, all while wearing a long undershirt that belonged to Tala. It barely came to her hip. Tala had watched her move in it like she was wrapped in bacon until she shooed Tala away.

Tala was surprisingly calm, dressed in black slacks and a heather grey polo. She sat on the couch, playing a game to help keep her awake. Tala slept when Citlali was at work, but woke up extra early to meet Citlali when she was done. Clearly, her girlfriend wasn't used to it, but insisted she'd work it out.

"Are you sure you're going to be okay for the day?" Citlali asked.

"Yeah, and if I'm not, I'm around more than enough drugs to find something to keep me awake." Tala waved the matter off.

Citlali chuckled. "Who told you to try to be funny?"

"I'm trying it on for size."

Citlali laughed. "Don't hurt yourself. Now, come eat."

Tala was up and at the table as soon as Citlali put the plate of pancakes down. She wasn't sure how many pancakes would fill Tala, but she made twenty just to be sure. She also scrambled six eggs and cooked a whole pack of sausage. Tala ate all of it along with two glasses of orange juice.

"That was great. It should hold me until lunch," Tala said.

"Which I also made you." Citlali got up from the table, grabbing the brand new lunch box she purchased for Tala and handed over it.

Tala's eyes went wide and those color bursts in her eyes popped. "Oh, wow. You didn't have to."

"Then you'll be really surprised by the tumbler of coffee." Citlali held up the twenty-ounce container.

Her jaw dropped. "I don't even own one of these."

"I bought you one."

Tala blushed and looked down, clutching the black and white striped bag to her chest like it was a precious treasure. Citlali sneaked a kiss, so she didn't have to say anything. Tala grinned as they pulled away. They walked to the door where Kyra was waiting.

"First step into the real world!" Kyra tossed confetti in the air and then threw her arms out, but Tala arched her eyebrow at the colorful bits of paper. Kyra had decided last week that she was going to go with Tala down to the pharmacy to help keep Tala from assuming the worst on her first day.

"Take good care of her," Citlali said.

Tala rolled her eyes. "I'm going to an internship, not kindergarten."

Citlali kissed her again. "Good luck. Show off that big brain."

Tala made a face, her blush deepening. Then, she was off with Kyra. Citlali sighed as she closed the door. She really wanted to go along, but Tala and Kyra deserved the moment.

Citlali texted Tala before falling asleep in Tala's bed. **Good luck. You're going to do awesome. Let me know how it goes**.

When Citlali woke up, she frowned at the response. **I think I screwed up, but nobody said anything because they expect the intern to be dumb**.

Citlali sighed. Anxiety was such a bitch. It was so much worse since Tala couldn't see anyone about it. Citlali did her best to be reassuring. **Sweetheart, if no one said anything, you're probably doing fine**.

While waiting for a text back, Citlali did the dishes. **They keep explaining stuff to me**. Tala's worries made her think something was wrong when someone was probably just doing what they should be doing with an intern.

Citlali made sure to respond back as soon as she could, wanting Tala to be aware she was interested. **What sort of stuff are they explaining to you?**

Just to warn you, my mom texted me that the family's coming over to celebrate my internship. Citlali could imagine Tala groaning and rolling her eyes, so she let her have that swift change of topic.

Good thing she warned me. She had other plans for when Tala got home, and they wouldn't be appropriate to do around family. **Poor baby. You just want to come home and game.**

And hold you.

That got a smile. **Aw, look at you being romantic! Your family's being supportive. I'll go shopping.** While the family would show up with supplies to cook, they wouldn't show up with napkins or snacks. Plus, she needed to make something, too.

Thank you.

Citlali got dressed and went out to do some shopping to prepare for Tala's family. It was nice that Rashida warned Tala, giving Tala time to mentally prepare for company. And, as she thought more on it, it was really great that Tala's family gave her space, even though they didn't understand it.

At the store, Citlali got the strange sensation someone was watching her. Fearing it might be Ruby, she called Daphne, who was by her side in less than fifteen minutes. Citlali was ever so grateful.

"What's all the grub for?" Daphne asked as she poked around the shopping cart.

"Tala's family is coming over to celebrate her internship."

"Her family sounds nice."

Citlali smiled. "They are."

Daphne pursed her lips. She was about to be a pest. "Make you think of your parents?"

"I get that my parents have a plan for me, and it freaks them out when I go off script, but they're still good parents." Citlali didn't realize her parents did that until they met Tala.

Daphne held her hands up in surrender. "Hey, I wasn't saying they were bad parents. I've spent more than enough time with both of them to know they're cool. Did they like her?"

"In the end, yes, but they had already ruined things with their attitudes. She's going to always think they hate her, and that bothers them."

Daphne gave her a sidelong glance as they wandered the aisles. "You told them how shy she is?"

"I told them all about her. The second my parents jumped on her, it was over. She folded into herself."

Daphne pouted. "Well, they have to make it up to her. I'm going to scold them over it."

Citlali wouldn't stop her. "Good. They deserve it. I scolded them already."

They continued moving through the store, Daphne keeping a sharp eye out. Citlali felt like she could still feel eyes on her, but she couldn't figure out who might be watching her. No one stood out. She definitely didn't see Ruby, but Ruby did have the money to hire someone to watch her. Maybe it was just her imagination, but the way Daphne glanced around, they both couldn't be having the same delusions.

"Are you all right?" Citlali asked.

"I am." Daphne sighed. "I'm just on guard for you. I'm sorry."

"Don't be. I'm glad you're here."

Daphne grabbed her hand. "I'll always be here."

So maybe it is my imagination and I'm just on edge right along with Daphne. "You want to come over to celebrate, too?" Citlali asked.

Daphne smiled. "Thanks, but this sounds like a family affair. Catch me when you two are just hanging out."

"True enough. Tala will be overwhelmed by her family, anyway. I can give her a lot of advance warning about hanging out with you."

Daphne grinned with her chin in the air. "That's probably for the best."

They parted ways in the supermarket parking lot. Citlali made it back to Tala's apartment to start cooking right before Tala's family came in. After a round of hugs and smiles, they got to work.

A huge meal was ready by the time Tala returned. Tala blushed, accepting hugs and pats on the back. Despite not liking company, Tala was content and comfortable with embraces from her family. Once she got through everyone, she jumped on the food and everyone followed. The conversation turned to how the day went, and just like Citlali had, Tala's family infused the conversation with optimism Tala could rarely find. It was a good night.

***

Citlali was happy. Work was going well after a week. She had feared there would be panic attacks and anxiety, but she picked it up like no time passed. The staff treated her the same. It was still like she never left, and she was more than thankful for that.

A tension had been wrapped around Citlali's belly like a well-tied knot, and she didn't realize how bad it was until it began to unravel. From past behavior, they all expected at least one night of Ruby demanding to be let in, but no. Nothing. It was like she learned her lesson. And every morning Tala picked Citlali up, to make sure she was all right.

"Hey, babe," Tala said, waving to the other staff members who had excited The New Moon with Citlali once the night was over.

Citlali's face lit up. That was the first "babe" she got from Tala. It felt so good she wanted to celebrate it somehow. Their relationship was going well. They split time between their places, so they balanced each other out.

"My place?" Citlali asked as she took Tala's hand.

Tala shrugged. "It's easier for me to get to the pharmacy from there."

Citlali chuckled. "Oh, is that all?"

Tala glanced around, distracted from the conversation. A slight wrinkle formed in her brow. Citlali gave her hand a little tug.

"Everything okay?" Citlali asked.

"Yeah. It's weird. For like the past week or so, I keep smelling this strange mix." Tala scratched her head. "But I can't find the source. It's like I'm imagining it, but I know I'm not."

Citlali's stomach dropped. She felt like someone had been watching her all week, too. Was it a coincidence? "Is it something bad?"

Tala wrinkled her nose. "It's a bad combination of smells. Let's just get home."

Citlali agreed, and thankfully they made it back to the apartment all right, but she couldn't shake the feeling that someone was watching her. Stalking her, almost.

Chapter Nineteen

WHILE LEAVING THE PHARMACY the next day, Tala pressed her hand to her forehead. A hint of wolfsbane lingered in the air again. She thought she was losing her mind. Then she caught a surprising whiff of Citlali's scent on the breeze. *Wait, is she here?* Yes, Citlali stood by her car in a stunning black dress. She waved, grinning. Tala's heart swelled. She never would've thought she'd enjoy a surprise like this, but she actually did.

Tala's attention got split between Citlali and noticing a woman in a hoodie approaching the pharmacy. She thought the woman was going inside, but the pungent scent of silver hit her. *Shit!* She twisted just as the woman lunged for her. A knife pierced her skin, white-hot pain shooting down her side, but she caught the woman's wrist before the blade could go in too deep. The silver ripped through her, like having barbed wire dragged across her insides. She yanked the blade out.

She swung her gaze to Citlali. "Run!" Tala's voice was practically a roar.

Citlali ran toward them. She moved fast in her heels and yanked out mace. *No!* Tala's instincts screamed for her to move away—werewolves were terribly allergic to mace—she wasn't fast enough. Her assailant got a face full of mace, screaming and falling back, but the spray was close enough that it got Tala, too. Now, along with a burning, itchy stab wound, her face felt like it was on fire. She couldn't see or smell. Her heart rate spiked. Terror filled her.

"Damn it, damn it, damn it!" Tala shook her head. Not surprisingly, it did nothing for the intense sting.

Someone grabbed Tala's hand and yanked. A car door opened and she got shoved inside, door slamming on her back. Another door opened, closed, and then the car was moving.

"Tala, I'm sorry I got you with the pepper spray! Are you okay?" Citlali sounded frantic.

"I don't currently have a knife with silver in it embedded in me, so yeah," Tala replied through gritted teeth. Her heartbeat pounded in her ears, intensifying each ripple of agony. She growled, anguish tearing at her face, senses, and abdomen.

"Here's water!" Citlali shoved a cold bottle into Tala's hands.

Tala used the water to wash her face as she righted herself in the chair. It didn't help much. She needed milk. Still, it was better than nothing. *This has to be what Hell feels like!* Just enough relief to recognize it as relief, but still so much burning torment.

"Are we being followed?" Tala asked, turning around as if she could make out anything. Her eyes stung just from trying to open her eyelids, and even when she succeeded, the world was a blurry mess.

"I think so." Citlali groaned. "What the hell just happened?"

Tala breathed through the pain. "If I had to guess, I'd say Hunters. I've been smelling damn Hunters for a week and thought I was overthinking it. How could I be so fucking stupid?" *Why the hell else would I be smelling wolfsbane?* "The pack probably gave them fucking permission to hunt me! Fuck!"

Tala bent over with a moan. Raising her voice made her wound throb like she had been punched in the gut with a spiked glove. Then the car rocked and she rocked with it, slamming her head into the window. A distinct grinding sound filled the cab. "Shit, did they just ram us?"

"Don't worry. I have it under control." The car rocked back and forth again.

"I am worried! You're in danger and it's my fault." Tala felt around for the door handle. She pulled it. Nothing happened.

"Did you just try to jump out of the fucking car?" Citlali asked, her tone a mix of outrage and concern.

"I don't want you to get hurt." She'd never forgive herself if her mate was as much as scratched because of her actions.

"Well, I don't want you to die, so sit the fuck back and let me think!"

Tala obeyed, which surprised the hell out of her. The car rocked again, shoving her to the side, and pain shot through her. Bright, white light flashed before her. It felt like her body had been pulled apart. Growling, she put her hand on the wound and tried to keep pressure on it.

"Should I call the cops? It's not like they can say you're a werewolf and deserve to die," Citlali said.

"No cops." Tala clamped her teeth around another moan. "You don't know who might be a Hunter. And there are werewolf cops."

"From your former pack. They'd just let you die, wouldn't they?"

"Yeah."

"Bastards. So, what do we do?"

The car was rammed from behind. The sound of Citlali slamming her foot down on the gas pedal thumped through the small sedan and Tala got pressed back in her seat. Tala's vision returned enough for her to see the blurs of traffic along with spots that might've been traffic lights. She had no idea where they were. Hopefully, Citlali did. The car lurched forward again and swerved.

Citlali grunted, righting it. "Damn it, they're trying to make us crash."

"You can't outrun them?" Tala took a slow, deep inhale. Attempting to breathe through the pain in her stomach wasn't doing as much as she hoped. *If we make it through this, stomach, maybe you'll remember real pain and stop freaking out over every little thing.*

"Hold on, I'm going to make a turn."

Tala barely had a chance to brace herself as Citlali hit a sharp turn, like they were in a movie. Not long after that, Citlali hit another turn, and then another. Tala bounced around her seat like a pinball, adding to her agony, but as long as they got away, she didn't care. With each turn, she could smell Citlali calm down, so she relaxed, too. Thank goodness her smell was back. Her face still burned, but she could open her eyes, if only a crack. Her world made a little sense again.

But her wound felt like there was acid eating through her flesh, like it was festering already. She coughed, and blood came out of her mouth. *Not good.*

"Babe, are you—" The words were cut off as a car slammed into the passenger side of the car.

Metal crunched against metal, a horrible tearing sound, and the impact made Tala throw up, a mixture of blood and bile. They came to an abrupt halt.

"Shit, sweetheart, come on!" Citlali grabbed her hand and yanked her out of the car. Tala trusted Citlali to lead her. Her vision could make out Citlali ahead of her; she was a blur, but there. She would feel better if she could smell Citlali again, but her own vomit filled her nostrils instead.

They ran. Tala didn't hear any traffic. Tall brown blurs shooting up into the sky could've been brick buildings for all she knew. Citlali pulled Tala into an alley. She shoved Tala through a door.

"Stay here. Don't say anything."

The sound of ripping echoed in Tala's ears. *The hell?* Hot, thick air pressed against her stomach. Okay, so Citlali had ripped off a soaked bit of her bloody shirt. Then, Citlali left. Citlali vanished for more minutes than Tala liked, long enough for Tala's vision to come back enough for her to see she was in some old decrepit building. Broken crates piled up to her left and right, a cracked window loomed ahead of her. A small warehouse? An abandoned storefront? She couldn't be sure, but dust tickled her already raw nose. Citlali came back.

"What did you do?" Tala asked, sniffling to avoid sneezing.

"Gave them a blood trail to follow. Let's go." Citlali grabbed her and leaned her against her for support.

"Good thinking."

Citlali winced. "Yeah, but I don't know what else to do."

Tala clutched her wound, blood oozing through her fingers. It felt like a million hot needles were being stabbed into her flesh. She gagged. "I have to get to my mom. I think I have silver poisoning."

"Where's your mom?"

Tears gathered in her eyes. "Fuck. It hurts. Gotta call her." Her knees buckled, too weak to hold her. The only reason she didn't collapse was because Citlali had her.

"Give me your phone."

Tala used her free hand to give up her phone. She didn't want to think about what would've happened if that knife had gone all the way in. Inside the wound itched. The area around it felt like it was liquefying, her flesh softening with each passing moment. That had to be wolfsbane at work, decaying healthy tissue and blood cells bit by bit, like snake's venom.

"Citlali, I gotta sit down." Tala tumbled, wanting to catch her breath. If she could just get a moment, maybe she could stop the pain.

Citlali caught her, wrapping her arms around Tala, pressing her close. "Tala, hold on!"

"I think I'll take a nap." Sleep always made things better. The wound could heal if she rested for a bit.

"Don't you dare!" Citlali moved them to a spot by the wall. Boxes blocked them from view of the door, but if Tala angled right she could still see out the windows. They both sank to the floor. "Don't you dare die on me."

Tala took a deep breath, tossing her head from side to side. It felt like lava coursed through her veins, burning her from the inside out. "I'm so hot. Are you hot?"

"No, but you're sweating a puddle. Just hold on. Your mom's coming."

"You called her already?" *When did that happen?*

"I texted her. She's coming, just hold on, please. She's coming." Citlali spoke the words like a prayer as she clutched Tala to her.

Tala sniffled. "How? She doesn't know where we are. We don't even know where we are."

"She can track your phone." Citlali gathered Tala in her arms in a way that was more comfortable. "So just hold on."

Tala wasn't sure if she could. Everything hurt. It was like having thorns wrapped around every inch of her, and each thorn had a thousand thorns that were being dragged across her muscles and bones. She was so damn tired. *I just wanna take a nap. Just for a second.*

* * *

Citlali watched Tala's eyes droop and grunted as Tala got heavier against her. It was already hard to hold Tala up, so much denser than her tiny size let on. Nothing good would come from Tala closing her eyes. She had to think fast. She tore her dress to press a clean cloth to Tala's wound and tried to keep Tala talking to keep her conscious.

"Hey, sweetheart, how was work today? You still like it?" Citlali asked as she looked out the broken windows, hoping to find some sign that it was safe to move. No shadows moved across the glass, no footsteps outside. She wasn't sure they really lost the people chasing them, and she didn't want to trap them in this abandoned building.

Tala licked her lips, which were darker than usual from pepper spray. Her hair stuck like glue to her face, weighed down by sweat. "It was good. I'm learning so much and...they're nice to me. Patient. And then you came." She sounded exhausted, like she was about to drift off.

Not good, so not good. Citlali had to keep up Tala's spirit, though. She forced the worry from her voice, making her tone light and airy. "You liked the surprise?"

Tala gave a weary smile, tears falling from her eyes. The color bursts in her eyes were washed out, like they were fading with her. "It's always nice to see you."

"Then when we make it through this, I'll surprise you again, but you have to keep your eyes open, okay?"

Tala nodded, but her breathing grew shallower than before. Citlali wanted to cry, but she had to hold it together. It wouldn't do them any good to panic. *What do I do?* Tala wasn't in any shape to move. She didn't like it, but they needed to stay put and hope Rashida showed up in time. *Trust her family.*

"I'm glad I met you," Tala whispered.

Citlali held back tears. "Even though you're in this mess because of me?" *All I had to do was watch out for Ruby. My damn hubris is going to get the sweetest person I've ever met killed.*

Tala chuckled, but it transformed into a cough. "You didn't get me into this, but meeting you showed me there's someone on the planet that got me. I grew up thinking I was wrong, something was wrong with me, but you've never treated me that way."

"There's nothing wrong with you. You have anxiety and you don't like a lot of socializing. It's not weird. You may notice I actually don't like a lot of socializing."

Tala opened her mouth, but then closed it again. She tilted her head and squinted, as if the realization just hit her. "Wait a—"

"Whatever it is," Citlali interrupted, not wanting Tala to waste her breath on worrying. "We'll talk about it as soon as we get out of this mess."

"She's not getting out of this," a woman's voice said. When Citlali turned, three individuals stepped into view. Two men, one woman. They were dressed in all black with tactical gear. She could see their faces through their face shields.

Citlali blocked Tala's body and glared at the trio. "Leave her alone."

"Move, so we can put this rabid dog down," the woman said, pointing a gun at them.

Tala growled, but Citlali stayed in front of her. She wasn't scared of them. She would protect Tala with her life, just as Tala had done for her. "To hell with you! This is an angel."

"You're really trying to protect this beast?" the woman practically spat at her.

Citlali opened her arms wide to block their view of Tala. "Fuck you!"

"We can just throw you out of the way." The taller man stepped forward.

Citlali held up her mace. "If you want a face full of pepper spray, come on." She also had a knife in her purse, but she'd need time to get to it.

"We can't harm a person," the woman said.

"Tala is a person!" Citlali glowered at all of them. How dare they!

"Tala's a vicious bitch who needs to be put down before she hurts anyone else," the woman said.

"Who the hell do you think she hurt?" Citlali replied.

"There are four people this monster hospitalized," the tall Hunter said.

Citlali couldn't believe this nonsense. "Are you fucking kidding me?" Maybe they weren't Hunters. They could be mercenaries. "You guys work for Ruby?" All this time Citlali had worried over Ruby coming after her, and it never occurred to her that Ruby would hurt Tala.

"We don't work for anybody. This is about justice." The taller Hunter stepped closer, drawing a handgun.

"No, you care about revenge," Citlali said, edging closer to him. If anything went down, she'd probably have to spray him first. There was an opening between his helmet and face shield. It would be a tight squeeze, but she'd make it work.

"A police report confirmed that story," the woman said, gun relaxed at her side now.

"Bullshit. Nothing Ruby and her gang told the police was true. They were attacking me. Without Tala, Ruby would've raped me," Citlali said.

The taller Hunter scoffed. "Rape you?" He said it like it was impossible.

"Her goons almost killed me, shooting up the room the way they did," Citlali said. He didn't seem moved, but the other two weren't pointing guns at her. A flicker of hope started in her chest.

"Because they were rightfully trying to put down a beast," he replied.

Tala growled again, eyes blood red, and the trio moved closer, all of their guns up now.

"Tala, calm down. Let me handle this." Citlali seemed to be getting through to at least two of them. It was a good start.

"My mate," Tala said through pointed, gritted teeth.

The taller Hunter laughed. "So, you're her bitch."

"At least I'm not a fucking moron." Citlali really wanted to spray him, but she didn't want to risk it since last time she got Tala, too. "You idiots are about to murder a hero on the word of an attempted rapist."

"Watch your mouth," the woman said with a sneer, gun aimed at Citlali now. Her lips pursed and her eyebrows knitted close together. She seemed to be their leader.

"Why?" Citlali locked eyes with the woman. "Tala isn't the villain here just because she's a werewolf. Tala is a hero because she's a werewolf."

The woman shook her head. "She's the villain because she attacked humans, and we're here because no one else is equipped to punish her. She'd tear through the average police force."

"She wouldn't have to do that because a police force wouldn't be coming after her—because she didn't do anything wrong." Citlali wanted to tear her hair out. "Let me tell you what happened, and then you tell me if you still want to shoot her." She might be able to think of some way out of this, or buy some time until Tala's mother showed up.

The tall one kept his gun trained on Tala. "So you can lie for her?"

"So you know the truth."

"We know the truth! That's a beast." He pointed at Tala using his gun.

"So, you're all comfortable with executing someone on the word of a liar? You're all just murderers then." Citlali couldn't do anything with that. "You're worse than whatever the hell you think Tala is."

"We read the police report, but fine. What do you claim happened?" The woman scoffed. "Just be aware we've been watching you both, so we know your relationship to her."

"Fine, but do you know Ruby? Did any of you do research about her? Ask around my job about her. She's been banned from The New Moon because she started the attack. She brought in armed men. Threatened me and the club to get me to a private room where she planned to have her way with me with her goons right there," Citlali said.

"Bullshit." The taller Hunter stepped even closer.

Tala moved, and the tall one fired. The shot boomed in the quiet space, but Citlali didn't see what the bullet hit and sprayed him with pepper spray. He screamed and lowered his gun. The other two Hunters yanked her away. She twisted, wanting to spray them too. They pulled her arm behind her back. Dagger-like pain shot through her shoulder. She stilled. If she moved the wrong way, they'd break her arm or shoot her.

"Let...her...go..." Tala crawled toward them, blood oozing from her eyes and ears. A bullet wound dribbled blood on her arm—the shot hit true. More shots rang out, but Tala kept coming, stumbling forward. Hopefully, she wasn't hit.

"Tala, stop moving!" Citlali jabbed her elbow into someone's neck. A grunt came from behind her and her arm was freed. She turned and tried to dash for Tala, but one of the Hunters pounced on her back. A heavy weight crushed her back, thick arms wrapped around her own, and she stumbled from the impact, falling to the floor. The Hunter landed on her back, and air left her lungs in a rush.

"Stop before you get hurt," the shorter hunter barked in her ear.

"To hell with you!" Citlali twisted again, doing her best to spray the Hunter. Blind luck and unlucky tonight. The weight never stopped crushing her, like a slab pressed on her back.

Citlali heaved herself up and grabbed her purse crushed against her chest, feeling for her knife, the same style she recalled Tala handing over to the police. She couldn't be sure how she managed to open the damn thing, but she did, and she stabbed the Hunter in the leg.

"Damn!" He slammed Citlali's head into the cement floor.

Citlali's head throbbed, her vision blurred, and her nose crunched. Pain splintered through her face. She didn't care. *I have to protect Tala.* She twisted the knife. The Hunter screamed. Before Citlali could do anything else, a knife pressed to her throat.

"How about we all calm the hell down?" the leader said. She glanced at Tala, who had fallen on the floor, wounds oozing, arm outstretched for Citlali. "Don't move."

"Don't." Tala coughed blood, it heaved from her. She needed help. Now.

"You don't call the shots here, beast. Your pack gave us permission to hunt you," the leader said. She pulled Citlali to her knees, knife still pushing against her jugular.

Tala chuckled. "My pack? You stupid bastards. My pack excommunicated me right after that happened. They can't give you permission to hunt me."

"Tala, don't talk. Don't move," Citlali begged. Tala needed to stay still, conserve her strength. The knife to her throat pressed closer to her neck.

"I think we all need to stop moving," Rashida said, stepping into Citlali's view with Rocky by her side. She clutched a bag, eyes wide. With luck, it was medical supplies.

"They have guns," Citlali gasped.

At that, Rashida dropped her bag and seemed to disappear. Rocky also vanished.

Citlali's assailant was yanked away from her, and she gasped. She looked up to see a massive, black-furred werewolf holding the shorter Hunter off of the ground. The other Hunter suffered the same fate, a russet werewolf gripping the Hunter with its long claws. The Hunters thrashed. Citlali scrambled to Tala, but Tala hardly noticed. Her gaze was locked on her parents.

"We have permission for this Hunt," the Hunter leader yelled.

"What did the Hunter Council say?" Rashida asked, voice a growl.

The Hunter man struggled, trying to kick at Rocky. "We didn't need their permission with the pack's permission!"

"Wow, you guys are young idiots," Rocky replied. "You can't hunt a werewolf that doesn't have a pack without the Council's okay. This Hunt is illegal."

What they said must have made sense because the Hunters stopped struggling. Rashida dropped her captive and changed back, her clothes in tatters, but hanging on enough for her to be decent. She grabbed her bag and rushed to Tala's side. The way the doctor winced didn't make Citlali feel comfortable.

"Can you transform, Tala?" her mother asked. "Your wolf form can heal you faster."

Tala shook her head, pressing her wound. Angry purple lines wove their way from the wound in her side, the flesh around it nearly black. "Silver. Wolfsbane."

"Animals." Rocky flung his captive down. The leader's helmet head cracked onto the floor. "Do you know what wolfsbane can do to us?"

"You can save her, right?" Citlali asked, tears burning her eyes.

"I'll do my best. Is it deep?" Rashida asked.

Tala shook her head. "Hurts, though, like battery acid in my veins. Burns. It burns, Ma." She sobbed, tears pouring down her face.

"Damn it." Rashida went to work. No one moved. Citlali could hardly breathe. If Tala didn't make it, the Hunters murdered her for doing the right thing. Talk about no good deed going unpunished.

Chapter Twenty

TALA WANTED TO SLEEP, but she couldn't, not until she got the all clear from her mother. She had been given an injection to counteract the wolfsbane. She had at least an hour before it kicked in. And that was if she was lucky. Sometimes, the injection didn't work. She tried to ignore the burning, itching just under her skin. Citlali sat with her, holding her had helped distract Tala. Her mother stitching her stab wound also helped.

"What type of sadist stabs a werewolf with a silver knife coated in wolfsbane," her mother muttered.

"It's a Hunt, not a cookout," the non-maced Hunter replied.

"Silver isn't going to kill a werewolf unless they are extremely allergic to it," her mother said.

"Hunters put it in bullets, so why not knives?"

"Because a bullet is typically meant to stay in the body. The silver is soft, will warp, so it's not likely to exit the body and it could cause problems. Putting silver in a knife is just torture. It just makes you want to tear at the stab wound. The wolfsbane on the knife is meant to kill her, but you designed a torture device to make her want to rip her own skin off as it rotted away." Her mother's face twisted.

"Also not legal. How young are you guys?" her father asked.

The leader of the Hunters paced, texting with someone. She had her helmet off, scowling at her phone screen. "Our age doesn't have anything to do with this."

"Really? Because I've dealt with more than my fair share of Hunters and it's never a shit show like this," her father said, waving his arms around. "Definitely never seen a Hunter hurt a human." He motioned to Citlali, whose face was bloody. Her nose was probably broken. As soon as Tala could move, she'd punch the idiot in the mouth for hurting Citlali.

"She stabbed me!" And thanks to the idiot opening his big mouth, Tala now knew who to go after.

"To be fair, you tried to kill Tala. You're lucky I only stabbed you," Citlali replied.

"I'll get you back for pepper spraying me." The taller Hunter's face was bright red and he hadn't opened his eyes.

"Shut up," the leader said as she looked up from her phone. "None of us will be paying anyone back."

"Wait, was this illegal?" the shorter Hunter asked.

The leader sighed. "Talking with our contact at the Council, if the werewolf Tala was excommunicated from her pack, they can't give us permission for anything. And according to his information, we shouldn't be hunting her in the first place."

The shorter Hunter paled. "So they're telling the truth? This doesn't make any sense."

"It makes all the sense, you morons!" Citlali pointed at them. "Tala used her powers to save me. Humans aren't inherently good and werewolves aren't inherently bad."

The Hunters glared at her, but they couldn't dispute that right now. Her mother handed Citlali gauze to wipe her face. Citlali did so.

Her mother glanced at the wounded Hunter. "If you wait, I'll look at your wound. I don't believe any of you can handle that."

"Hey, we're professional," the leader said.

"Yeah, professionals who were felled by a club manager with mace and a knife. I can only imagine how you managed to actually stab Tala," her mother said.

"Thought she was going into the pharmacy," Tala said. She didn't want her parents to think she couldn't take care of herself.

"And I think she was distracted by me surprising her," Citlali said. That was definitely true.

"Ah, so they got lucky." Her father shook his head. "What kind of Hunters endanger a human life?"

"She wasn't supposed to be there! We're not heartless," the leader said.

Her mother scoffed. "No, only careless, which is equally dangerous."

That silenced the Hunters again. Tala's mother finished with her stitches, put ointment on the wound, and then bandaged it. She gave Tala a couple of pills, which she took dry, and her mother kissed the top of her head before moving onto Citlali. Tala wanted to tear through the Hunters for what they did to Citlali, but she could barely move. Exhaustion wrapped around her like a blanket.

Tala watched the Hunters while her mother worked. They sat in a semi-circle, nursing their own wounds, waiting for their Hunter Council contact to come and debrief everyone. They had really screwed up, and it was probably because they believed Ruby. She couldn't figure out the reason for it. If Ruby said the sky was blue, Tala would look up to check, but others actually believed the redhead.

By the time the Council contact arrived, Tala's mother had bandaged everyone up and Tala was struggling to keep her eyes open. The contact introduced himself as Lee, and he seemed familiar with her father. They laughed over something while shaking hands. Lee shook her mother's hand, Citlali's hand, and her hand as well.

"First things first, I'd like to apologize for this group of Hunters. They're trying to make a name for themselves," Lee said, pinching his nose and glaring at the trio. "Any experienced Hunter would've checked to see why a pack would give you permission to hunt one of their own. It takes extreme negotiations to do what you just did. Sometimes it can take months to get packs to let Hunters do their jobs, and usually it's because the wolf has gone on the run."

Tala growled at the group of idiots for not knowing the basics of what they do. The sound was as weak as she was, though. Citlali caressed her forehead, as if to calm her down.

"They also made a silver laced knife dipped in wolfsbane," her father said.

Lee's eyes were so wide they were about to fall out. "They did what?" He glared at the Hunters. "So, cruel as well. Who even authorized you to carry such a weapon?"

The group winced. Tala couldn't believe what she was hearing. "You almost killed Citlali, and you don't even know what you can and can't do as legit Hunters? Asshole doesn't even cover it."

"Calm down." Citlali stroked the side of Tala's head.

"Better training and education on how packs operate sounds like it would be helpful," her mother said.

Lee shook his head. "How did any of this even sound like a good idea?"

Tala definitely wanted to hear that. They should've aborted the mission the second Citlali was involved, yet they doubled-down on it, like she was acceptable collateral damage. And of course, there was the car chase. *For people who are supposed to protect humans, they endangered a lot of humans today.*

"The woman she attacked found us, begging for justice because the police didn't believe her," the leader replied.

"We got a chance to read the police report and four people backed her," the taller idiot added.

Damn police report. It probably blamed the whole incident on Tala and imaginary prostitutes.

Lee rubbed his eyes. "But none of you bothered to ask why it wasn't an official case among the Hunter Council? It was investigated, and we found that the werewolf Tala was not the cause for the incident. We actually think her pack reacted poorly in excommunicating her, but we don't have a say in that. All you had to do was talk to me about it. Or even talk to the detective in charge."

Wow, Detective Letran wasn't just being an asshole. Tala would thank him, if only he actually arrested someone for harming Citlali.

Citlali laughed. "Told you. Tala's a hero."

"And all you've done is made her life harder for doing the right thing. Now, what happens if she sees a person in need and she can help? She might hesitate thanks to you three loose cannons." Lee pointed to them.

"But—" The leader tried to chime in.

Lee held up a hand. "I'm not done. You've also allowed yourself to be used by her former pack and exposed our organization to a woman who threatened to shoot up a club to try to rape someone. You attacked a werewolf just because she's a werewolf, like this was medieval times." Lee sighed and put a hand to his forehead. "This is going to take so much time to clean up, and you three will help me every step of the way."

Tala didn't much care about this mess. The important takeaways were that Hunters had actually cleared her of wrongdoing, and her former pack had set her up to die. *Why? To punish me and my family?* She didn't understand, but she also didn't have the energy to do any heavy thinking. Her eyelids were too heavy to keep open. She finally fell asleep.

***

Citlali sighed as she flopped down on Tala's couch. Her face throbbed, but they were safe. She was barely down before Kyra pressed a warm bowl in her hands. Spices hit her throbbing nose almost immediately.

"Thank you for protecting her." Kyra smiled at her.

"Always," Citlali said.

Kyra sat next to her. "It's good she has you."

Citlali stared down at the bowl. Beef stew, brown rice, and red beans. A biscuit soaked up gravy at the side of the bowl. "Are you sure? This all happened because of me."

"No." Kyra put a hand on her shoulder. "This happened because Ruby isn't used to being told no. I can't believe the pack elders were alright with killing Tala. I know they don't like her, but not to this extent."

Rashida came into the living room, mug of tea cupped in her hands. "The good news is the pack technically didn't sanction the Hunt. They told the Hunters they didn't care what happened to Tala, which the group took as an okay to go after her."

That was a little better. Citlali looked at Rashida. "How do you know?"

"While the pack lost all of this, there are still members who are close to us. You can't break that bond on command. So my mother talked to a few people. Tala's safe. They're not trying to have her murdered." Rashida caressed the top of Citlali's head. "You should eat. And maybe we should go to a hospital over your nose."

"I trust you." While it hadn't been the best job when they were in the abandoned building, Citlali got proper medical attention the second they stepped into Tala's apartment. She had a guard across her nose and plugs in her nostrils.

Rashida nodded. "Then eat and get some sleep. We'll handle the rest."

"And Ruby?" Citlali wasn't sure what they could do, but there needed to be something. Ruby wouldn't stop.

Rashida smiled. "We'll handle the rest."

"I want to help." She wanted to close this chapter of her life.

Rashida nodded. "Get your strength up then."

"I will." Citlali turned her attention to her food and Rashida stepped away, going into the kitchen with Rocky and her mother.

Kyra stood up. "Take it easy. You're part of a good group here, a good pack. We'll take care of each other, and that means we care about you."

"Thank you." Citlali wasn't sure what to say beyond that. She didn't need to say anything it seemed. Kyra left her to eat.

Citlali didn't realize how hungry she was until her bowl was empty and she wanted more, but she was exhausted. She went into the bedroom, stripped, and crawled into bed next to Tala. She texted

Daphne she wouldn't be in for work. **Ruby hired thugs to attack me and Tala. We're fine.** She muted her phone after that and fell asleep wrapped around Tala's warm, small body. She wanted to protect Tala from every possible ill in the world. *I won't let Ruby hurt you, or us, ever again.*

***

Citlali clung onto Rocky as he leapt from one building to another. Ruby managed to bring werewolves and Hunters together in a way they hadn't expected from what Citlali could tell, and they all needed to know how that was possible. Tala's parents, Lee, and the Hunter leader traveled together. Rocky held onto Citlali while jumping over to Ruby's balcony. They all entered Ruby's condo through the open sliding glass door. They knew she'd be home. Alone.

"What the hell is going on?" Ruby jumped off of her sofa.

"Sit down," Rashida said with a snarl that was so convincing Ruby sat right down. The rest of them lined up behind Rashida. Rocky put Citlali down.

"Your actions caused a lot of damage," Lee said.

"How did you people get in here?" Ruby glared at them.

"You people?" The Hunter leader laughed. "Hardly two weeks ago you were throwing money at me and mine to hunt Tala."

"She's a monster." Ruby glared at them.

Rashida curled her lip at Ruby, a challenge in the werewolf community.

"You're the monster," Citlali told Ruby. "And you almost got her killed because you can't take no for an answer."

"We've come to help with that." Rocky grinned, showing off a mouth full of sharp teeth.

Lee stepped forward. "Hunting werewolves is serious business. This isn't putting down a rabid animal. It's about taking on a criminal normal law enforcement wouldn't be able to handle. In this case, you were the criminal. Your world might believe your lies, but you've exposed yourself. No one will forget what you've done. We won't allow it."

"This stone you've cast will ripple for the rest of your life," Rashida said.

Ruby sneered. "I'm not scared of you freaks."

Rocky chuckled as he bulked up right before her eyes. Extra inches and extra muscles along with his canine teeth.

Citlali's eyes widened. Apparently, they could control how much they transformed.

"It's not just us," his voice was deeper now, like a low growl. "Maybe one of your drivers is a werewolf. Maybe a bartender at a club you like is a Hunter. Maybe when you're older, the business contact you need used to frequent The New Moon. You'll never know, but we're all out there. And we all know what you are."

"You're bluffing," Ruby said, but her voice trembled a bit, like she knew the hornets' nest she kicked.

Lee laughed. "If only! The world is littered with us. The patrons might be less unforgiving, after time, but not the Hunters or werewolves. We're all waiting for you to step a tiny bit out of line. Or we're all just waiting for the moment you're by yourself. Who knows?" He shrugged.

"Live with it," Citlali said. Now, Ruby got to look over her shoulder and have anxiety gnaw at her gut.

And they were gone as quickly as they came. They regrouped on the ground several blocks away. Lee and Rocky shook hands.

"Sorry about your kid again," Lee said, and then he glanced at the Hunter leader. She had the decency to blush and glance away.

"Thanks for trying to protect her," Rocky replied.

Lee shrugged. "I'm just trying to do the right thing, just like her. Never would've thought a jackass like you would have such a good kid. Take care of them."

Rocky did a thumbs up. "I got this." Rashida cleared her throat and Rocky laughed. "We got this." He pointed between the two of them.

They went their separate ways. Rocky and Rashida accompanied Citlali to Tala's apartment. Tala was still bedridden, and she'd been asleep for the better part of two days. Her mother went to check on her, and Rocky and Citlali lingered in the living room.

"You did good standing up for Tala." Rocky patted her shoulder.

Citlali shrugged. "Well, I love her."

"That's good, because you're stuck with her for the rest of her life, and let me tell you, it would suck for you to have her being all amazing to you and you can't muster the same emotions."

He spoke from experience. She couldn't imagine not having feelings for Tala. The emotions she had for Tala, the desire, she only wanted those things to grow. She wanted a life with Tala.

"Is that why you can't love her mother?" Citlali asked.

Rocky sighed. "I love her to death. I just don't have that bond with her. Tala is our bond now, but it's not the same."

Tala mentioned a bond, how Citlali wouldn't feel it like she did. Citlali bit her lip. "Do you think not being able to have that bond with Tala will affect me?"

He snorted. "Nah, I think you loving her will be more than enough. You both know firsthand what you'll do for the other."

She hoped. "Do werewolf/human couples happen often?"

"Not often, but that doesn't mean anything. You'll be fine." He grinned. "Promise."

Citlali laughed, and she sort of understood how Rashida fell for him. He was just the right amount of dork. He probably embarrassed Tala every time they went out. Rashida stepped out of the bedroom.

"That kid is resilient." Rashida looked at Rocky. "I know they try to blame her being an introvert on you, but I'm pretty sure the toughness and extra strength comes from you."

Rocky shrugged. "I'll take it."

"She's getting better?" Citlali asked.

Rashida nodded. "She's healing well. She's upset she can't go to her internship. She's scared she's going to get fired."

"I'll talk to her boss about things. I'm sure they'll be sympathetic to find out we were robbed right outside the pharmacy and Tala was stabbed." That was the story they were telling. "I'll go in person, so they can see my face."

Rashida snatched Citlali into a tight hug. It hurt a little, but it was a good hurt. "Thank you for standing with her."

Citlali returned the embrace. "I'm lucky to have her."

"If you need anything, don't hesitate to call any of us," Rashida said. "Although, I've already told Kyra to pop in and check on you both at least once a day."

Citlali smiled. "Well, thank you for caring. I'm sure we'll be fine."

After that, they were gone, and Citlali went to work taking care of Tala and herself. She took a hot shower, washing away the tension of seeing Ruby. She wasn't scared of Ruby now. In fact, she was certain if she ever saw Ruby again, she'd punch her.

She heated up some food. Kyra made sure they had enough meals to last almost two weeks. Entering the bedroom, she set up the tray and then eased into bed.

"Your eyes are black," Tala said.

"Your mom said to expect it with a broken nose. I'm fine. How about you?" Citlali asked.

Tala groaned. "Better. I'm sore, can't move, kinda itchy in places I can't reach, but it doesn't feel like my whole body is filled with lava."

Citlali kissed her cheek. "Good. You should eat and then sleep some more."

"Can you go to work like that?"

"I can help set up and do paperwork, but only if you promise to sleep and get better while I do."

"Will someone see you home?"

"I'll leave with Kyra or have Daphne follow me. I'm also going to let your internship know why you won't be in."

Tala's eyes drooped and she nodded. Citlali helped her eat, and then Tala fell asleep. Citlali cleaned their meal up.

In the morning, she went to Tala's internship and explained what happened. Tala would be welcomed back whenever she was healthy again, as long as she had a doctor's note. Easy enough. As for Citlali's job, she was given the rest of the week off once Ruby's name came up. When she went back to Tala's house, she found Tala still sleeping.

Citlali collapsed on the couch and called Daphne. She caught her up on the latest drama.

"This thing with Ruby has to go away eventually, right?" Daphne asked over the phone.

"It should be over." Right now, it depended on if Ruby wanted to try a group of werewolves, and she didn't seem to be in the mood anymore.

"Good."

With luck, they wouldn't have to deal with Ruby again, but if they did, they were in this together, and she felt like nothing could stop them. *Is this what they meant by having a pack?* She was more than open to learning.

***

Tala was surprised her internship kept her on after missing almost two weeks. More than that, they hired her when the internship was over. She had a job as a pharmacy technician, which would allow her to learn more about being a pharmacist as she finished school. So as the weather changed, the air a little crisper as autumn rolled in, her family had a backyard barbecue to celebrate. Kyra and Tala's father fought over grill duty, until her mother forced her dad away. Citlali brought Daphne, who the whole family immediately embraced. Citlali made herself comfortable on Tala's lap, handing her a beer. Tala smiled.

"Congratulations, sweetheart," Citlali said as she clanged her bottleneck against Tala's.

I should've known she'd want to sit on me. It was becoming a thing. Citlali seemed to delight in the fact that Tala had no problem holding her weight. "Thanks, but you know what's even better than being one step closer to the job of my dreams?"

Citlali laughed. "You're not going to get me with the 'having you as my girlfriend' line."

"I was going to say having the girl of my dreams as my girlfriend."

Citlali groaned and hid her face in Tala's shoulder. "I should've known!"

Tala kissed Citlali. She used to be against public displays of affection, but months with Citlali taught her why people did such things. It was fun to kiss Citlali, regardless of location or who was around.

"Girl of your dreams, huh? So you'll move in with me?" Citlali asked.

Tala pulled back. "'Are you serious?"

"Very. We already basically live together."

That was true. They split their time evenly between their homes. They had keys to each other's places. They came and went as they pleased. Hell, their best friends came and went as they pleased as well. It wasn't a strange sight for Kyra to cook in Citlali's kitchen, or for Daphne to have show ideas spread out on Tala's table. One place would be easier, and Citlali's was definitely the better choice since it was bigger.

"Should we sell my furniture?" Tala asked. She was only attached to her game system, but Kyra would salvage her cookware.

"Was that a yes?"

Tala decided to play it cool, even though she wanted to dance inside. A flutter started in her chest, but not from her stomach butterflies. Her heart was light. She gave a playful shrug. "I guess."

"Oh, you!" Citlali kissed her again.

"Did you tell her about the celebration we're doing for her?" Daphne asked.

Rashida perked up. "You're doing another celebration for Tala?"

"It was a surprise!" Citlali glared at Daphne.

Daphne scoffed. "We've all gotten to know Tala at The New Moon, so when Citlali said she got hired, we all wanted to do something. Citlali set the menu. And you guys can see our new show!"

Citlali nodded. "It is our best to date. Amazing."

Tala's family jumped at the offer. Tala would go for the food and company as always.

"I'll give you a private show later, so you get the gist of it." Citlali nipped her earlobe.

Tala grinned. "You know that'll be more than fine by me."

The End.

About S. L. Kassidy

What is there to know about me? Not much. I was born, bred, and raised in New York and I have no desire to live anywhere else. One day, I would like to travel to a few places, but for now I am content where I am.

I started out writing poetry in junior high and continued to do so for ten years. I wrote short stories, usually fantasy and romance stories, for my own entertainment throughout high school and college. Back then, I wrote strictly for me and those stories remain locked in the back of my closet in little notebooks, written in my almost unreadable, tiny handwriting. In between writing those stories and poetry, I managed to get a college degree in history.

After graduating college, I had a semester off before graduate school and I didn't really have anything to do with my time. So, I took a chance and wrote a fanfic and dared to upload it to the Internet. I was surprised that other people enjoyed my work and I've been posting ever since. I had quite a bit of fun with fan fiction and eventually decided to try my hand in original fiction. I suppose it was sort of like coming back around to what I had been doing in high school and college, except this time the stories were for whoever wanted to read them. I uploaded my first original story a few years ago and haven't looked back. I plan to continue writing as long as I continue getting ideas for stories and it continues to be fun.

Connect with Shea
Email: slkassidy@gmail.com
Facebook: S.L. Kassidy

Note to Readers:

Thank you for reading a book from Desert Palm Press. We appreciate you as a reader and want to ensure you enjoy the reading process. We would like you to consider posting a review on your preferred media sites and/or your blog or website.

For more information on upcoming releases, author interviews, contests, giveaways and more, please sign up for our newsletter and visit us at Desert Palm Press: www.desertpalmpress.com and "Like" us on Facebook: Desert Palm Press.

Bright Blessings

Manufactured by Amazon.ca
Bolton, ON